TACKED TO DEATH

TACKED TO DEATH

MICHELE SCOTT

THORNDIKE
CHIVERS

This Large Print edition is published by Thorndike Press, Waterville, Maine, USA and by BBC Audiobooks Ltd, Bath, England.

Thorndike Press, a part of Gale, Cengage Learning.

A Horse Lover's Mystery.

The text of this Large Print edition is unabridged.

Other aspects of the book may vary from the original edition.

Set in 16 pt. Plantin.

Printed on permanent paper.

LIBRARY OF CONGRESS CATALOGING-IN-PUBLICATION DATA

Scott, Michele, 1969–
    Tacked to death / by Michele Scott.
        p. cm. — (A horse lover's mystery) (Thorndike Press large
    print mystery)
        ISBN-13: 978-1-4104-0870-9 (alk. paper)
        ISBN-10: 1-4104-0870-1 (alk. paper)
        1. Bancroft, Michaela (Fictitious character) — Fiction. 2.
    Horse trainers — Fiction. 3. Polo players — Crimes against —
    Fiction. 4. Large type books. I. Title.
    PS3619.C6824T33 2008
    813'.6—dc22   2008015027

BRITISH LIBRARY CATALOGUING-IN-PUBLICATION DATA AVAILABLE

Published in 2008 in the U.S. by arrangement with The Berkley Publishing Group, a member of Penguin Group (USA) Inc.
Published in 2009 in the U.K. by arrangement with the Author.

U.K. Hardcover: 978 1 408 41263 3 (Chivers Large Print)
U.K. Softcover: 978 1 408 41264 0 (Camden Large Print)

Printed in the United States of America
1 2 3 4 5 6 7 12 11 10 09 08

Thank You to the best writing coach around,
Mike Sirota.
You've been along for the ride and never let me give up on myself.
This one is for you, Yoda!

Cheers,
Kid

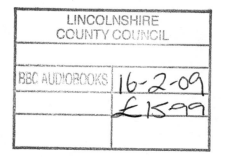

ONE

The man standing across from Michaela Bancroft gave her the creeps. Sterling Taber was handsome by most women's standards: He had that tall-and-dark thing going on with brooding brown — almost black — eyes, his cheekbones were something Michelangelo would have been proud to sculpt, and his longish black hair hung slightly in front of his eyes. He'd been voted Coachella Valley's most eligible bachelor and Michaela had heard the word *mysterious* used in regard to him. Her word was *repulsive.*

Sterling set the ropes on the glass-topped case, which inside held equestrian-related jewelry and various sets of spurs and silver belt buckles. Michaela and her friend Camden had recently delved into the venture of owning and running a tack store. Today was not only opening day, but Camden had convinced Michaela that an accompanying fashion show and charity polo match would make this an opening to remember, an *event* even.

"So, isn't it true that you rope?" Sterling asked.

"No. I rein." If he'd listened at all to her in the past few months, he would've known exactly what Michaela did. She'd spent plenty of time around Sterling as of late. He was one of the bigwigs on the polo team, and in less than an hour she'd be on the field playing against him in the charity event.

"That's right. Reiner. You look pretty good up on a polo pony. Good technique." He fiddled with the ropes. "I like watching the ropers. Real cowboys, those guys."

"Yes, they have great technique." Michaela narrowed her eyes, wishing he'd buy the ropes and get on with it.

"You plan on continuing with polo when this thing is over?"

She almost laughed at the thought. "No. It's been fun and hopefully we raise a lot of money for the autistic riding center, but I don't plan to continue."

He snapped his fingers and pointed at her. "Right. You run that place. That handicapped riding place."

She nodded. "It's for kids with autism."

"Handicapped" was not really how she saw the kids with whom she worked. They had special needs, sure, but they were capable, loving children, and just the way he'd said the word *handicapped,* as if it were a bad one, bothered her. Again, if he'd taken the time to listen when they'd had meetings regarding today's event he'd be on top of it, but she got the feeling that he knew all this already. If anything, he enjoyed this head game she felt he was playing with her. She sighed.

"You sure do look good up there on those ponies," he said again.

"Thanks. But I can't afford polo and it's pretty rough." Granted, Michaela had inherited a large sum of money and her uncle's ranch when he was killed, but much of it was tied up in the ranch, establishing her center for the kids, and now in the tack shop that Camden promised she'd run, since Michaela was already busy with plenty of commitments. "Speaking of polo, we should probably hurry up. You want to buy these?" She wasn't sure what Sterling needed a set of ropes for. He wasn't exactly the rugged cowboy type. She was trying hard to be nice, silently reminding herself that this was a business she and Camden were running and he was a paying customer.

Sterling leaned against the counter and folded his arms. A large diamond in a ring on his finger caught her eye. It was on his right hand, and for some reason it only annoyed Michaela even further that he was there. Show-off. He winked at her. "You bet. I've got some plans with these. You know that there are other things that ropes can be used for besides steers." He winked at her, held up the ropes, and set them back down.

She didn't comment. She picked the ropes up off the counter and scanned the price into the computer. Sterling handed her a credit card and she slid it through. It came back denied. She put it through again — still denied.

"Is there a problem?" he asked.

"Do you have another card?"

"Why?"

She felt her face flush. "This one's been denied."

"That couldn't be. Put it through again."

"I put it through twice already."

"You did it wrong then."

"No, I didn't."

"The card is fine. I own nine polo ponies; I think my card works. It's your machine."

From the back room, where the office and kitchen were located, Michaela heard raised voices. She recognized them immediately and knew she needed to put out a fire, because the two who were arguing were not exactly the most amicable of personalities. She tossed Sterling the ropes. "Here, take them. They're yours." She was done dealing with him.

She started out from behind the counter as a smug smile spread across his face. "See you on the field. I'm looking forward to it."

She walked quickly past him feeling like she'd just seen a cockroach crawl across the floor.

Michaela found the cause of the commotion in the kitchen.

"Oh no, no, no! I don't want spaghetti, Pepe. You can't do this to me!" Camden tossed her copper-colored tresses behind her shoulders and screamed at the rotund, older Italian man. He appeared to be matching her temper for temper, with his arms crossed and a look on his face that said he didn't care one iota about Camden's complaints. "You promised me that we would have veal scaloppine and chicken parmigiana. You said it wouldn't be a problem. I could kill you for this! Do you know how many people are coming to this event? I can't believe I already paid you up front!"

Michaela watched Camden's face contort

with rage. Next to Pepe Sorvino stood his twenty-year-old daughter, Lucia. It was hard not to notice that Lucia turned heads when she entered a room with her pale green eyes, long, wavy dark hair and voluptuous body — a young Sophia Loren in the making. She stood about Michaela's height at five feet six inches and she could see by the fire in the young woman's eyes that she was about to explode, along with her father.

"You didn't pay my father enough. Not for all these people."

"Wait a minute," Michaela interrupted. "What's the problem?" They would need to get it solved sooner rather than later. Sorvino's was catering the Sunday afternoon event, and people would be arriving shortly expecting hors d'oeuvres and champagne while they watched the polo match and a catered lunch during the fashion show.

"The problem is," Camden shouted, "these two are trying to rip us off."

Lucia took an aggressive step toward Camden. "Whatever. I don't think so. You're a cheap ass. That's the problem."

Camden pulled an arm back. Michaela grabbed it before she had a chance to swing.

"Did you see that?" Pepe said, his Italian accent growing thicker in line with his anger.

Michaela placed a hand on Camden's

shoulder. "Why don't you take a breather? Let me work this out."

Camden held up a finger, her face the color of her hair. Michaela shook her head at her best friend, and then nodded her toward the front door. Camden glared at Pepe and his daughter, but heeded Michaela's advice and left. "Go see Dwayne," Michaela suggested, knowing that her assistant trainer and Camden's fiancé was helping set up the tables for the lunch outside. If anyone could calm her down it would be him, with his Hawaiian philosophy and mellow attitude.

"I cannot work with her. She's crazy. You see how she yelling at me, and swearing at me, she saying she gonna kill me!" Pepe took his index finger and made the loopy sign around the side of his head. "Crazy!"

Michaela took a step back. "Listen, Pepe, I agree that my friend can be a bit temperamental —"

"A bit temperamental?" Lucia said. "She's a bitch. We're not doing this thing, and we're keeping your deposit money."

"Wait a minute," Michaela said.

"What's going on?" Mario Sorvino, Pepe's son, walked in with a boxful of tomatoes in his arms. "Oh great. My sister and father giving you a hard time?"

Michaela mustered a smile. Could it be there was a levelheaded individual amongst this clan? Mario set the box down on the counter and put an arm around Lucia, whom he towered over. He was definitely one of the tallest Italian guys Michaela had ever seen — long but muscular, his dark hair slicked back into a ponytail, and an apron covering his barrel chest. "Bella, run along and be a good kid. Leave Michaela alone. We'll work this out."

Lucia opened her mouth to say something, but Mario cut her off. "Go. There're tables to be set." She stood her ground a second longer. "Now!"

Pepe watched as his daughter skulked away. Mario looked at his dad and shook his head. "Papa, she doesn't need to be trying to run things. She's a stupid kid, and you give her too much freedom. Now, what's the issue here?"

Pepe frowned at his son but didn't retort. It appeared as if Mario Sorvino pulled the strings in the family.

"That other lady, that Camden, she's a hothead and she doesn't want to pay what they owe us." He pointed at Michaela. "We gonna make spaghetti and that's it."

"Yes, well, you see, we do have a contract." She directed her reply to Mario. "Your father agreed to make chicken parmigiana and veal along with spaghetti, so I'm confused as to why there's a mix-up."

He crossed his arms. "You not pay me enough, that's the mix-up."

"No, that's not true. We paid you exactly the amount you quoted us." He was beginning to try her patience. No wonder Camden had lost it on him. Everyone knew Pepe had a tendency to be cheap.

"It's not enough."

Mario held up a hand. "Okay, Dad, if there's a contract and you didn't estimate properly, it's not Michaela's problem."

She sighed. "No, it's not our fault if you miscalculated the price."

"Not gonna do it."

She looked at Pepe. "I don't have time for this. I have to be on a horse in an hour, swinging a mallet in front of a hundred or so people, who afterward expect to have a gourmet Italian meal while they watch a fashion show. I know that you would not want those *influential* people to walk away hungry, thinking poorly of Sorvino's, now would you? Those are well-to-do folks out there." She rubbed her finger and thumb together. "Cha-ching. *Capisce?* I'm certain that a man with your business sense and your talent will want to impress the people

15

and have them come back to dine at your divine restaurant." Yeah, so she was pouring it on, but she could tell she was getting to him as the downturn at the corners of his lips started to relax. If his son couldn't convince him, she'd give it her all. "I mean, after all, you do make the best veal I have ever had. Really." She leaned in closer. "And, I heard that a food critic from the *L.A. Times* may join us today. Oh, and I believe *my friend* Joe Pellegrino and some of his cousins might be around, too."

She knew it was not very nice of her to mention Joe. He'd been a friend of hers since childhood and he owned the local hardware store. It was rumored he had some unsavory *family* ties. She had made a conscious decision not to ask him about those rumors. Joe was a good friend, and he'd saved her butt on more than one occasion.

At the mention of Joe, Mario shot her a dirty look. "You'll get your veal and chicken. The Sorvinos don't go back on their word. Right, Papa?" He said it so that his father didn't have much choice but to agree; however, Michaela got the distinct feeling that tossing out Joe's name helped.

"Hmph. *Capisce.*"

Pepe stormed out of the kitchen and

Mario said, "Sorry about that. My family can be overbearing sometimes. I'll make sure they stay in line for the rest of the day." He took a tomato from the box he'd brought in.

"Thank you." She started to walk out.

"Michaela?"

She stopped. "Yes?"

"One thing about my family though, is that threats, subtle or not, don't usually sit well with us."

"What?"

"I don't miss much, in case you hadn't noticed." He smiled. "Mentioning Joe Pellegrino was unnecessary. I know why you did it, but I didn't like it."

"I'm sorry."

"We're even then. You'll get your food and you now understand how I operate." He picked up a sharp knife and sliced through the tomato. For some reason Michaela felt like he was taking his time cutting that damn tomato and it sent a chill down her spine. He eyed her. "I think you should be careful the names you toss around and threaten people with. It could get you into some trouble."

Michaela winced. "What is that supposed to mean?"

"Take it as you like," Mario said and

slammed the knife directly through the tomato, squirting seeds and liquid onto the wall. He looked at her and then at the mess he'd made. "Sorry about that. I'll get it cleaned up."

Michaela walked away shaken and unsettled, with the definite decision to never again hire the Sorvinos for a damn thing.

Two

Hopefully Michaela had really doused the fire in the kitchen. Between Sterling Taber, Camden, and the Sorvinos, she was already exhausted; now she had to go and get on a horse, run it full speed with balls flying this way and that, and pray to God she didn't somehow get clobbered with a mallet. Sure, she could ride. She'd ridden horses all her life; but the sport of polo was a whole 'nother ball game altogether — literally.

She took a few minutes to splash water on her face and pull her long blonde hair back into a low ponytail in order for her helmet to fit over it. She slathered on a good-sized dollop of sunscreen across her already sun-kissed, freckled face. She didn't have freckles like many redheads did, but enough years in the sun on horseback had dotted them across her nose, giving her a somewhat younger appearance than her thirty-three years. After a few more minutes of pulling on her boots and breeches and changing into the light yellow polo T-shirt her team had chosen to wear for the event, she figured she was as ready as she'd ever be to play the match.

She spotted Camden as she was leaving the shop, which wasn't exactly a tack shop in the true sense; rather, it was like a department store with equine-related equipment for sale. Her friend had gone over the top, like she did with everything in her life. The place had hardwood floors and faux cream and butter yellow paint on the walls, which gave it an almost marblelike look. The tack was organized by event, announcing the section with wooden engraved signs: hunter jumper gear here, dressage over there, western upstairs. Yes, there were two stories to the place — and the apparel section, which Camden definitely enjoyed best, was displayed in a large section in the back of the store. At first Michaela found it ostentatious, but she was proud of Camden for putting it together. Only five months earlier Camden could barely bring herself to go out to the horses' stalls. But since becoming engaged to Dwayne, she'd taken it upon herself to learn everything she could about horses and the lifestyle. To her credit, she was doing a good job.

Still, Michaela pondered on a regular basis — especially after the way her morning had gone — as to how in the world had she been roped into this idea with Camden. She should've known better, even in her buzzed state that night over margaritas, four months earlier. She really should have known better when she committed to the two-thousand-square-foot place that Camden had turned into the Saks Fifth Avenue of tack stores. Everything from jazzy jeans to highly polished leather saddles, stationery and art featuring the beautiful animals, to protective leg wraps for equines was available at Round the Bend, and lately Michaela found herself hoping that the opening day would be as lucrative as Camden promised. Having so much cash tied up in inventory was extremely uncomfortable for her.

She knew they'd need to turn a profit quickly, so she'd thrown herself full throttle into helping put the event together. But the kicker was this charity polo event. Camden had come up with the idea to get some of the team players to mix it up with some of the locals. But the prerequisite of being a local was that you did have to know how to ride; thus, Camden had hit Michaela and Dwayne up to be involved, and Michaela had turned around and hit up her childhood friend and veterinarian, Ethan Slater. Ethan did have an advantage: He'd played a bit of polo in his younger years. He was playing against her on that jerk Sterling's team.

Because she didn't want to make a complete fool of herself, Michaela had been taking lessons from the polo team's coach for the past three months. She'd played with the other members, like Sterling and her coach, Robert Nightingale, but she still felt like she didn't have a clue as to what in the world she was doing. What she did know after a few experiences with being hit by a mallet was that it was definitely a rough sport. At least she had convinced the polo team and the other riders that, instead of having a match of polo players against other types of riders, each team should be evenly mixed. She was afraid some of the macho cowboy types who had never before swung a mallet in their lives just might wind up seriously injuring someone in the knee, or worse, the face.

She located Camden and told her, "The Sorvino thing is handled. I've got to get over to the field. Are you coming?"

"Yes. Thank you. I owe you."

"Yes you do."

Michaela walked outside, breathing in the

faint smells of orange blossom and honey-suckle that hung on into the Indian summer, even in early November. This was the desert, and thankfully today it was tolerable — beautiful actually, reaching only eighty degrees. Rolling hills and peaks surrounded the valley, hued in golds and a rustic clay-like color she found stunning against the manicured kelly green of the polo fields.

Having been cooped up inside the tack shop for most of the morning, she hadn't witnessed the festivities' setup progression. A large white tent was in place in the parking lot for the fashion show. She peeked inside and took a step back. Everything was gorgeous. Camden would be pleased. There were about a hundred tables topped with cream-colored tablecloths, with vases of pink bud roses placed on them for the centerpieces, and a catwalk and stage lined with clusters of more roses, spread out in front of where the guests would be seated. A crew worked with the sound system. No doubt that this would be some event.

She saw Dwayne plugging in the stereo system. He glanced up and immediately smiled and waved at her. He wore his breeches and polo T-shirt. The number on the back of his shirt was 2. She sported 1. He was the other amateur rider on her team. Each team consisted of four members, two who had been at it for some time. She couldn't believe that Camden had been able to talk both her and Dwayne into playing the charity match. Like her, Dwayne trained reiners and working cow horses. It wasn't that either one of them had to learn much in the way of riding per se — both sports required agility and a good seat in the saddle. And both of them were fast. The difference all came down to that ball flying through the air, and the mallet with a bamboo shaft and hardwood head. If that sucker connected with any body part, it hurt like hell.

Michaela still found it pretty unbelievable that her assistant trainer and Camden were planning their wedding. They definitely fit the old adage that opposites attract.

Dwayne came over to her. "Got my girl calmed down a bit."

"I appreciate that." Michaela enjoyed hearing the melodic sound of his voice, accentuated by his native Hawaiian tongue.

"Sorvino sounds like he be difficult to deal with."

"Yes." She didn't add that although Pepe was difficult, his son kind of frightened her.

"You heading to the field?" he asked.

"Yes."

"Me, too, in a minute. I got to help one of the guys move a speaker first. I be right over."

"See you in a few." Even though the field was just across the street from the tack shop, it entailed a bit of a walk because the grounds were so large. She decided to drive her truck over. As soon as the match was finished, she'd have to get back in a hurry to help with the last-minute touches before everyone made their way over for the fashion show and lunch.

She pulled up, and parked under a row of trees that shadowed the unmarked dirt parking lot. She knew that she'd already find the ponies she was to ride saddled up and ready to go. Technically, the horses weren't really ponies; they were horses that averaged fifteen hands. A "hand" is a four-inch measurement used to determine the horse's height. Michaela had learned from her coach that when the British discovered polo in Persia, the average polo pony stood only about twelve hands high, which is the customary size for an actual pony today. Contrary to the thinking many nonequestrians share, ponies are not baby horses. The first height limit for polo ponies was set in 1876 at fourteen hands. In 1896 the limit was raised to fourteen hands two inches.

Limits were abolished in 1919. Polo ponies were not actually a breed but a crossbreed. Players looked for agility, speed, and intelligence. Many times the cross they'd found to fit their criteria was between a Thoroughbred and quarter horse. The Thoroughbred had the stamina and speed to last, and the quarter horse maintained the agility and intelligence.

But real-world players didn't own just one polo pony; they owned several because of the wear and tear on the animals. Michaela would ride three different ponies today, but she knew that Sterling would ride six and she was pretty sure that one of the pros on her team, Zach Holden, would also use six horses. They would be exchanged between chukkers, which lasted seven minutes. There were always six chukkers to a game, with three-minute breaks between chukkers and a halftime where spectators would rush out to stomp down the divots. The rules stated that no horse could be played for more than two chukkers, thus Michaela's three school horses.

She got out of her truck and looked around the parking area — Sterling's Porsche was there as well as a few other cars. It didn't look like she was either the first or last one to arrive. She grabbed her gloves and mallet from the backseat. She'd pick up one of the school's helmets from the office. The helmet she used at her place was different than what they used in polo. It reminded her of one of those safari hats that elephant tamers sometimes wear. She turned around to head over to the stable and heard a car door slam, then another. An engine roared and the next thing she knew a car raced past her and down the gravel road. What in the world? She squinted to get a better look. She could've sworn the BMW that sped down the road belonged to the polo coach's wife, Paige Nightingale. Then she saw Sterling climbing out of his Porsche. Had Paige been in the car with him? She didn't see anyone else around. It struck her as odd. What reason would Paige have to be in Sterling's car? And what were the slamming doors and screeching tires all about? She wondered where Robert was.

She certainly didn't want Sterling to spot her. He was the last person she wanted to talk to, so she picked up her pace and headed to where the horses awaited. Who really cared what that had been about? She'd met her stress quota for the day.

The three horses were lined up at a long hitching post. Her favorite was a bay mare named Rebel. The mare had the kind of eyes that Michaela liked on a horse: intelligent.

"Hey, Rebel," she said, patting her on her rump. "You look good." The horse glanced at her with a baleful eye, and then turned back around. "Uh-huh. That's what I like about you. Not one for small talk." Michaela laughed. She knew the horse had no clue what she was saying — for the mare it was probably like a Charlie Brown cartoon where the kids listen to the teacher and all they hear is "Waa, waa, waa, waa, waa, waa." But she did know that horses liked to be talked to. They were social animals, and the sound of their rider's voice could put them at ease, or wind them tight — depending on the person and the tone.

She gave the other two horses a pat and a few words of encouragement — again knowing they could care less what she had to say. She headed over to the office on the grounds — a decent-sized trailer — needing to get her helmet.

Robert sat inside the trailer on a tattered, blue velour couch, pulling on his boots. "Oh hey, Michaela. You ready for this?" He pulled up his other boot and sat back, running his hand through his light brown hair, which appeared to be thinning on top. Michaela guessed him to be somewhere in his mid to late fifties. He was known for his intensity on and off the polo field but he'd been nothing but nice to her, and she found the rumors of his brusqueness to be just that so far. She'd had a soft spot for Robert and Paige ever since she'd learned that their only son had been killed in a car accident a few years earlier. She couldn't imagine ever enduring that type of pain. Although she tried not to let it bother her, she still wondered why Paige had left the grounds in such a hurry, either trying to get away or leaving Sterling Taber behind. Again, Michaela reminded herself that it was none of her business.

"Uh, no. I doubt I'll ever be ready." She laughed.

"You're a good rider. You'll be fine up there. Don't let any of my guys intimidate you. Plus, you got a couple of your buddies out there, too."

"Yeah, but I'm the only woman."

He waved a hand at her. "You'll be fine. Got your helmet?"

She picked through the bin where the school helmets were kept, and held one up after making sure it was the right size. "I do now."

They walked out of the trailer together and back over to the horses. Dwayne had shown up and she saw Ethan pulling into the parking area.

She wondered if his wife, Summer, was with him and breathed an audible sigh when she didn't see anyone else get out of his truck. Michaela loved Ethan. They'd known each other since they were little kids. Camden insisted Michaela was *in* love with him, but that wasn't true. It *couldn't* be true, because Ethan was a married man. Married against Michaela's wishes, but that was only because she knew Summer was not right for him. The woman had strung him along, left him at the altar where Michaela picked up the pieces left behind, and then had the audacity to strut back into his life, get pregnant, and manipulate him into marriage. Now Ethan was the proud daddy of little Joshua, who was also her godson, most certainly against Summer's wishes.

"Hey, Mick, Robert," he said.

Robert shook his hand. "Good to see you, Ethan. I'm going to make sure everything is a go. Looks like all the riders are here. I don't see one of the umpires, though."

"Sure. Do your thing. This is gonna be fun," Ethan said, "even for an old guy."

"Old guy? Please." Ethan was only a couple of years older than her. Michaela had noticed him aging a little in the last year, but he was far from old — a wrinkle

30

here and there above the forehead, a few around his eyes. She liked it. It added character. Not that he needed any. Ethan had plenty of character with a slightly crooked nose from a pony kicking him in the face, but he was still a good-looking man.

He looked at her with his dark green eyes. "I don't know about going against you, Bancroft. You might kick my ass."

"Sure." She laughed. "Who else is on your team? I know Sterling Taber is, and Tommy Liggett is the other pro rider, right?"

Ethan nodded. "Yeah, and I got a buddy of mine . . . do you know Lance Watkins?"

"Sure. He trains show jumpers. Wow. He's going to ride today?"

"He is."

"Impressive."

"What do you say we get on the field? Looks like the grooms have everyone ready," Ethan said.

"Ah, the luxury of playing polo."

"Yeah, really. Good luck."

They both laughed, knowing that because of the wealth surrounding the sport, it was a rarity that any of the players ever actually groomed and tacked up their horses. Today, even the locals like herself and Ethan were being treated like kings — and supposedly polo had been dubbed the sport of kings.

Michaela mounted Rebel and they headed onto the polo field, which was three hundred yards long and one hundred and fifty yards wide. She would be playing the most conservative position as the number four, or back, player. Her job was to play defense and guard the goal to keep the opposition from scoring. Dwayne was playing first position, which was offensive, along with the number two position, played by a longtime pro in the sport and owner of the polo field, Ed Mitchell. He would have to play aggressively, his goal to break up the defensive plays of the opposition. In third position was Zach Holden, a young guy and good friend of Sterling's, but totally opposite from the pompous ass. Michaela liked Zach. He was congenial and generous — always giving her tips and advice. Zach would be the pivot man, kind of like the quarterback on a football team. He would be making the long-ball shots and be the key playmaker for the team. Michaela admired his playing ability. He was also the player who would most likely be hitting any penalty shots.

The two umpires and a referee, all on horseback, were ready to go, along with the scorekeeper and time recorder. Michaela's heart pounded as a wave of nervousness coursed through her. She looked out at the crowd, all in their designer outfits, champagne flutes in hand, and couldn't help but question her sanity.

Then, one of the umpires tossed the ball into the center, and everything began to move. Michaela forgot the crowd, the morning, what was on tap next, and just played the game. Once the ball was in play it traveled at speeds upward of one hundred miles per hour. The ball came flying toward her as she guarded the goal. Sterling had hurled it toward her, and when she stopped the ball with a forehand by swinging her mallet forward on Rebel's near side, she almost whooped out loud. The pounding of hooves drummed in her ears as clumps of dirt kicked up around them. She had just sent the ball back into play when it came back down the line, and before she could blink Sterling was next to her, his mallet hooked with hers. She got it undone in time to save another goal from being scored, this time on a shot from Ethan.

The ball had once again turned around and Dwayne had it down the line. Michaela squealed when Dwayne hit it past Ethan's pal Lance Watkins. She could have sworn she heard Sterling down at the other end scream an obscenity at Lance. How immature.

Before Michaela knew it, they were into the last chukker and she had changed to her third horse, a white speckled gelding named Snowman. Her team was ahead by two points and Zach yelled to her, "Nice work out there!"

"Thanks." She wiped the sweat off her brow and one of the grooms gave her a leg up onto Snowman. They were back in play, horses going at a full canter, well-toned athletes moving with grace and speed, carrying riders who depended on the sound mind of their animals to keep them in the game. The ball flew between thin, fine legs — riders bumping shoulder to shoulder, mallets hooking and clanking around one another, red nostrils of the horses flaring, and the smell of sweat and dirt and grass hanging in the air. Shouts from the crowd and curses from the riders who missed a goal contrasted the whoops of joy when one team scored. Michaela wasn't sure she even breathed the rest of the game, it was so intense. And in the end, her team won by one point after Lance Watkins fouled and Zach was allowed to take the penalty shot, zipping it past Dwayne.

The losing team congratulated Michaela

and the others. Sterling rode up next to her on a beautiful black gelding. He had to have been from Argentina, where many of the best polo ponies came from. "Looks like lady luck was the key, huh? Or maybe the guys were just taking it easy on you. Granted, Watkins plays like a girl, but that's what I'd expect from some guy who trains jumpers."

Sterling didn't realize that Lance Watkins and Ethan were directly behind him and within earshot. Michaela didn't reply; she simply turned her horse, walking him over to Ethan and Lance. "That guy is an asshole," Lance said. "I'd like to bump him off his high horse. I'm sorry, Michaela. I don't mean to be rude. Nice to see you. Great playing out there."

"Thanks." She didn't know Lance well, but she couldn't blame him for being irritated with Sterling. "You guys played hard, too. I don't know about this polo thing."

"It's not for me," Lance replied. "I need to take off. See you two later."

"You going to the fashion show and lunch?" Michaela asked Ethan.

"I wish I could, but Summer has something she needs to do and I need to get home and be with the baby."

"Oh." She tried hard to keep the disappointment out of her voice.

They talked for a few more minutes, until Dwayne rode past and reminded her that they didn't have much time to get back over to the shop for the rest of the day's festivities. She said good-bye to Ethan and dismounted her horse, giving him a pat and handing him over to one of the grooms.

Zach Holden was over by the stalls with one of his horses. "Good game out there," he said.

"Thanks. You did a good job yourself." He couldn't have been over twenty-five and was from money, like most of the people on the pro team.

"She did do well." Sterling Taber approached them. "Lucky for her we had that pain-in-the-ass show jumper on our team." He laughed. "That guy is clueless. He wasn't on his game at all."

Michaela tried to maintain a smile, but Sterling was such a jerk. Lance Watkins had an excellent reputation in the show ring, and although she'd only met him a few times, he was always pleasant and, as Ethan had indicated, he was a good guy. She chose not to respond to Sterling's comment. Ignoring him was taking the higher road, by far.

Funny thing: Sterling did seem to have

enough of something — be it charisma, charm, she didn't know exactly what — and whatever it was, he always appeared to have plenty of friends, like Zach.

Sterling swung his mallet back and forth. "Well, like I said, dumb luck or lady." He winked at her. "Just kidding. You did well out there. I gotta run." He pointed at her. "See you at the show. Hey, anyone seen Tommy? He was supposed to catch a ride with me over to the shop."

"Yeah, but I think he already went on ahead."

"Okay. Thanks."

There was another friend that Sterling had in his entourage — Tommy Liggett, who again, by all accounts, was a decent guy. And he hadn't been born with a silver spoon in his mouth like the rest of the crew.

Sterling waved at Michaela and Zach, as if they wouldn't see each other in only a manner of minutes. They watched as he slipped into his Porsche Carerra and zipped it around the gravel road that led to the tack shop. She noticed Zach staring after Sterling, a scowl on his face, and if she wasn't mistaken, she could've sworn she recognized hatred in his eyes.

THREE

"Aren't you in the show, too?" Michaela asked Zach.

His expression softened. "Uh, yeah. I just wanted to make sure the groom put this new liniment on my horse's right front suspensory. He's sore and favoring that side."

"I think Ethan already left. Do you need to call him back?"

"No. I don't think so, but I'll come back later and check. I should probably hurry, too. I'm sure Camden is beside herself. We shouldn't be standing around chitchatting."

She nodded. "Yep, you better go. The makeup lady should be ready for you guys."

"Makeup?" Zach said.

"Camden's idea."

"Okay, I'm gone. Sure you don't need a ride?"

"No. I'm good. I've got my truck. I'm going to drop off the school helmet to Robert and I'll be right over."

She headed to Robert's office. The door was propped open a crack, but she still went the customary route and announced herself before entering. When she didn't get a reply she figured that she'd go in and drop the helmet in the bin. The bin stood near Robert's desk, which was a mess. Piles of equine magazines and books filled one side of the desk, and papers were stacked high. She knew that Paige helped him with the business, but it looked as if they were getting behind. God, how she could relate.

Odd; a sharp letter opener was stuck right down the center of the papers. Why would Robert would do that? Maybe it was to keep the stack from blowing away as people walked in and out.

She put her helmet in the bin. Before leaving, she noticed that the paper on top on the stack was an invoice to Sterling. He owed quite a bit in board and training. In fact, it looked as if he were several months past due. But it wasn't the numbers that astounded her so much; it was the fact that across the statement someone had written *SCREW YOU!*

"Hey Michaela, what's up?"

Michaela spun around as Robert walked in. "Uh, I was just returning my helmet.

You going to the fashion show? I know Paige was really excited about it."

Robert waved a hand as he sat on the sofa. "Nah. I think I've had my fill of charity for a while. Fashion shows are not my thing."

Michaela nodded, not sure what to say, still processing the scrawled message on Sterling's invoice.

"What about you? Don't you have to get over there?"

"I sure do." She checked her watch. "Definitely." She reached for the doorknob and turned to tell Robert good-bye.

"Hey, before you go, can I ask you something?" the older man said.

Uh-oh. Had he seen her peering at his paperwork? Before she could reply, her cell phone rang. She glanced at Robert.

"No problem. Answer it," he told her.

Saved by the bell. She flipped open the phone; Camden was in hysterics. "Where are you? I need you now. We've got a huge problem!"

Michaela started to ask her what it was, but Camden hung up. "I'm sorry," she said. "I've got to go. There seems to be a problem at the store."

"Go. It's no big thing."

She walked out of the trailer. Another problem; great.

FOUR

Camden's face was flushed the color of magenta; her arms flailed in obvious frustration as Michaela entered the back room of the tack shop. A handful of models clustered around, all eyes on a petite, dark-haired, gothic-looking young woman, her lips painted a purplish black. Michaela had an odd thought: dark fairy from beyond, or a woman trying hard to resurrect 1985.

Camden grabbed Michaela by the arm and pulled her aside. "That's Erin Hornersberg."

"Okay."

"She's our makeup artist and she's the best, but she is refusing to do the models' makeup. She's packing up her stuff. Do something!"

This was the crisis? Oh boy. "Camden, hold on. First of all, I am not a mediator to every little problem that springs up."

"Yes, but you have a way with people.

Now go over there and convince her to stay."

Michaela sighed. "What, is she claiming that we didn't pay her enough, too?"

"No. It's about Sterling."

"Sterling?"

Camden nodded. "She won't say what, but within two minutes of him sitting down, she started screaming for him to get the you-know-what off her chair and the hell out of here. When he refused, she told me to forget it. She's saying that she's not about to do *anyone's* makeup for the show."

It was only makeup. Couldn't the models do their own? "Just ask Sterling to leave. I need a few minutes to shower and set my things in the office." She held up her mallet and purse. With so many people milling around she hadn't wanted to leave the polo mallet in her truck, and definitely not her purse. Although she had no intention to play the sport any longer, the mallet had been a gift from Ed Mitchell, and she wanted it as a keepsake.

"Are you kidding? You don't have time. You have to talk to her now! Sterling was voted the most eligible bachelor from Indio to Palm Springs and probably all the way to L.A. Most of the women here today came to see him. I can't do that."

"Right. Do you know what he might have

said or done?"

Camden shrugged. "I don't have a clue. I wanted to put on the best show from here to flipping Timbuktu, and dammit, it's all falling apart."

Michaela turned back to see Erin locking up her makeup box. She walked over to the woman, still holding her mallet and purse, both starting to weigh on her. How was it that purses got so heavy? It needed a good dumping-out, and the mallet wasn't exactly light to begin with.

"Hi, I'm Michaela Bancroft, part owner of the store, and I'm sorry to hear there's a problem. Can we talk about it?"

"Nothing to talk about. He's an ass. I want him out of here." She pointed at Sterling, who stood drinking a Coke, seeming not to care at all about the drama swirling around him.

Michaela leaned in closer to her. "I agree with you. I think he's a pompous piece of you-know-what. Look, can you just come outside with me? We'll see if we can work something out."

Erin shook her head. "Nothing to work out. I want him out of here. It's simple."

"Okay, look, what if I make sure he's not anywhere near you and you won't have to do his makeup or even see him?"

43

Erin eyeballed her. "And you'll make it worth my while? You know, it's a pain in the ass to have to take all my stuff out and now I had to put it back, and then I'll have to take it back out again, and —"

Michaela held up a hand. "I'll see what I can do." Great. Erin and Pepe Sorvino must have gone to some sort of lecture on how to screw a client prior to an event. If her instincts were right, she'd be paying out more money than they'd planned to the makeup artist. But she was still curious about what Sterling had done to get under the woman's skin.

"I *could* use a smoke."

"I'm sure you could."

And right about now, she could use one of those shoulder massages Jude Davis was famous for. She wished he wasn't away for the week on a Caribbean cruise with his daughter, Katie. Michaela and the detective had been dating for a few months. It wasn't anything serious, not yet anyway, but she realized that she missed him. His calm demeanor in stressful situations like this would have been exactly what the doctor ordered. Needless to say, there wasn't much more she could do than play diplomat. Tonight though, when this thing was over — one long hot bath, oh yes.

She followed Erin to the door. Camden looked at her wide-eyed and tapped her wrist several times, indicating that the clock was ticking. "I'm doing what I can," Michaela muttered. Never again would she agree to something of this magnitude — for charity or not. She'd rather get smacked by a polo mallet than deal with this.

Erin pulled out a pack of Marlboros from the black apron holding a variety of makeup brushes in the front pockets. She lit one and took a deep drag. Michaela knew time was of the essence, but she also understood she was likely dealing with someone who, when push came to shove, could shove back pretty hard.

Michaela tried to subtly wave away the toxic plume. "So, Sterling was being an ass to you." She presented it more as a statement rather than a question, and decided to keep going along those lines. "He's a real jerk. You should see that guy up on a horse playing polo. He whoops and hollers when he scores, as if he's made the winning touchdown in the Super Bowl."

"Yeah, I bet, like his shit don't stink." Erin snorted.

"Exactly. He gets under my skin. Who would have ever voted him most eligible bachelor?"

"Eligible? Isn't he hooking up with that Juliet chick? The one whose folks own the club?"

"It looks like they're dating to me. But you know, I haven't seen them hanging out this past week at the field. They're usually all over each other. So, I don't really know. I'm not interested in his love life." She had to wonder though, if Juliet and Sterling were together, then how *did* Juliet feel about her boyfriend being considered an "eligible bachelor"? Juliet Mitchell was Ed's daughter. Michaela knew Juliet from the field because she also rode. She seemed like a nice girl. But it was a wonder how she tolerated Sterling. Juliet was from a privileged family and Michaela doubted she would tolerate playing second fiddle.

"Yeah, probably her and about a hundred other stupid chicks are dating him."

Michaela nodded as she let Erin speak. She was pretty sure she'd won the woman's trust.

Erin continued: "I've seen him around, you know. At clubs. He works a room. Got all the girls after him. He *thinks* he does, anyway."

Michaela hoped this was going somewhere. "I'm sure he does. You've seen him out and around then?"

"Uh-huh. And he's seen me. He made a point of letting me know it, in there." She pointed to the tack shop.

"I take it he said something rude to you?"

Erin nodded. "About me and my girl-friend."

"Girlfriend?" Michaela tried not to allow shock to creep into her voice. Did Erin mean girlfriend or *girlfriend?* Either way, it didn't really matter. She didn't know why, if Erin had a *girlfriend,* this would surprise her, but in a way it did. She would have pictured this woman having a tattooed, biker-type boyfriend. So much for stereotypes.

"Yes. Sheila. She's my girl." She arched her brows. "I'm gay."

"Oh."

"Don't tell me you're one of those red-neck homophobes, too."

"No. Not at all. I just didn't expect that."

"Why not?"

Oh great, now *she* was making waves with the makeup artist. "I don't know. But it doesn't bother me. Look, I don't know what Sterling said to you. I can only imagine it was something nasty. But right now, we're running short on time. I promise that you won't have to deal with him again. The jerk can do his own makeup as far as I'm concerned."

Erin tossed down her cigarette, stubbing it out with her boot heel. "Double my pay."

"Double?"

Erin nodded. "I'm the best and, right now, the only one you have here. You're in a freaking bind, lady, and you know how life can be unfair sometimes. I think your friend Camden in there might have a nervous breakdown if I walk."

She had one thing right: Michaela *was* in a bind. She still felt the models could apply goop to their own faces, but she thought about Camden and how much this meant to her. "Fine. I'll double your pay."

"Give it to me now."

Michaela sighed. "Tell you what. I'll go back in and ask Sterling to dress elsewhere. You can get started on the next model and I'll write you a check."

"Fine. Here's my card. My last name can be hard to spell." She took a card out of her apron. "Oh sorry, there's an address on the back, but I don't need it anymore. Anyway, that's my last card."

"No problem." Michaela took the card and marched back in to confront Camden. "You need to get Sterling Taber out of here *now.*"

"No! What? Why? I already told you that he's the star of the show."

48

"Here's the deal, sis. Your star said some disrespectful things to the makeup girl and she's ready to walk. I've convinced her to stay as long as she doesn't have to deal with him, along with some extra cash on top of it."

"Why, that little bitch," Camden replied.

"That little bitch is extremely offended by Mr. Taber. And, as you mentioned, she is the best and you seem to think we need her."

Camden looked mortified. "What am I supposed to do?"

"I don't know. You and Sterling seemed to be buddy-buddy. I think you can figure it out."

"What does that mean?"

"Nothing, really. I just noticed during the course of putting this thing together over the last few months that you got along well with him."

"Everyone gets along with him. He's a great guy."

"Whatever you say." From what she had seen, not everyone got along well with Sterling at all.

"Michaela, are you implying something? I'm engaged, for goodness' sakes. I would never cheat on Dwayne."

"I know that. You better not anyway. Why

even say something like that?"

Camden's face softened. "I don't know why I'd say something like that. Of course you know that I would never cheat on Dwayne."

"Didn't cross my mind. For one thing, Sterling is just a kid, what twenty-five or something?"

"Twenty-six."

"Right. Get him out of here. I've done what I can to make this go smoothly. It's time for you to use your finesse."

Camden shrugged. "Okay, I'll get him out of here. Now, can you tell Erin to get in here and get the other models finished?"

Michaela watched as Camden approached Sterling, who was talking to Tommy Liggett. After a few minutes, Camden had succeeded in luring Sterling out of the area and Erin came back in to finish her work.

Michaela needed to grab a quick shower and wash the perfume à la equine off her. There wasn't much time, but it was necessary.

On her way to check on the silent auction items, she spotted Robert Nightingale and his wife, glass of wine in hand, engaged in conversation with Ed Mitchell. Robert must have changed his mind about coming to the event. Interesting. She'd be sure to avoid him. She didn't want to answer any questions about what she'd spotted on his desk. Facts were, it really was none of her business. Though she did wonder if it had been Sterling who'd written the unpleasantry across the invoice, or maybe Robert had written it in anger because the bill hadn't been paid.

She wound her way through the crowd and entered the back room of the tack shop. The storage area was a mess with discarded clothing, purses, and backpacks scattered all about, the remains of the flurry to dress the models and get them ready to strut their stuff up on the catwalk.

Michaela headed to the private office area that she shared with Camden and set her purse and mallet down. She'd already hung up the outfit she wanted to change into when she'd gotten there this morning — a teal-colored sheath dress, simple and casual but also classy. She brought it with her to the bathroom off to the side of the office and kitchen, and took a quick shower. Getting out, she thought she heard a door shut. There was no door to the kitchen, only swinging panels. The only doors were either the back one or the office. Must've been Camden grabbing something.

She dressed and headed back to the office

to find her hairbrush and some lip gloss. Placing the key in the lock, she discovered that the door was already open. Hadn't she locked it when she showered? She didn't want anyone going in there, especially with her things around. Maybe in her haste she'd forgotten.

Michaela opened the door. It took a second to sink in that what she was looking at wasn't just a pile of discarded clothes . . . oh, she was looking at a pile of clothes, all right, but not just clothes — clothes with someone in them. Blue jeans, white T-shirt with red sprayed across it. Red. No. Blood! Everywhere. Michaela looked down again. A polo mallet. Next to the clothes. *Her* polo mallet. Oh no. Next to a body. Sterling Taber's body. And the back of his head all bashed in.

FIVE

Michaela knew that Sterling was dead and all she wanted to do was get the hell out of there, but her conscience made her check just to be sure. She bent down next to his body. He was not breathing. His eyes were rolled back, showing the whites. She scrambled backward, ran out of the office and into the bathroom, where she threw up several times.

She faced the bathroom mirror, blinked her eyes repeatedly. Was this really happening? Then it hit her: What if whoever did this was still around? What if they were hiding in her office or just outside the bathroom door? She had to find Camden. No, she had to call the police. No, she had to find Camden. Hell. Security guards. Yes. They'd hired a couple to man the tent outside. Start there. No. The police. *Shit!* She stepped out of the bathroom hesitantly, then ran to the front of the store. They'd locked the doors when they'd started serving lunch, except the back door for the waitstaff going in and out of the kitchen. Dammit, why didn't she just go out the back door? Her mind raced with confusion. She turned and headed to the back of the store again, everything she passed a blur of colors.

"Michaela?"

Mario Sorvino was walking through the back door as she reached it. He looked at her oddly. "Is everything okay? You look a little pale."

"We have to call the police. St-Sterling Taber has been . . . murdered in my office."

"What? No." He shook his head.

She nodded.

"Stay here," he said. He headed toward her office.

Michaela suddenly realized that she wasn't too comfortable staying put. Mario Sorvino hadn't exactly proven to her that he was a good guy with his earlier remarks. No way. She was out of there.

Once out through the back door, she stopped the closest guest walking by. "Do you have a cell phone? I need to use it. It's an emergency."

The woman, dumbfounded, handed her a phone and Michaela dialed 911. "There's been a murder," she said, her voice shaking.

The operator took down the details and told her that help would be on the way. She then went to find Camden, who was marching models onto the stage.

"Michaela! Have you seen Sterling? Jeez, I hope that little stunt the makeup girl pulled didn't chase him away. It's not good. See all those women out there? They are here to see *him*," she wailed.

In a sort of fast-forward daze, Michaela was aware that Camden had pulled back the drapes inside the tent where the show was going on and pointed to the crowd, but she couldn't see anything. It was all a blur. Oh God, she thought she might be sick again.

Camden turned to Juliet, who had just tripped over one of the acoustic cords, and said, "Hurry up, get out there. You need to be up there." Then she asked, "Have you seen Sterling?"

Juliet shook her head. "No, I haven't. I don't know if I can do this. I've never modeled before! There's a ton of people out there. I didn't know I'd get so nervous!"

Zach Holden was just coming off the stage. He looked at Juliet and asked her if she was okay. She nodded. "I'm fine."

Camden reached across a table for a large tequila bottle. She handed it to the girl.

"Take a swig of this and get your ass out there. You'll do great."

Juliet shook her head. "No thanks. I'm good."

"Great. Never figured that one for nerves. I mean, hell, she comes from what, one of the wealthiest families around. She must have done this kind of stuff before. And I thought for sure that she and Sterling were doing a little . . . you know . . . in the back room, because I couldn't find her for a few minutes either. I've noticed those two flirting quite a bit."

Michaela listened to this as if she were outside of her body, as if time had stood still, and she wondered if this was what being in shock felt like. Then suddenly, as if someone slapped her, she blurted, "Sterling is dead!"

Camden shook her head. "What? What did you just say?"

She took a deep breath and felt emotion rise in her throat. Sure, she hadn't cared for Sterling Taber, but he'd been brutally murdered and no one, not even a jerk-hole deserved that. "Listen to me." She strained to get the words out. "The police are on the way. Sterling was murdered in our office. I found him."

Camden's face drained of color. She

shook her head. "No. Oh no. No, no, no. That can't be. What? What the hell?" She nearly knocked Michaela down as she raced toward the tack store and into the back office. Michaela tried to catch up to her when she realized where Camden was headed and the horror she was about to see.

Mario, walking down the hallway, tried to block her, but as big as he was, Camden dodged past him. "Camden, please stop. It's awful! Don't go in there!" he yelled.

Camden was at the door, opening it, when Michaela grabbed her arm. Too late. The door had swung open. Camden's scream echoed throughout the tack store. She ran to where Sterling lay, kneeling down by him. Her eyes brimming with tears, she stroked Sterling's hair. "Oh, no, no, baby, I am so sorry."

Baby? Michaela placed a hand on her friend's shoulder. "I'm sorry. I know that you were friends. I wish you hadn't come in here."

Camden looked up at her, tears streaming down her face. "I've known him for years and we . . . we've been more than friends."

Six

Before a stunned Michaela had the chance to further question her distraught friend, the police arrived and asked them to wait outside the office. By this time word had gotten around, and Dwayne was now at Camden's side. Mario also lingered. He'd called the police from his cell phone just before Michaela did. His appearance, so soon after finding Sterling, bothered her.

Camden rested her head against Dwayne's chest. Michaela's stomach churned with confusion, shock, and horror, not only from finding Sterling's body, but from Camden's comment about her and Sterling being more than friends.

The police separated everyone, and no one was allowed off the grounds until each person had been questioned and their contact information recorded. The process lasted well into the evening, with many people becoming agitated over being detained for so long.

A forensics team was brought in, and Michaela was questioned a number of times in a grueling manner by a detective who was nothing short of a hard-ass. She recognized him from dropping off lunch to Jude at the station one day. The detective, Mike Peters, acted as if he'd never seen Michaela before, until he'd finally closed his notepad and looked at her with his dark brown eyes. The look in them was not friendly, and Michaela felt uneasy. He ran a hand through his thinning silver head of hair. Cracking a grim smile, he shook his head. "Your boy won't be too happy about this, Ms. Bancroft."

"Excuse me? What? My *boy?*"

"Yeah. Davis. He isn't going to be too happy that you found yourself a dead man. Your reputation precedes you."

"If you're finished with me, I'd like to lock up when the forensics team is done. From the looks of it, your crew has pretty much allowed everyone else to go home."

"I'm done with you for now." He shook his head. "But don't it seem odd to you that you somehow stumble across dead carcasses a little too often for comfort?"

Michaela didn't reply. His insinuation was unsettling and insulting. "Again, if we're finished here, I'd like to start locking up."

He held the palms of his hands toward her. "Sure. For now."

She clenched her jaw. As the police left, she started to lock up. Camden and Dwayne had already gone home. Michaela really needed to talk with her friend.

A handful of police were wrapping things up outside as she headed toward her truck and unlocked the door. A crescent moon hung in the sky, surrounded by bright stars lighting up what on any other occasion would be a peaceful night. A cool breeze had dropped the evening temperature along the desert floor and Michaela wished she'd grabbed her poncho from the shop. Then she realized she'd left it in the office. Well, it wasn't really a poncho, the old-school kind with the drawstring around the neck. It had been a gift from Camden; it was cashmere and so soft, a pretty rose kind of beige color, and every time Michaela put it on, she felt good. But in all of the craziness, she'd left it in her office and she wasn't about to go back in there. Not right now anyway. She just wanted to get home. Then, just feet away from her maroon-colored truck, she heard someone approaching.

"Excuse me, Ms. Bancroft?"

She swung around to see a sullen Erin Hornersberg, makeup box in hand. Michaela brought her hands up to her neck in surprise. "You scared me!"

"Sorry. Hey look, I left some of my brushes in the back room where I was doing the makeup. Can you set them aside for me and I'll pick them up later?"

"I can just unlock the door and we can get them now."

"No. That's okay. I just want to get home and I have extras at the shop. I'll call you tomorrow and see when it's good to swing by."

Her attitude had softened in light of the events. "It's horrible about Sterling."

"Whatever. Good riddance," Erin said dismissively.

Michaela took a step back. "I know he wasn't the greatest guy in the world, but don't you have any feelings? I mean, at least show some respect. The man was brutally murdered."

"Like I said, whatever. I'll be by for my things."

Michaela watched Erin drive off. So much for a softer attitude.

Michaela made it home and ran a tub of water for a hot bath. When she'd pulled in, the lights had been off in the guest house where Dwayne and Camden lived, and she decided that their conversation would have to wait until the morning. She contemplated walking out to the barn to say good night to her horses but found herself too tired. Dwayne would've fed them. Poor kids, though; they had to have been starving even by the time he got there, since the police had kept everyone for so long.

She lay in bed going back over the day, from Sterling acting so slimy when buying the ropes, which he really didn't buy since his card hadn't cleared; her confrontation with the Sorvinos; to Paige tearing off the grounds and then showing up later at the fashion show all smiles, with Robert on her arm. There was the polo match, where Sterling was more than rude to Lance Watkins, and also toward her. And what was the deal with the way Zach had looked at Sterling when the game was over? Had they had a falling-out? Then there was the invoice with the not-so-pleasant note written across it in Robert's office. Finally, the discovery of Sterling's body. Who had done that to him? And now Michaela could not help the guilt feelings welling inside her over her distaste for Sterling. Maybe she hadn't given him a chance. Was she simply too judgmental? What was it about Sterling that she hadn't liked? For one, it was his poor sense of sportsmanship. In the sport of reining and working cow horses, other riders were typically supportive of one another. Sure, men dominated the field and they had their own feelings about a woman doing well at the sport, but most of them had been taught respect for women while growing up. They typically kept their feelings either to themselves or within their tight circle of friends. Michaela had been able to gain a lot of respect from the men in her sport. But Sterling came across as a chauvinist with superiority issues.

She couldn't think on it any longer. Her head hurt from it all. She willed herself to sleep after a short prayer to help rid her of the day's trauma.

She didn't know what time it was when the banging woke her up. At first, she thought she was dreaming. But the banging grew louder, and then the doorbell rang. Michaela rolled out of bed, noticing that it was just past four in the morning. What in the world?

She pulled on her robe and tromped down the stairs. She really did need to get a new dog. She'd lost her old lab, Cocoa, a while back, and it was time to look into getting a puppy. She didn't like opening the door to someone at this hour, but because it was so late, she knew that whoever and for whatever reason they were on the other side of her door, it could not be good.

She peered through the peephole. Her stomach sank. Detective Peters stood there. What did he want? "Ms. Bancroft, open the door, please."

Michaela swung the door open. A uniformed cop, who Michaela recognized as Officer Garcia, stood behind him. "How can I help you? You do realize it is the middle of the night?"

"Turn around, Ms. Bancroft," he said, reaching behind him for his handcuffs. "You are under arrest for the murder of Sterling Taber."

SEVEN

"Wait, *wait!*"

Garcia started reading Michaela her rights. Peters abruptly turned her around. "What are you doing? What is this about? I didn't kill Sterling Taber! You can't come into my home and do this."

"I'm afraid we can," Peters said.

"Can you tell me on what grounds you're arresting me?"

"Your polo mallet."

"My mallet? We went over this before."

"Yes we did, but your fingerprints are the only ones on it. And you *discovered* the victim and you had motive."

She shook her head. "Motive? What motive? I had no reason to murder Sterling Taber. This is insane! What motive are you talking about? And my fingerprints on my mallet — of course they were on my mallet. It's *my* mallet, for God's sakes! What about other prints? Weren't there any other prints?

And again, what motive? It wouldn't be very smart of me to use my own mallet to murder someone."

"It might be smart for you to stop flapping your mouth, because I'm arresting you and, like Garcia said, you have the right to remain silent . . ."

This was no nightmare . . . well, not one she was sleeping through.

Camden raced through the door in a pair of short pajama bottoms and T-shirt, Dwayne at her heels. "What's going on?" she asked. "The flashing lights outside our window woke us up. What are you — ? Wait a minute! What are you doing?" She looked at Peters.

"We are arresting Ms. Bancroft on suspicion of murdering Mr. Taber this afternoon."

"Oh no, no, man. You be wrong. This girl, she good people. She didn't kill nobody," Dwayne said.

"There has to be a mistake," Camden added.

"No mistake, ma'am. Now if you'll excuse us."

"Wait," Michaela said. "I'm in my robe. Can I at least change?"

Peters nodded. "Go on up with her, Garcia. You got three minutes."

"I didn't kill him," Michaela muttered as Garcia followed her up the stairs. There was no love lost between her and the officer. They'd dealt with each other in the past, when a good friend of hers had been murdered, and Garcia had caused some problems for her and Jude. It wasn't a secret that Garcia had a thing for Jude, who at that moment Michaela wished wasn't on vacation.

"That's for a court of law to decide," Garcia replied.

Michaela ignored her and quickly dressed, everything seeming so surreal at that moment. What in God's green earth was this all about? Someone had come into the office, picked up her mallet, and killed Sterling with it. Someone who had gloves on. Could it have been another player? They all wore riding gloves. But it could have also been a socialite with a pair of white gloves, showing herself off to the polo elite. Oh jeez, it could have even been a server. Didn't they all wear gloves?

Peters yelled up to them, "Let's go."

This could not be happening. But it was, and moments later Michaela found herself in the back of a squad car, Garcia at the wheel, surely with a satisfied look on her face. Camden and Dwayne followed them to the car. "We'll get you out. I'll call Ethan."

"No." She didn't want Ethan to find out about this. "Call Joe. He'll be able to help."

She thought about her parents for a minute and was thankful that the two of them had taken a well-earned vacation for their fortieth wedding anniversary. They were on an African safari — something her father had always wanted to do. She could straighten all this out by the time they returned. But it wasn't good that Jude was also gone. She needed him right now.

Emotion rose up in the back of her throat, making her feel like she was choking. She swallowed it, refusing to allow any of this to get to her. This was one big mistake. One helluva mistake, and she would find the answers, because she refused to be framed for murder and spend her life in jail.

This was ludicrous. Peters and some other detective — a woman named Singer — had her inside an interrogation room. They were throwing questions at her right and left. She felt like a boxer inside a ring — right hook followed by a double left. If she could only pass out and then wake up to find them all gone.

"When did you meet Mr. Taber?" Peters asked.

"I don't know. I think four months ago. It was about the time I started taking polo lessons. Robert Nightingale introduced us."

"And what was your relationship like?"

"We didn't have one. We were acquaintances. That's it. I saw him at the polo grounds on occasion and we played polo together."

"So, you never spent any other time with Mr. Taber outside of the polo grounds?" Singer asked. She was an attractive, short-haired blonde who looked more like a soccer mom than a hard-nosed detective.

"Once, actually. A group of us went over to Sorvino's for dinner one night after practice. Ed Mitchell, the owner of the grounds, wanted to meet with us about the charity event."

Singer didn't respond. She left the room.

"Think about it, Ms. Bancroft, is there maybe another time or two that you *associated* with Mr. Taber?" Peters asked.

She tried to find the right answer to get him off her back. "You know what? No. What is this about?"

Singer came back in holding a set of ropes that looked like the one she'd given Sterling yesterday. "Do you recognize these?" she asked.

"Sure. I sell them at Round the Bend. They're roping ropes."

"Uh-huh, and did Mr. Taber get these from you?"

"He did."

"But I thought that you said that you didn't have a relationship outside the polo facility with Mr. Taber."

"I didn't."

"Do you want to explain the ropes?"

Michaela detailed the incident that had led Sterling Taber to walk out of her shop with the ropes.

Singer and Peters eyed each other. "You and Mr. Taber never used these ropes *together?*"

Michaela sat up straight, aghast at the question. "Are you kidding me? First, we could not have had time, considering he got them just before the polo match, and as far as spending any time with him, that wasn't going to happen. I didn't even like the man. He was repulsive to me . . ."

Oh how stupid. How could she have allowed herself to say such a stupid, stupid thing? Oh no, no, no. She could tell by the looks on the cops' faces that she'd helped put another nail into her coffin. Coffee!

Maybe coffee would help her brain connect at this ungodly hour.

Singer and Peters looked at each other again. "Ms. Bancroft, we have it from a source close to Mr. Taber that the two of you had a sexual relationship and that Mr. Taber had certain fetishes." Singer held up the ropes.

Michaela's jaw dropped. Now not only was she as dumb as paint on a fence, she was speechless.

"Do you care to comment?" Singer asked.

It took her a few seconds. *Brain connect. Brain connect.* "What source? You are kidding me." She shook her head. "No, no. This is some kind of joke. Who told you that?"

"We can't reveal sources. But this person claims that Mr. Taber frequently discussed your relationship."

"Well, whoever it was is lying. That is not true. Not even close."

Peters sat down and pulled the chair up, his face now only inches from hers. Michaela could smell coffee on his breath. Her stomach soured as he spoke in an accusatory tone. "Is that why you killed him? Because he was spreading rumors that the two of you were sleeping together? Or did you kill him because you were having sex with him and he was dating another woman?

71

Did you murder Sterling Taber because you were jealous? As I said, we have your fingerprints on the mallet. They match what's in the computer. Lucky for us when you applied for a license to teach autistic children, you were fingerprinted by the county."

"I did not kill him. I never slept with him. That's crazy. It's just not true!"

"Why would he say it then?"

"I don't know!" Michaela now knew what it must feel like to be a cornered dog — one being kicked and beaten for no reason. And, as her brain further connected, she realized that it looked like she needed a lawyer, and panic started to set in.

"Ms. Bancroft, you still have the right to contact an attorney."

"I think that would be a —"

Before she could finish there was a knock at the door. Singer opened it. On the other side stood a shorter version of her friend Joe. The man stretched out his hand. "I'm Anthony Pellegrino. I'm counselor for Ms. Bancroft here."

Yes, the man was definitely related to Joe. Same last name, same round stomach, wavy black hair slicked off his face, and warm brown eyes. A first cousin was her guess. It looked like Camden had called Joe, and he'd obviously gone to work rapidly, round-ing up one of his cousins to save the day. Anthony looked to be doing well for himself. He wore a pinstriped silk navy suit, crisp white button-down shirt with a rose-colored tie — Italian, for sure. Joe had a barrage of cousins. He blamed it on his devoutly Catholic family. He claimed there were some he hadn't even met.

Michaela had learned over the years that Joe's many cousins worked at anything from garbage truck driver to chef . . . but an attorney? That was a new one on her. Still, at that moment she felt grateful, albeit a bit surprised, to see Mr. Anthony Pellegrino enter the room to represent her.

The attorney removed a handful of papers from a leather briefcase. He took his time — deliberate and slow, almost achingly so for Michaela. She wanted to get out of there. "It's my understanding that you've charged my client with murdering a Mr. Sterling Taber."

"That's correct," Peters said.

"On what grounds?"

"The murder weapon belongs to your client and her fingerprints were on the weapon."

"The murder weapon being the polo mallet I read about in your report," Pellegrino said.

"Yes."

"Of course her fingerprints are on the mallet. It's her freaking mallet. I don't see what that's got to do with anything." Pellegrino shook his head and looked as if he were about to laugh. Michaela wasn't sure how to take it, because she was about to cry. "You are so joking here. You do realize that it would take nothing for the real killer to slip on a pair of gloves and there you go? No wonder Ms. Bancroft's fingerprints are the only ones. Anyone can see that. You don't have to be detective to figure that one, eh, folks?" Pellegrino smiled. "You, my friends, have a weak case and I'm sure that you know it. I'd like to confer with my client alone."

Both detectives left the room. Pellegrino stuck out a hand. "Joe sent me over. I'm a cousin."

"I figured. I would normally say that it would be nice to meet you, but . . ."

He waved his hand at her. "I understand. So, did you off the guy?"

It took her a few seconds to process his question. "Of course not!"

"You can tell me, I'm your lawyer."

"No way. I didn't kill anyone."

"Yeah, Joe says you're a good lady. I think I did pretty good with them cops, huh?"

What did he mean by that? "Yes," she said. "I think so. Wouldn't *you* know? I, uh, have never been in a situation like this."

"Oh yeah, me either. Crazy, man. Kinda cool, like one of them cops-and-lawyer shows."

Michaela crossed her arms and stared at him. "What kind of law do you practice?"

"Who, me?" He pointed at himself and then flattened down his silk tie. "Yeah, well, I'm a tax attorney, you know."

"Perfect." She put her face in her hands.

"Don't cry on me. I don't do so good with tear jags."

"Out of all the cousins you guys seem to have, there's no criminal defense attorney?"

"Oh yeah, there is. That'd be Pauly, but he's out in Chicago, you know. But look, I can get you out of this. Like I said, it don't take a genius to see they got a weak case. We just gotta get your bail posted."

"Right." Anthony Pellegrino may not have been a criminal defense attorney, but he was all she had right now.

"Okay, so here's the deal. They got your prints on the murder weapon. But it was your mallet, so they gotta prove you had time. They got a motive with this thing, though."

"Uh-huh, me sleeping with Sterling. Do

you know who told them such a thing?"

Pellegrino looked down at his notes. "Do you know a Lucia Sorvino?"

"What? Pepe's teenage daughter?"

"Says here she's twenty."

"I know who she is. We're not friends. But she's served me a platter of lasagna from time to time at her father's restaurant. I had a little disagreement yesterday morning with her father before the event. She was there and her brother showed up. I don't even really know the girl. Why would she say something like that?"

"I don't know, but the police have it on file."

"This is craziness!"

"I'm going to level with you. This Peters dude, he's a jerk, a real uptight cop, and I think he'd like to wrap this thing up because Taber was from a highfalutin family who lives up in Santa Barbara. He don't want no heat, so if you look like a good suspect, then that's the angle he's gonna pursue for now. But Joe says you got a friend here in the department."

She nodded. "Jude Davis. He's a homicide detective."

"He might be able to help us out. Have you spoken with him?"

"No. He's on a cruise with his daughter.

He won't be back until Friday."

"Huh. Five days. Okay, so while we're waiting for your friend to come back from his vacation, there is a hearing arranged for first thing this morning. The judge will likely set bond, but it won't be cheap."

"How much?"

"Murder case? You're looking at a quarter mil."

"Two hundred fifty thousand dollars! I don't have that kind of cash right now."

"You only have to come up with ten percent of it."

Michaela sighed. She didn't even have *that* amount of liquid assets at the moment. She'd put most of her cash from her inheritance into building up the autism riding center and for the special equipment needed, along with the extra horses she'd bought. The money that hadn't gone into the center she'd invested in the tack shop, and she was working on just enough capital to keep her business running and pay her bills. Oh God, she couldn't turn back now. She'd been down the road toward bankruptcy a few short years ago, and she refused to go back there. "That's still a lot."

"What about your parents, friends, property?"

She cringed at any of those thoughts.

Definitely not her parents. She couldn't ask any friends. She wouldn't do that to them. But her property? Uncle Lou's place. That was her only option. "My ranch. If I have to."

"Good. I talked with your friend Camden and had her pack an outfit for you for this morning. By the time they take you back to your cell, the clothes should be there."

Her eyes stung with tears. *Her cell.* The one hour she spent inside the jail cell in the wee hours she'd paced back and forth, her mind full of rage, fear, and shock. Then Peters had come for her and she'd been in the interrogation room ever since.

Pellegrino smiled warmly at her. "It's gonna be okay. We'll get through the morning. You'll be home by noon. That's my job, and after that we'll get to work on your defense and I will get to work on these clowns here and continue to remind them that everything they have is circumstantial and weak."

How was he going to work on anything? He was a *tax attorney,* for crying out loud, but she didn't have it in her to bring that up right now. All she wanted was to get the hell out of there. She nodded and tried to smile back in return, but she wasn't sure at all how she was going to make it through the morning.

EIGHT

It wasn't twenty-five grand that got Michaela out of jail but rather fifty, and the thought of leveraging Uncle Lou's place made her ill. Apparently the judge thought she was a flight risk because she had the financial means to "get away." Please! Where would she go? She had a barn filled with horses that were family to her, a handful of children she gave riding lessons to whom she adored, parents who lived two miles from her that she saw at least once a week, and a circle of friends she couldn't live without. She almost laughed when the old curmudgeon of a judge brought up the idea that she might flee. It was as ridiculous as the notion that she had been sleeping with Sterling. She had every intention of speaking with Lucia Sorvino to find out why in the world she was spreading such vicious lies. That girl had some explaining to do. Didn't she know what rumors could do to a person's life? Try on *destroy it* for size!

Joe showed up at the courthouse to take her home, while her new attorney shook her hand and said he'd be in touch with her by the end of the day. "I'd go with you, but I want to see what I can line up for you before we talk again. Joey, take care of her."

"Always do." Joe opened the passenger door to his minivan. Once he was behind the wheel, he looked over at her. "What the hell happened, girl?"

"I wish I knew. One minute I'm riding in the match, the next I find Sterling dead in my store, then when it's all over with, I head home and just as I've finally fallen asleep, it sounds like a herd of my horses are trying to break the door down, and outside stand Starsky and Hutch."

"At least you haven't lost your sense of humor."

"I think I'm still in shock. Look, I'm in trouble, Joe. I can see it in Detective Peters's eyes. He thinks that I did this and so does that woman cop. I can't go to jail. I didn't kill anyone. And by the way, thanks for sending in Anthony . . . but a tax attorney?" Michaela felt something under her on the car seat and picked up a half-eaten cheese-burger, which she'd sat on. "What in the . . ."

"Sorry. I know, the kids. They got a problem picking up after themselves. We're working on it."

She spotted a few French fries on the floorboard and pointed. Joe glanced down. "Throw in a Coke and I might have a meal."

"That Joe Jr.! Anyway, of course you didn't kill no one. I've known you since we was kids, Mickey. I know Anthony isn't exactly what you need. But it was the best I could do on short notice, and he did get your bail posted."

"Yeah, he did do that."

"You could eat a little more these days. I'd tell you to eat that burger but I don't know how long it's been here. Why don't we stop and get a bite?"

"It does look partially dehydrated. Eating isn't always a priority for me. I've been busy. And right now I just want to get home and shower."

"Never too busy to eat." He rubbed his large belly. "I think you get overwhelmed with all you got going on and you are the last person you take care of. You handle the horses, the kids at the center, that crazy broad Camden you live with, and then some. You need some *you* time."

She smiled at his comment. Ah, the big bro she never had — technically, because

Joe had become everything a big brother is for a sister. She knew it drove Jude nuts that they were such good friends. He liked Joe, but his family ties made Jude uncomfortable. They didn't bother Michaela, who had seen plenty of Joe's softer side. She'd seen him with his little girl, Gen, Michaela's first autistic student and the reason she'd agreed to open the riding center in the first place. She adored the little girl, who loved to be around horses. No, she was not about to lose any of it — her animals, her friends, the kids, her ranch. She'd fight whoever had set her up. "We've got to get a handle on this. You and I both know the cops won't help me."

"What about Jude? The guy is crazy for you."

"He's on a cruise with his little girl."

"Oh."

"Oh is right, and he won't be back for five days. I can't wait for five days while Peters attempts to burn me at the stake. I've got to find out who did this, who murdered Sterling Taber."

"Oh no. I see where this is going."

"It's not like we've never been down this road before. We make a good team. You know we do, and this time I *really* need your help."

He didn't comment for a second, just sort of frowned, then nodded. "Where do we start?"

She sighed. "By questioning that Sorvino brat. Pepe's daughter, Lucia." Joe turned the corner into Michaela's ranch. A slight sound escaped from her lips. "Oh my God."

"You can say that again. I don't think we start with Lucia."

NINE

A local TV news van was parked out in front, with a blonde-headed woman reporter all miked up and ready to interview, along with her cameraman. It looked as though Camden and Dwayne were trying to chase them off the property, but they were being completely ignored. Now they turned their attention to the oncoming minivan. "This isn't good," Joe said. "I can run them over."

"No!"

"Just kidding. Maybe I can flip a U-ee and we'll make a run for it."

"No, don't do that! What do they want?"

"I think we are about to find out. Keep your head down and walk to the house. I'll get rid of them." Joe parked the van and got out first, asking everyone to back away. He did his best to keep his hulking self in front of her while the reporter shouted obnoxious questions at her: "Did you kill Mr. Taber? Were you in love with Sterling Taber? What about your riding center?"

Michaela turned around and faced the reporter — a statuesque blonde with a crisp navy suit and heels.

"What are you doing?" Joe asked.

"I'm telling them the truth. For the record, I barely knew Mr. Taber. I did not kill him. My riding center will remain open. I ask that you respect my property and my privacy and please leave."

She turned around and headed toward her front door. The cameraman and reporter ran in front of her and were now in her face. The reporter shoved the microphone at her. "How did you meet Mr. Taber? Can you tell us about the mallet?" She tried to push the camera out of the way, which caused her to trip and nearly fall as she reached the front porch step.

Joe lost it at that point. "Get the hell out of here, or I will call the police. You are on private property and Ms. Bancroft will charge you with trespassing. She's made a statement, and has kindly asked you to leave. I won't be so kind. Get the *hell* out of here!" he bellowed.

One look at Joe and the newspeople understood he was serious. Michaela finally made it through her front door and heard her phone ringing. Joe eyed her as she reached for it. "Let me answer it." He grabbed the phone before she could. "No!" he yelled, slamming it down. He looked at Michaela, who set her purse on the kitchen counter. "Reporter."

"Ah. Great! As if I'm suddenly like Angelina Jolie adopting a new kid. At least instead of making *People* magazine's most beautiful list, I'll only have the honor of making Indio's most wanted list. Just what I need — star status. Yeah. Great. Why do they have any interest in me?"

Camden walked in with Dwayne like a lap dog at her heels. Michaela still needed to have that one-on-one with her, and the sooner the better. She had to get to the bottom of what Camden had said after finding Sterling's body.

"The media likes a juicy story, and you are apparently it," Camden said. "Remember that Sterling was voted most eligible bachelor by the women's league of social activities in the desert."

"Oh, what an honor. He was a regular Colin Farrell." Camden made a face at her. "I didn't do jack. I'm a horse trainer. I teach children how to ride. I barely knew that guy, and now this. And I plan to find out who did it. Speaking of that 'most eligible bachelor' thing, weren't he and Juliet Mitchell a couple?"

Camden shrugged. "I wouldn't know."

Sure.

The phone rang again and again Joe answered. "What? No, of course not. Now listen, Rhonda, you've got to be reasonable here. That's ludicrous. Yes." He paused.

Michaela turned her attention to Joe. Rhonda was the woman who headed up the autism society, had been the one to help Michaela get a license, and worked with her on teaching the kids. She had recommended many children to her, and Michaela was now working regularly with seven children, including Joe's daughter, Gen.

"Okay." Joe sighed. Oh, this could not be good. "Yes. No. I'm sure that she'll understand and we will get all of this worked out." He hung up.

Michaela crossed her arms. "Work out what? *What* will she understand?" Joe looked down. "What is it, Joe?"

"Rhonda received a call from channel 8 and they wanted a quote from her for tonight's six o'clock news about your arrest, whether or not you would still be working with the autistic society, and if they would still recommend children to ride with you."

"What? No! Oh no, no!"

Camden placed a hand on her shoulder.

Michaela, near tears, shook it off and walked into the kitchen, where she took a pitcher of water from the fridge. She needed to think. "What did she say?"

"She wouldn't give them a quote. But . . ." He paused. ". . . she did ask that in light of the negative publicity that for a while, until everything is worked out, you not work with the kids. She's pretty sure that when the parents hear about this, there'll be some fallout to deal with."

Michaela slammed the pitcher onto the counter, spilling water on the floor. "Those are my kids! Those kids are everything to me, along with my horses. She can't do this! She has to know that I'm not guilty."

"Of course she knows, but look at it from her point of view, Mick. She's gotta cover her butt."

Michaela frowned as she said, "Unbelievable!" She grabbed her purse off the counter.

"Where are you going?" Camden shouted.

"To see Lucia Sorvino . . . but first, I want to talk to you. Upstairs. Now."

"Now?"

"Now." Michaela motioned for Camden to head up first. She wasn't about to let her get out of this.

Camden turned around to look at her.

"What's this all about?" she asked when they'd closed the bedroom door.

"The comment you made yesterday about Sterling right after he was killed, about being more than friends. Do you want to elaborate?"

Camden sighed.

Michaela's stomach sank. "Please tell me that you weren't cheating on your fiancé!"

"No, no I wasn't."

"Thank God." Michaela plunked down on the end of her bed atop a coral tropical-flower print.

"But I did sleep with him." Camden tossed back her red hair.

"You better explain this one, my friend."

Camden sat down next to her. "Look, here's the deal. It was a long time ago. A very long time ago."

"Like how long ago?"

Camden scowled. "Do you remember George?"

"Your first husband?"

"Uh-huh."

"Yes. The golf pro."

She nodded. "Sterling was his caddy."

"Oh no. I can already tell that I am not going to like where this is going. Wait, George? That was what, eight years ago?"

"Nine."

"Nine, and Sterling was twenty-six when he died, which means that you and he . . . when he was seventeen!"

"He told me that he was nineteen."

"Oh my God! You . . . you're like a regular Mrs. Robinson. That is really disturbing!"

"Hey, I prefer more like an Eva Longoria on *Desperate Housewives* during that first season, when she was sleeping with the gardener kid. He was a senior in high school. Really good story line."

"I don't watch TV, and I don't care who you think you're like. That's just gross."

"He said he was a virgin and he wanted to know what it was like because he was going off to college. Kind of like a soldier going off to war."

"You've got to be kidding me. You're delirious, Cam. You believed him? Young guy like that waiting until he was nineteen? Even at seventeen, I'm pretty sure Sterling Taber did his share of the cheerleading squad long before he graduated. Wait. How did you even meet him?"

"Golfing one day with George. He had those dreamy eyes and his body, wow . . . And George was already messing around with Debbie, who became wife number four, so I figured, no harm, no foul —"

Michaela cut her off. "It doesn't matter.

What I want to know is, were you sleeping with him again?"

"I told you that I wasn't. God, Mick. I just said that it was a long time ago. I'm engaged to Dwayne."

Michaela cocked an eyebrow. "Like that really stopped you in the past. I just want to be sure."

"This is different. I love Dwayne and you know that. I'd never do anything to hurt him."

"Then why even have Sterling close by? Why have him in the show? If you love Dwayne like you say that you do, then why tempt yourself?"

She sighed. "I'll tell you everything from the beginning."

"I wish you would. But, you can leave out any more details from your Mrs. Robinson days. I don't think I want to hear about any of that."

Camden took a sip of her tea before going into her saga. "I hadn't seen Sterling in years. He'd moved to L.A., then back home to Santa Barbara, and then I think he came back here, he said, when he was twenty, but I'd moved on and so had he. We only had a fling —"

Michaela held up her hands. "Forget that. What I want to know is what had been going on between you two as of late."

"I'm getting to it. His family is some well-to-do, high-society-type bunch."

"I thought you said he was seventeen when you met him, but his family lives in Santa Barbara."

She nodded. "He had some ups and downs with his parents. They tried military school and then finally agreed to let him move out here and live with an uncle, who got him the caddy job. If I remember right, the uncle passed away not long after Sterling turned eighteen, but I really don't know. I wasn't in his life at that point. I only caught bits through the grapevine of what was going on with him."

"Okay, and . . ." Michaela motioned for her to continue, finding herself growing impatient.

"I first saw him a few months back, when that spread ran about him being the most eligible bachelor in the desert and how he rode down at the polo fields. I went to visit him. I thought he'd be a great attraction for the fashion show. It was his idea to do the charity match in the first place."

"Sure, and you want me to believe that you just went over there for a howdy-do, and to ask him to be in the show." Michaela rolled her eyes. "I've known you for a very long time. You're not fooling me, and please don't try. This is my life on the line here."

"Okay, so maybe I was a little curious. We had some good times together. We were friends. But trust me, I had *no* plans to cross that line again, and I *didn't*."

Michaela studied her. She actually believed her. One thing that Michaela knew about her friendship with Camden was they were brutally honest with each other. "You're telling me that Sterling came up with the idea for the charity match?"

"Yes. I don't understand why you didn't like him."

"He was a show-off, and he made me uncomfortable. I don't like overbearing men and he was one."

"He was just confident."

"We don't need to get into the reasons why I didn't care for your friend. The facts are he didn't deserve his fate, and I certainly don't deserve to be charged with his murder."

"No, you don't. I know you didn't do it."

"Did he talk to you at all about his personal life, anything that might have been going on?"

"He did. I told the police yesterday what he told me only a few weeks ago."

"What was that?"

"We met for lunch at the polo lounge. He called me, sounding upset and asked if I'd come and meet him. He said that he felt like someone was watching him. He thought someone wanted him dead."

"Did he say who?"

"Juliet's father."

"Ed Mitchell?" Michaela knew Ed fairly well after riding with him at the polo fields. He'd been the one to give Michaela her mallet. He'd told her it was a gift from the club. She couldn't see a man of Ed's prominence murdering anyone.

"Yes," Camden replied.

"Okay, wait, so he had this girlfriend, Juliet. But he was also considered an eligible bachelor. I've been wondering about that. Do you know what the deal is there?"

"That's why he thought her father might want him dead. He and Juliet started going out after he was voted most eligible. We talked. I even spoke with Juliet and she seemed okay with it at the time. We decided that it would bring in a larger crowd to the show if we promoted him that way. I think, though, that Juliet may have had second thoughts, and it upset her. Especially when Sterling was approached by one of those reality TV dating shows. He didn't agree to do it, but Sterling told me that Juliet freaked

95

out about it. And Sterling told me that if Juliet is upset, her daddy becomes even more upset. And I guess Daddy Warbucks also has a bad temper. I told the cops all of this yesterday, too."

"What did they say?" Michaela had caught wind that Ed was protective of Juliet and that he occasionally lost his temper. But she still couldn't see him as a killer.

"All the detective said was thank you. I didn't know at the time that Peters was going to arrest you; if I had, I would've pushed the issue further."

Michaela stood up and paced across her bleached hardwood floors. She needed to think. "Can you do me a favor?"

"Sure. Anything."

"Can you see if you can locate any article, or whatever else you can on Sterling? I know he did some acting in L.A. and other modeling gigs. Maybe there's something there. Can you do that for me?"

"Why?"

"Please, can you just do it?"

"What are you looking for?"

"I'm not sure yet. But the mystery lies with the dead guy, and maybe we'll learn something about his past, his life, anything that will give us answers as to who really killed him, and why."

"Michaela, don't tangle yourself up in this."

She let out a sarcastic laugh. "I don't have a choice now, do I? Peters wants me behind bars. I'm in this mess whether I want to be or not, and this time I'm fighting to keep my sanity and my freedom."

TEN

Michaela pulled up in front of Sorvino's, which was on the hill overlooking the polo fields. To her dismay the restaurant appeared to be closed. Only one car stood in the parking lot — a silver convertible Mercedes. She was pretty sure Ed Mitchell drove a car like that. Maybe Sorvino's was open, but normally it was packed; one car in the parking lot didn't exactly constitute *busy.*

She didn't know where Lucia Sorvino lived and had hoped that she would be here at the restaurant. Maybe it was for the best if the girl wasn't around, at least for her sake, because Michaela's anger had only deepened as she'd wiped away angry tears on the drive over. How could anyone think she could have murdered Sterling? And now her students — *her kids* — not coming for lessons because of the negative press! It had been one thing that she owned the damn murder weapon and only her fingerprints were on it. But Lucia had sealed the coffin shut by making up the bizarre lie about her and Sterling. She would get to the bottom of it.

Even though Sorvino's might be closed, she decided to walk around the building. Maybe someone was there and she could ask them when Lucia might be in. Typically, a clear blue sky in November would have made her grateful to be alive. She'd have taken in the surrounding beauty of the grass field below and the majestic mountains in the background. But there was not a whole lot to appreciate at the moment. One minute it was Sunday afternoon and her team had won a polo match and raised a nice chunk of change for her riding center, then by Monday she'd been arrested for murder. All she wanted to do was be vindicated and get back her life — a life that seemed to have drastically changed in the last twenty-four hours.

She went up to the front doors and pulled on them but they were locked. She started to walk around to the back of the restaurant, passing some of the large picture windows, which allowed patrons to enjoy the view. Something caught her eye and she peered inside. Pepe Sorvino was talking to Ed

Mitchell. So, it *was* Ed's car. They looked to be having a drink and laughing about something and did not notice her. Michaela continued around the back to knock on the door, but hesitated. Ed stood up from the bar and pulled something from his pocket. She squinted to see what it was. It looked to be a jewelry box. Pepe opened it, and took something out: a diamond ring. Michaela could tell by the way the light caught it. Why would Ed Mitchell be giving Pepe a diamond ring? Okay, jewelry was Ed's business, but wouldn't they conduct a transaction like this in *his* store?

She had to hustle as she saw the men make their way toward the back door. How would she explain being there? She didn't mind running into Ed, but she wasn't prepared to deal with Pepe again. She raced for a shed that stood behind the restaurant. It was open; she went inside and crouched down. From what she could tell, the shed was used to store catering needs like large platters, a cappuccino maker, extra plates and . . . a wig. What? A *wig?* Michaela picked up the long blonde wig. Strange. She set it back down again and listened as Ed and Pepe walked to the parking lot, still laughing.

"My wife and I loved what you did for

our last party. You've got a knack for this, and when we open up the restaurant in Palm Springs, your business will only grow."

"I thank you for investing in this with me. This will be good, Ed. And I plan to have my daughter helping out in this restaurant here while Mario and I get the other one off the ground, now that she isn't so distracted by . . . other things. My apologies for that. I know Juliet was hurt by that incident with Sterling."

"The good news is that neither of us have to worry about Sterling Taber being a problem for us or our daughters again."

"This is true." Pepe laughed. "Is the Realtor meeting us at the restaurant?"

"Yes. She should be there before us. We better get a move on." With that, both men climbed inside Ed's Mercedes and zipped away as Michaela picked her jaw up off the ground.

ELEVEN

Michaela remained in her stupor on the drive home. The question running through her mind was the obvious: Did Ed Mitchell and Pepe Sorvino have something to do with Sterling's murder? Neither one of them was upset by his death, that was for sure. What was the ring all about? And the restaurant in Palm Springs? Were they going into business together? It seemed like an odd pairing to her, but Ed was a good businessman and Sorvino's was a profitable restaurant. Oh boy, did she need to talk to Joe — someone whom she could tell everything she'd heard, seen, experienced. Maybe he could help her sort through this. She called his house and got voice mail, then tried his cell with the same result.

A wave of exhaustion hit her and she felt like she was on autopilot for the rest of the drive home. What she needed to do was think, and the best place to do that was on a trail ride.

She parked over by the barn and went into her office, where she kept an extra pair of riding jeans and boots. Moments later, she had Rocky hooked up to the cross-ties. She groomed him faster than usual, hoping not to have anyone notice that she was back. She needed a game plan and she didn't need anyone clouding her mind with their own thoughts.

Once up on her sorrel gelding, she and Rocky headed out onto the trails behind her ranch. Passing by the pasture that in the future she prayed would be home to champions, she sighed and breathed in the fresh air. The sun was beginning to set and its brightness cast shadows across the boulders on the mountainside. Rocky stepped out, seeming to appreciate being able to stretch his legs as much as she was to be free and away from the insanity. Much of the time her riding skills and that of her horses were expressed inside the arena, but there was nothing like getting out on the trail to remind a person exactly what the meaning of freedom was. *Freedom.* The clean, dry air perfumed by chaparral and the earthen floor. The sweet songs of larks here and there. She might even spot a predator bird looking for his prey; a hawk, or on occasion a golden eagle, soared on by. She sighed and gave Rocky a pat as she leaned slightly out of the saddle and forward while he worked to climb up the mountain's crest.

But what if her freedom were suddenly ripped out from underneath her? It had been, briefly . . . and what if it got worse? What if Joe's cousin couldn't remedy things as he'd insisted he could? She didn't see how any of this was simply going to resolve itself. She had to tell Peters what she'd overheard while in the shed behind Sorvino's. But what did it mean? She again analyzed what she'd seen and heard. Neither one had actually said that they'd done away with Sterling. They were pleased he wouldn't be a problem anymore. So, if she went and explained this to Peters, what would his likely reaction be? Probably the detective would do nothing. Ed Mitchell was well known and a bigwig in town, one of the wealthiest. The last thing the police would want to do would be to rock the boat with one of the movers and shakers. And Michaela still couldn't see Ed as a murderer . . . still, what about what Sterling had told Camden, about being afraid of Ed? That was weird, too, because Michaela couldn't see Sterling being intimidated by anyone.

She knew she still needed more information, and talking to Lucia was a must. She decided to make a mental list of all the players and see what her brain could turn up. She knew that Robert might have a motive and it was possible that he'd had time, unless he'd been with his wife when Sterling was killed. Then there was Zach and the way he'd looked after Sterling; the vibes coming from him were nothing short of hatred. Oh, and Lance Watkins. Sterling had been rude and disrespectful to Lance. And, Erin Hornersberg — the makeup artist with an attitude — who definitely was not happy with Sterling. Her strange behavior last night in the parking lot bothered Michaela. What about Sterling's pal Tommy Liggett? She knew Tommy, but not well. What was the old saying — keep your friends close and your enemies closer. Right now it looked as if that was what Zach was doing — for what reason she didn't know, but what if Tommy had a reason, too? They always hung out together. At the very least, she'd need to talk to Tommy since he was Sterling's best friend. Maybe he'd know what had been going on with Lucia and why she would lie about Michaela and Sterling.

And Camden: She hadn't killed Sterling; she'd only slept with him. Michaela squeezed her hands tight around the reins. Rocky sensed her stress and sped up due to her shift in the saddle. "I'm sorry, bud. It's not you. Definitely not you."

They reached the top of the mountain and stopped. Michaela got off the horse to let him rest. She rubbed his face and he nuzzled her shoulder, his weight nearly throwing her off balance. "Hey, easy buddy."

She looked down across the vista spread below her, peppered with small ranches and homes — some plush and green with horses in their pastures. A few were weathered, aged, and in need of attention, but the landscape gave her a sense of security. This was her home — where she'd grown up, and knew people. It was where she belonged. She lingered there, taking it in, but knowing she should get back. She realized that to get through this she was going to need to suck it up and move forward. Typically, moving forward would've meant that she would work with her students, exercise her horses, and manage her ranch. Now, *forward* meant unraveling a murder mystery.

Another thought weighing her down was Jude. She didn't want him to come home to this mess. She should've gone with him and Katie on this cruise. He'd asked, but the timing had not been good.

Only a few days earlier — last Friday — Jude had taken her to dinner. They'd sat out on the patio at the restaurant eating shrimp cocktails and each having a glass of wine. The sun was setting, reflecting a myriad of colors across the desert sky, and candlelight flickered in the tea lights on the table.

The evening had been romantic from the get-go. Jude had shown up with a dozen red roses in one hand and a dozen pink ones in the other. Then he'd taken her to a gourmet restaurant, and she'd figured that she was pretty much being swept off her feet.

He had leaned across the table and taken her hand. "I wish you could go with me and Katie on this cruise."

"I wish I could go, too."

"Then come with us. Please. I'll pay for everything. Come on. You deserve a break. And Katie would love it. This is her week off with year-round school, and we've been looking forward to this for months. It would be over the top for her if you came along."

He smiled his devilish smile, which made her heart skip a beat. His smile and the way his skin around his blue eyes crinkled got under *her* skin in a very good way. She sighed. "You know I can't. I have the charity match and we're opening the store. I couldn't skip out on all of that. Plus I have kids to teach. It would be irresponsible."

"For once in your life, you should try on irresponsibility for size."

She laughed. "Sure. Come on, you know I would go if I could."

"I know. I understand. Next time though." He shook his head.

Jude had been right, because if she'd for once hadn't been so responsible she wouldn't be in this mess. She climbed back up on Rocky and they eased on down the mountain. She didn't know where things were headed with Jude, and now she was more uncertain than ever. Not because she didn't have feelings for him, but because she was in a hell of a lot of trouble, and she was concerned how he might react. Maybe that was the real reason she wasn't picking up the phone to call him. This wasn't her first rodeo. She'd found herself in the midst of murder and mayhem in the past and she really wished she could lead a quiet, simple life.

Ah, so much for simple. As she rode onto her property she knew simple didn't exist. Ethan's truck stood out front, and the last thing he represented in her life was simple.

TWELVE

Normally Michaela would be happy to see his truck parked in front of her house. But not this evening. Ethan was waiting for her in the stable office, and he had Josh with him. Michaela spotted him before he saw her. He'd set Josh down on a blanket with some toys and was bending down, wiping something off the baby's face.

She decided to bite the bullet. Ethan never stopped by without a reason any longer. Michaela was pretty sure that Summer was behind that. Back in the day, Ethan would pop in after a long day of work and they'd have a beer together. They'd talk about his cases for the day and how her training sessions had gone. They'd known each other since they were three, and the comfort level between them was both intimate and special. Not many people had the kind of friendship that she and Ethan did. "Hey look, it's my favorite boys."

"Mick, what is going on?"

"You've heard."

"Heard? It's all over the news. You and Sterling Taber? I thought you were dating that detective — Jude."

"I am! You don't believe that crap? What, do you think I killed him, too?"

"No, of course not." He walked over and put his arms around her. She sank into him, leaning her head on his chest. "What are we going to do?" he asked.

"We? *We* don't have to do anything. I have to find out who killed him."

"That's the cops' job."

"You would think, but I am apparently the prime suspect and from everything I can tell, the cops have zeroed in on me and think they have the killer."

"Oh come on, that's absurd. They can't believe that, and you can't go around trying to figure this out, Mick. The last time you got yourself involved in something like this, you nearly got yourself killed."

She pulled away from him and threw her arms in the air. "I don't know what else to do."

He shook his head. "The police have to be looking at other folks. I know that guy was popular with the women, but he also seemed to have enemies, or at least I know that there were some people who didn't care much for him."

"Did you know him?"

"No. Other than playing that match with him. I met him a few times before that and never thought much of him. He was an ass; you know that and so do I. Look at the way he acted out on the field with the other players."

"What do you mean though, about enemies?"

"I don't know if you'd actually call them enemies, but the day I was out there I overheard some of the grooms grumbling about him, and we both know that Lance couldn't stand him. Remember yesterday after the match the way Sterling was talking trash about him?"

"I couldn't blame Lance for saying what he did about him."

"Yeah, well, before the match I was talking with Lance and he said that he couldn't wait until the charity event was over. He said that Taber was a miserable SOB to ride with. That the guy was always doing stupid stuff on the field, like cutting him off when it was unnecessary and just being a real ass to him. Then he caught him trying to flirt with his wife, who Lance said blew him off, but he wasn't real happy about it. The wife was pretty offended, too."

"I imagine. I think their dislike for one another went both ways."

"Right, no love lost there, huh? But that's what I mean; this Taber guy wasn't well loved by everyone."

"Do you think Lance Watkins might have killed him?"

Ethan shook his head. "You know, I've known Lance for a long time. The guy doesn't strike me as having an evil bone in him. He's always low-key. He's kind to his animals. His wife and daughter are really sweet people. I can't see it. But you never really know someone enough, do you? People will surprise you. I only know him through treating his horses and we've had a few beers together over the years, but no, I don't think so. Lance is a good guy. I'm only telling you this because if Taber could've gotten under someone's skin like Lance's, who knows who else he's pissed off. I think the police have their heads up their asses."

"Join the club."

"Tell me what you need, anything."

She smiled. "I appreciate it, but your plate is full." She pointed to Josh and bent down. "Hey, bubba, what you doing besides growing?" She picked him up and kissed the top of his head. "I've missed you. Ethan, why don't you take Summer out for dinner this weekend and I'll watch him." She wanted to try and divert him. She knew that his desire to help her would probably cause a rift between him and Summer, and she didn't want that for the baby's sake . . . or Ethan's. He'd made a commitment to Summer, and Michaela wouldn't come between that.

"No. You've got plenty going on. You don't need to be babysitting for me. That's the thing with you: You always try and help other people out and all it does is add more pressure for you. You've got to stop it."

"It'll help me take my mind off of everything." But she knew the real reason Ethan wouldn't have her watch Josh likely had more to do with Summer's feelings toward her than anything else.

"Maybe. But you do have to start thinking about yourself."

"I am. Honestly. I'm thinking about how in the heck I'm going to prove that I didn't kill Sterling Taber."

"And I want to help. I want you to keep me in the loop and tell me what I can do." He rubbed his eye. "Damn. Something in there. Been bugging me all afternoon."

"Let me see. Sit down on the couch, and I'll take a look." She set Josh back down on his blanket and handed him a set of plastic baby keys, which he eagerly went back to playing with. She leaned over Ethan, who lay his head back on the couch. "Whoop, yep, there it is. Eyelash." She gently removed the lash and then brushed it off his face. She went to back away but nearly tripped over the baby, who had rolled over next to them.

To avoid hurting Josh, she fell forward onto Ethan. Right into his lap. "Oops. Sorry." She scrambled to get up, her face burning. Ethan was looking at her in a way that he hadn't before. At first there was a slight curve on his lips and then as a second passed, the look in his eyes became one of intensity, almost as if were looking directly into her heart and soul, as if he knew her at her very core. Another second slipped by. Michaela shifted uncomfortably. She lifted herself and braced her hands against the couch trying to get all the way back up. They both started to laugh. The tension eased.

Ethan quickly reached down and picked up the baby. "That's okay. Better than falling on you." He poked Josh's chest and tickled him. The baby giggled. Ethan stood. "Promise you'll keep me in the loop."

Uh-huh. She believed that Ethan was

there to support her, but Summer might not have too much of a problem with her being locked away. "I will. Thank you." She kissed both of them on the cheek and helped Ethan put the baby toys back in the bag.

Once they were gone, she went back out to the barn to take care of Rocky. Now, here was a male who understood her. She leaned her head against his neck and sighed, her mind spinning at not only the prospect of being a murder suspect, but also at the fact that something had just happened between her and Ethan. She couldn't deny it. It was something that had never happened before. When they'd looked into each other's eyes for that second, a powerful surge of electricity had shot through her — straight to her heart. It had been nothing like she'd ever felt before, and she knew Ethan had felt it, too.

THIRTEEN

Michaela went to bed with her mind in a jumbled mess. Between Sterling's murder and her confused feelings over Jude . . . And then — dammit — Ethan had once again messed up her head. That slight but intense moment they'd shared had her wondering about her feelings for him. They were feelings she could never act on, and she knew they were futile. It was silly, really. So, she'd kind of fallen on him and he'd looked at her in the way a man looks at a woman he wants to touch, to kiss — to love — but none of that mattered. She wiped the thoughts from her mind.

Not unhappy to see the sun rise, she made an organized list in her mind as to the order in which she planned to see people today. She figured that no one would be at Sorvino's until closer to the lunch hour, so Lance Watkins was up first. Even though she'd overheard that odd conversation between

Ed Mitchell and Pepe, she couldn't get out of her mind the animosity that existed between Lance and Sterling. Ethan's conversation with her yesterday had only disturbed her further and made her more curious as to what the real situation between the two of them had been.

Michaela pulled up to the exquisite facility that Lance Watkins owned and operated. She got out and looked around. There was a dressage ring to her left, marked in the shape of a square and surrounded by trimmed date palms. Beyond that was a large green pasture where a handful of horses grazed and soaked up the sun, not to mention eating plenty of grass. She watched one lie down and roll. It was always a sight to see such large beasts rolling around in the grass, maybe scratching their backs, but more than likely doing it because it felt good. Not all horses took the pleasure in rolling, but many did and it brought a smile to her face to see a horse just being a horse.

There was a row of stalls and a barn to her right, painted a traditional brick red and trimmed in white. Adjacent to them were sets of pipe corrals, likely for people who boarded their horses. Michaela knew that Lance earned a nice income by simply setting up a room and board facility. As far as training with him, that was expensive and only the cream of the crop fit into that category. His facility looked traditional and well kept.

She walked up a small embankment to the jumping arena and saw that Lance was working a strong and forward-looking warm-blood over a set of cavallettis. The horse stood over seventeen hands high and was a gorgeous dapple gray. Lance handled him beautifully, his patience and connection with the animal obvious. Together the horse and trainer moved elegantly, with the rider in perfect balance as the animal bent and worked his way through the training session, seemingly to want to please his rider, which is what every trainer desires.

Lance worked the gray repeatedly over the cavallettis, a row of wooden poles on the ground spaced a few feet apart from one another. The idea of cavalletti training is to get the horse to move over them with agility and precision. It also allows them to start to connect with the idea that they want to avoid the wooden pole. Once the animal can maneuver the cavalletti with ease, it is likely ready to graduate to a higher jump. It took several goes at the cavallettis, but when the horse did it correctly, Lance knew it was time to stop pushing him. He gave him a pat on his neck and let his reins hang loose, allowing him to stretch his neck after working those muscles so intensely.

Lance spotted Michaela. "Hey, to what do I owe this pleasure?" he asked.

"Thought I'd pay a visit. Great horse."

He rode the gray over to the side of the arena. "He's a sweetheart." Lance nodded. "Hey, sorry I was so rude at the polo field, then after what happened to that guy I felt really bad. I also heard about the cops arresting you. What a crock."

"Yeah, well." She shoved her hand into her jeans pockets. "About those ruffians and the polo grounds . . ."

"Uh-oh. I don't like the sound of that." He slid his right leg over the horse, dropped lightly to the ground, and loosened the buckle on his Troxel helmet.

She mustered a smile. "Sterling didn't make it easy for many people to like him."

"Ah. No, he didn't."

She noticed he wore the polo shirt from the event. She squinted. There was a dark reddish-brown spot on the sleeve. Before she thought, she blurted out, "Is that blood on your shirt?"

Lance pulled the sleeve up slightly off his arm and looked to where she was pointing. "Yeah, it is. How the hell did that get there?

Oh, yeah." He bent down and undid a wrap around his horse's front leg. "He's got a nasty gash here, which I cleaned earlier. He clipped himself while being shod yesterday. Good thing he didn't get the shoer. I must've smeared some of the blood on my shirt when I was cleaning his wound."

"Oh." The cut was clean but it could have bled quite a bit. Michaela still couldn't help but notice that her mind was heading down a track she didn't like. She was here, so she needed to do what she came for. "Hey, so I wanted to ask you about Sunday. As you said, I'm no killer and I'm trying to see what I can find out. Not to put you on the spot, but I got the sense from Sterling that there was an issue between the two of you."

He chuckled again. "I didn't care for him, no. But, if you drove out here to ask me if I killed him, I can tell you that I didn't."

"No. That's not what I'm implying at all. I'm only trying to gather information. You were there. I wanted to know if you saw or heard anything."

"I wasn't at the show when he was killed. I'd taken off right after the match. Actually the guy pissed me off even more so after I rode away from you and Ethan. I won't deny that. He came right up to me afterward and told me that I played like a girl with my hands tied behind my back."

"Ouch."

"Yes. Ouch. You know, it irked me, but the thing that really bugged me was that it wasn't like we were playing some huge tournament for cash and prizes. We were playing for charity. A charity I believe in." He twirled his horse's mane around his fingers, his other hand holding the reins loosely. "You know, I hope the police find who did this. It's not fair that you've had to close your center. That money could do a lot of good. My wife's good friend's son is autistic. I know that he's involved with horses down in San Diego and it's been great for him."

"Don't worry, we'll be up and running again. I am sure of it. If the police don't find out who did it, then I will."

"Like I said, I'm not your man. In fact, if it would make you feel better you can ask my wife and daughter. They were both there on Sunday and once I was done the three of us took off, right after the confrontation with Sterling. My family was standing there when he went off on me like that, which I thought was classless. Hell, my eleven-year-old daughter was standing right there listening to this guy rag on me. I've got to tell you, I'm not surprised he's six feet under.

Not that anyone deserves that kind of death. But I heard him being horrible to Juliet Mitchell right before the match."

"You did?"

"Oh yeah. He was giving her a hard time. Something about how she needed to listen to him because she was wrong and didn't know what the hell she was talking about. She kept insisting that her dad was going to find out about it and she told him to leave her alone. He grabbed her then, and I started toward them. So did Zach, who pushed Sterling off of her."

"No kidding?"

Lance nodded.

"What happened after that?"

"Juliet walked away and went back to her horse. Zach started talking real low to Sterling and didn't look too happy with him. I thought I heard him say that he didn't want anything more to do with him. That he was only playing nice for the day because of the event, but when it was all said and done they'd need to talk some more."

"Wow."

Lance shook his head. "Make anything of that?"

"Maybe. I thought those three were good friends."

"Yeah, well, one never knows what goes on behind closed doors. Juliet Mitchell seemed to know something ugly about her boyfriend and she knew her father would go nuts when he found out about it. Whatever it was, it was enough to make Juliet walk away from him, and from what I could tell, Zach, too."

"Okay. That's food for fodder, isn't it?"

He nodded. "I wish I could be more help. You know I'm in your corner. Whatever you need."

"Thanks. One more thing: Tommy Liggett was also on your team. Do you know him at all?"

"He's okay. Kind of walks in Sterling's shadow. You know the type — not as good-looking as his friend, not as rich, not all the girls hanging on him, so he's kind of the wing man. But the guy is nice enough. I never had an issue with him. I know he doesn't come from money and he puts most of what he makes into his horse and his lessons with Robert, so he's really into the polo. That's about it."

Michaela thanked Lance and walked back down the hill to her truck. She'd doubted he had anything to do with killing Sterling. It didn't fit. But she couldn't shake having seen the spot of blood on his shirt. Was it

Sterling's blood? It was the same shirt he'd worn at the event. It was light colored, so even if he'd washed it, blood would've stained. But why would a killer be wearing the same shirt he'd killed someone in? And he was adamant about his wife and daughter being with him afterward. The only hole she could see with Lance was his *alibi:* Was it for real? Would his wife lie for him, and could his daughter not have a concept of the timing, being fairly young? She hoped not.

An altercation between Lance and Sterling had been something that Lance supposedly had been able to laugh off and then go home with his family. She really wanted to believe him. She liked Lance Watkins, and Ethan had told her that he couldn't see Lance hurting anyone. It was all super damn confusing.

On top of it, what Lance had told her about Juliet and Zach added to the mix that they could somehow be involved with Sterling's murder. Whatever they had argued about with Sterling seemed far more emotionally charged than the issue between Sterling and Lance, and Michaela aimed to find out if it had driven one of the two of them to murder.

FOURTEEN

Lunchtime: About time to locate one Lucia Sorvino. Michaela was suddenly famous, but not with the kind of fame that anyone cares to have. As she walked down the steps into Sorvino's, all eyes fell on her. The women with their glasses of white wine, rows of pearls across their necks, and fine designer wear scowled at her. The men, on the other hand, seemed to be looking at her with a sort of awe. She wanted to scream, "I didn't kill him!" but decided that would garner even more attention, and the last thing she wanted was any more of that. This was either the ballsiest thing she'd ever done or one of the stupidest. But dammit, she was innocent.

Sorvino's at the polo lounge had a classic Italian feel, with crystal chandeliers, hunter green and cream décor, and photos from a bygone era of Palm Springs and the surrounding desert. It was kind of Frank

Sinatra-ish, which fit, since Frank liked to hang out thirty minutes away in Palm Springs back in the Rat Pack days.

Michaela asked a busboy where Lucia Sorvino might be. He told her in the office. She asked him to show her the way. He did, also wearing that expression of awe. Michaela's stomach clenched. The busboy tapped on the door.

"Who's there?" a woman's voice asked.

"Uh, Miss Sorvino, there is someone here to see you."

"Yeah? Who?"

Michaela held a finger to her lips and shook her head, then shooed the busboy away. His eyes grew wide, as if she scared the hell out of him.

"Gino? Who is it?" Lucia demanded and swung open the door. She gasped when she saw who stood on the other side. Michaela quickly shoved her foot in the door and held her hand out to prevent Lucia from shutting it. It didn't stop her from trying, and they played push and shove for a few seconds until Michaela's strength won out and she was able to open the door all the way, storm inside the small office, and shut it behind her.

"I'm gonna scream!" Lucia said. "You better get out of here now, or I'll scream."

"I wouldn't do that if I were you." Michaela took a threatening step toward her. "You lied about me and I want to know why."

"Get out! Get out!"

"Why did you tell the police that I was sleeping with Sterling? That's a bald-faced lie."

"You killed Sterling. Everyone knows you did it. You need to get outta here because my papa will come in here and have a heart attack if he sees you."

Michaela took another step forward. "Spare me the drama. Someone told you to say that. You're just a stupid kid, and if I had to guess, I'd say you were sleeping with Sterling and you don't want your papa to find out about it. What do you think your brother would say? Or wait, maybe they already knew and killed him themselves for *tainting* you! You know that I didn't kill Sterling. What I want to know is why did you tell the police that I was sleeping with him?"

"Get the hell out of here, you screwed-up bitch!"

Michaela was getting right under the girl's skin. She could see panic in her eyes and felt pretty sure she was on the right track as far as something going on between her and

Sterling.

"I'm only curious as to what a twenty-six-year-old hotshot polo player has in common with a what, twenty-year-old chef's daughter? Wait, maybe Sterling started to feel the same way and blew you off, so *you* killed him. Now you're trying to cover your tracks by making up stories about me. Maybe you're not as dumb as you look. You got into my office, you used my mallet, and now you can tell everyone I was sleeping with him. I think you need to start talking."

"Get out! I told you to get the hell out of here! Papa! Mario!" she screamed.

"The cops may be fooled by your big green eyes and crazy lies, but I'm no fool. And when your family sees you for who you are . . . well, I think you've got yourself in some hot water."

The door flew open and Pepe Sorvino thundered into the office, nearly knocking Michaela over. "You get outta here. We don't want you here."

"Thank you, Papa, she was harassing me. She scared me."

"*Harassing* you? Oh my God. You are one lying little —" Michaela blurted.

"Out!" Pepe screamed.

"Fine. I'll leave, but I am going to find out why you're lying about me, Lucia. And if it's what I think the reason is, your life will be turned upside down like you've done to mine."

"Go!"

"I will find out what you're hiding." Michaela turned on her heel, nearly running into Mario Sorvino.

Mario followed Michaela to the front door until she turned to him and said, "I'm leaving."

"Hey, between you and me, that prick deserved what he got."

"What?"

"Yeah. Taber. Man was nothing but trouble," Mario said.

"Really? And you knew him?" Her hands shook.

"Who didn't know him? Hotshot dude, come in here and never pay his tab. I wasn't surprised that someone killed him." Mario crossed his arms. "I want to give you some advice. You may want to be careful around my sister and my father. They got hot tempers. I'm only letting you know."

"Mario!" Pepe approached the front door.

He winked at her and retreated into the restaurant. "Be careful, Michaela. It's that simple. Be careful."

She got back into her truck feeling as if the Sorvino family had more ties to Sterling

Taber than just Lucia Sorvino being his *friend,* and that Mario Sorvino was more than making small talk with her. If she was right, Mario had subtly threatened her with the "stay away from my father and sister" line. And he'd already warned her about making threats toward his family. She couldn't help wondering how Mario Sorvino tied into this and if she was spot-on when she'd told Lucia that maybe her big brother had done away with Sterling to protect her. He seemed the type to do something like that. And how about running into him right after finding Sterling dead on the office floor? He was on the kitchen staff. He had had the opportunity.

Did he also have motive?

FIFTEEN

Why would Pepe's son even come after Michaela? What was his point? She would have to see what Joe might find out about the Sorvinos' ties with Sterling, but right now she had another stop to make. Her stomach sank as she parked her truck next to the stalls at the polo fields. This was not a conversation she wanted to have, but it was necessary. She had every intention to fess up to reading the invoice that had caught her eye and confront Robert Nightingale about it. This was her life she was dealing with and there were some obvious issues between him and Sterling.

She tapped on the office door, which swung open almost immediately. To Michaela's surprise Paige, Robert's sweet but eccentric wife, answered the door. Her eyes looked red, as if she'd been crying. Michaela noticed that the back of her hand had a smudge of black, likely from mascara that she'd wiped off her tearstained face. Paige tried to smile, her brown eyes taking Michaela in. She had cropped blonde hair, which framed her round face. She was on the heavy side and tended to wear drapey, flowy kinds of clothing. Today she had on a purple billowy blouse and black pants.

"Oh, Michaela, hello. Did you come for a lesson?"

Had Paige been the only one to not hear that Michaela was a murder suspect? "No. I wanted to talk to Robert. About Sterling."

"He's not here." She sniffled. "I don't know where he is or when he'll be back. I don't know if he's coming back." She started to cry. "Oh yes, Sterling. Oh dear, I'm sorry that you're having so many troubles over his murder. Goodness knows you would never do such a thing. It's just so horrible. An outrage."

Michaela took a step back. Whoa, this was unexpected. "I'm okay. I'm sure that this will all work out and the police will get to the bottom of it."

"It's not that. It's not you."

Now Michaela was really confused. "Oh, okay. Um . . ."

"Oh no, I don't mean to sound insensitive, but of course the police will exonerate you, it's not that, it's . . ." She wiped her tears and sat down on the sofa. "Nothing. Nothing at all. How selfish of me to carry on when you're obviously having problems of your own. Forgive me."

"You don't need to apologize, Paige. What's wrong?"

"Nothing. Nothing." Paige looked up at her, the tears starting again.

"People don't cry over nothing." Michaela reached into her purse and dug through it. She knew she had tissues somewhere in her bag. She found a packet and handed one to Paige.

The woman blew her nose. "Robert is leaving me. Actually, he's left me."

"What?"

Paige shrugged. "I don't know. I really don't know."

Michaela sat down next to her. "Do you want to talk?" She didn't know Paige all that well, but she couldn't leave her here like this.

Paige put her face in her hands. "I've lost so much in the last few years. First Justin, and now this with Robert, and of course Sterling."

"Sterling? You were close with him?" Michaela now felt certain by the way Paige was talking that it had been her who'd hurried away from the polo field grounds after getting out of Sterling's car.

"Oh, yes. He was Justin's best friend."

"Justin? I'm sorry, Paige; I don't know what you're talking about."

"We don't talk about it much. Only people in our small circle ever even whisper about it. I hear them sometimes and see the looks on their faces. The ones that say they feel sorry for me."

Michaela suddenly understood. Paige was talking about her son, who'd been killed in a car accident. She'd never known his name, but she'd heard about the tragedy.

Paige blew her nose. "Justin was our son. I'm sure you know that he died five years ago in a drunk-driving accident after a party. He'd had too much to drink and hit a tree. He was twenty."

"Oh, I am so sorry. I had heard, but I knew it wasn't something to ever discuss with you."

"I know, dear. It's kind of an unspoken rule that no one talks about it, but it's not my rule. Robert won't talk about it. People tiptoe around him all the time. I think he's lost it. He left me a note this morning that said we were through and he was leaving."

"And you don't know why?"

"I have an idea. It has to do with Sterling." She started to cry again.

Michaela waited patiently for a few seconds and then asked her, "What about Sterling?"

"Robert found out that I have been giving him money."

She would have to be careful here. Paige was giving Sterling money? Odd. From everything that she had ascertained about the man, he appeared to have plenty of money of his own and he was doing just fine with that, along with the money he earned with his modeling gigs. "Um, I hate to pry, but why would you give Sterling money?"

Paige smiled, her eyes reflecting nothing but sadness. "I told you that Sterling had been Justin's best friend. It was how Sterling started riding polo. Justin got him into it. And yes, he does come from a wealthy family in Santa Barbara, but they recently stopped providing him with money. Not the kind of money he needed to live on, anyway. I think he'd gotten himself into debt by overextending. He had been receiving twenty thousand dollars a month from his family and then they cut that in half. You can imagine how difficult that would be if you're used to having more."

How much did he need? Ten thousand dollars a month for a single guy sure sounded like plenty. "Why did the family decide to do that? Do you know?"

Paige shook her head. "He wouldn't talk about it. He said that it was too painful. All I know is that last summer he went back home, then he returned, and within a few months his family had sort of disowned him. And, because he was a link to my son, I didn't want him to suffer."

"You became a mother to him."

"Yes. He filled the gap in my heart that was missing my son . . . and now they're both gone!"

"Robert didn't feel the same way about Sterling as you did?" Michaela assumed this.

"No. He liked Sterling fine, but I think he might've blamed him for Justin's death. They were at the party together and Robert feels that Sterling should have stopped him from driving home that night. But Sterling was with a date and claims he didn't realize that Justin was intoxicated."

"Did Robert tell you that he blamed Sterling?"

"No."

"Oh. So you were giving Sterling money? I assume that Robert didn't know about it?"

"Not until Sterling told him."

"He told him?"

"Yes. Sterling was not paying Robert for

the training and boarding bills here. I went to talk with him about it. I explained that the money I'd been giving him was from an insurance policy that we had on Justin and that he needed to use the money to pay Robert, and for his rent and education."

That must have been what Michaela witnessed between the two of them the other day. Paige had tried talking to Sterling about this. "I didn't know he was going to school."

"He was taking acting classes. It was his dream to be an actor and he would've been wonderful at it. He promised me that he'd get caught up with his bills with Robert. He went to talk to Robert. Things heated up, I guess, and Sterling lost it and told him that it didn't matter that he owed him money. Sterling laughed at Robert and told him where the money was coming from. Robert was so upset. He came to me and asked me what I'd been doing. I told him. I explained that Sterling was like a son to me and that I was trying to help him. I got him to calm down after a bit. Sterling had auditioned for a play and had promised to pay me back because he'd gotten the part. Robert was still angry, but not as much. Then this morning I found the letter. I guess he changed his mind."

Michaela was more than confused. This would take some time to digest. Sterling had played poor Paige. He *was* an actor. She felt sorry for the woman on so many levels.

She stood and tried to see if the invoice she'd spotted on Robert's desk was still there. It wasn't. She sighed.

"I'm sorry to have rambled on. I shouldn't have troubled you," Paige said.

"No. Not at all. I'm glad I was here for you." She put a hand on Paige's shoulder.

Paige nodded. Michaela said that she had to go, as she had a riding lesson to give. She walked out of the office, her brain twisted in frustration, for she had no real clue as to what had just taken place, or the significance of any of it. But if working around animals had taught her one thing, it was that trusting your intuition usually meant that you were on the right track. *Her* intuition told her that Sterling Taber had maintained some interesting and complicated relationships, and that more than one person had reasons to want him dead.

Sixteen

Michaela needed a breather and had about an hour before she had to be back home to give a riding lesson to Joe's little girl. Thank God that Joey believed in her innocence and had no plans of removing Gen from the riding center.

She walked down the stalls at the polo field to say hi to Rebel. Someone had moved the horse and at first she couldn't find her. She'd been moved all the way down to the end of the row. The bay mare walked over to her as soon as she called to her from the other side of the barred stall. "Hi, gorgeous, how are you today? Tell you what, I've been better. Why'd they move you down here?"

The horse's ears popped forward and she stared at Michaela as if she were listening intently. The beautiful thing about these animals was that they provided total and complete therapy, and all for no money down. Well, that wasn't entirely true when you broke down board, feed, and training, not to mention show fees, vet bills, horseshoeing bills, etc. No, hardly free, but they were really good listeners.

Michaela opened Rebel's stall door and slid through. She stroked the mare's neck and scratched under her chin, which made her toss her head about. The chin was typically sensitive and the scratching caused Rebel to bare her teeth with her top lip turned up, as if she were smiling or laughing at Michaela. "Oh, so you find my woes amusing. Wish you could talk; bet you know something about all the strangeness that goes on around here."

She continued to pet the horse. She rounded behind the animal and saw that her back leg had been wrapped. That was not unusual. Horses acquired cuts and scrapes at times that caused the grooms to have to treat the superficial wounds and then wrap them to keep the flies away and prevent the area from getting infected.

Michaela noticed that the wrap was partially off. She bent down and rewrapped it, uncovering a fairly deep cut. Looked as if maybe she'd rubbed up against something sharp. Kind of like what had happened with Lance Watkins's dapple gray gelding. Rebel had probably gotten the scrape in the other stall and that was why she'd been moved. Michaela retightened the binding. As she started to stand, something shiny caught her eye. She bent back down and brushed away the shavings to get a better look. She stared for a moment as her mind registered what it was. Then she picked it up. Oh, wow! Someone would be looking for this: a tennis bracelet. Each diamond had to be a carat and had obviously cost someone a lot of money. She started to stand when she heard voices in the corridor.

Juliet Mitchell sat astride her chestnut gelding, and Zach Holden walked next to them. Neither noticed Michaela. "You did good out there," Zach said. "All you need is to relax. He can tell that you're tense." He gave the horse a firm pat on the neck. Michaela was about to step out of the stall and say hello.

"Tense! Of course I'm tense! How the hell could I not be stressed out?"

Michaela shrank back inside the stall. Maybe now wasn't the best time to reveal herself. She'd never heard Juliet so . . . edgy. The girl was always well mannered, typically soft-spoken, definitely upper crest. It was possible that, like her father, the young woman had a hot temper hidden beneath her polished exterior.

"Think about it, Zach." She slid off her horse. "We have to get that letter out of Sterling's apartment. Do you know if the crime scene tape has come down?"

Oh boy. This was mighty interesting. No way was Michaela going to announce her presence now. What were these two talking about? A letter? What letter? She ducked back down, the bracelet gripped in her hand.

"I don't know why you even sent him that. What was the purpose?"

"Look, I know it was stupid. Really stupid." She started to cry. "I don't even know if it's there anymore. I had to send it to him. I was scared of him and I thought that was the best way to get him to leave me alone. I tried to send an e-mail but I thought a letter would be more final, more to the point. I had no idea it would wind up like this."

"It's okay. I understand. It has to still be at his place. You mailed it on Friday? Maybe he hadn't gotten it by Saturday. Or maybe he didn't read the letter. It might still be in his mailbox."

Michaela watched the two through the stall bars.

"What if the police find it? The things that I wrote in there . . . it was bad, Zach."

142

"The police are focused on Michaela Bancroft."

Michaela bit down hard on her lip.

"We both know she didn't do it," Juliet replied.

"But until we get that letter, we have to let the police think what they want. We can't tell them anything. It will ruin your life, *our* life, and so many others in your family."

"It feels wrong."

"I know," Zach said. "But we can't afford not to be protective right now. Not until we know for sure. And then we can decide what to do."

Michaela watched as he pulled Juliet into him. "You didn't do anything wrong."

Juliet nodded. Zach lifted her face up and kissed her. "We'll get through this together."

Get through what *together?* Michaela had no idea what they were up to. She started to sink down lower in the stall as she saw Zach turn her way.

"I promise it's going to be okay, Jules. Trust me." He smiled and brushed a piece of hair out of her face. She smiled back at him and nodded. "Look, I've got to check on Rebel. One of the grooms said she had a cut on her leg. Hang on. I know she likes to try and pull her wraps off."

Rebel. *Rebel! Oh shit, he was coming into*

143

Rebel's stall. As he approached, Michaela lifted her head. Zach jumped back.

"Oh hey," she said. "Didn't know anyone was here." She knew she didn't sound very convincing. "I came to visit Rebel and saw that she had a gash on her leg. Silly mare had her wrap off. I redid it."

"Oh. Yeah, I was going to check on her. Gosh, we've been here for a little bit." Zach glanced back at Juliet, who had a wide-eyed look on her. "You didn't hear us?"

"No. I didn't. I was bent over treating the horse, and you know, I've been having sinus problems lately. My ears seem clogged. I don't know . . ." She shrugged. "Maybe allergies." Michaela was fairly certain that neither Zach nor Juliet were buying her story. "I'd better go." She slipped out the stall door. "I've got a lot going on, you know."

"Yeah, sorry about all that. We heard. We know you're not a killer." He frowned.

"No I'm not. You two have a good day." Michaela walked quickly out of there. She knew she wasn't a killer, but after overhearing those two chat, she wasn't so sure that either one of them couldn't have murdered Sterling.

SEVENTEEN

Michaela didn't know what to make of Zach and Juliet's conversation. What were those two hiding? Of all the gall for Zach to say that it was okay for the cops to focus on Michaela when they both knew she hadn't killed Sterling. They were so certain about it, too, and yet they didn't really know her all that well. She was pretty sure that, upon first impression, she didn't come across as a homicidal maniac. But, were they so certain for some *other* reason that she hadn't killed Sterling? Was it because one of *them* had done it? She recalled Juliet stumbling out onto the stage and appearing flushed at the time and apparently not knowing where Sterling was. It had surprised Camden. What did they not know for sure? What did those two have to make decisions about?

One thing was for certain, there was a letter that Juliet Mitchell had written to Sterling Taber and it was damning to her in some way — which meant that Michaela had to find the letter before they did.

She needed to make a stop at the tack shop and see if a new helmet she'd ordered for Gen had arrived. The girl's birthday was only four days away, on Saturday, and she'd promised to get some things together for Joe and Marianne to give Gen. She couldn't let them down. As much as Joe and Marianne had done for her, she had to come through for them. They were like family.

Camden was helping a customer with a pair of boots. Boy, she'd come a long way form the hopeless shopaholic who didn't care much for anything other than designer clothes and cocktails shared with a good-looking guy. She'd always been a good friend to Michaela though, and it was a delight to see her making such positive changes.

She checked the back room and found that the helmet had been delivered, but not the charm that Marianne had asked her to get for Gen. When Camden was finished with her customer, Michaela asked her if she'd signed for any jewelry that might have come in.

"No jewelry. Some clothes, a box of horse wraps, those leg wraps."

"Sports medicine boots?"

"Yeah, the Professional's Choice ones everyone's asking for. How are you today? I tried to get online this morning to see what I could find out about Sterling, but the Internet is down. I called the cable people."

"Thanks. I'm okay. I'm trying to get through this, figure it out. So far, all I can determine is that I'm not the only one who didn't think much of Sterling."

Camden frowned.

"I'm sorry. I don't want to speak badly of him, especially considering the circumstances, and I know you didn't feel that way about him, but try to understand where I'm coming from."

"I know. I do. I'll get online as soon as I can. I've got several things to do around here as well."

"You do what you need to here first. I'm weeding through what I've found out."

She didn't go into what she'd overheard and seen in the past couple of days, because Camden had a propensity to worry, and she had enough on her plate in trying to manage the new store. They'd made the decision to go ahead and open their doors on Monday once the crime scene investigators had cleared the scene, because they didn't really see another option. "How's business so far?"

"Not too bad. I didn't know what to expect after what happened. I think there are some people who have stopped by just to see where a murder took place, but most of the people coming in are buying things. You know who did stop by?"

"Who?"

"That Erin Hornersberg, still as rude as ever. She said that she wanted her makeup brushes. I didn't know what she was talking about. She insisted they were in the storage room, but I checked and didn't see anything. Then she wanted to go back and look herself. At first I wouldn't let her, but finally I went back there with her and stood over her shoulder, but we still didn't find them. She says we'll have to pay for them. She wrote down her address for us to send her a check." Camden handed it to her. "I told her she had to be joking. She says she left four brushes here and she wants more than two hundred dollars for them."

"I don't think so. Give me a break! Since when did makeup brushes cost fifty bucks each?"

"Actually, if you buy the good ones, like the professional ones, they can be expensive."

"Fifty bucks?" Camden nodded. "Like I said, I don't think so. I'll stop by her place and see if we can't work this out. I have a few things to ask her about anyway. Maybe her brushes will turn up."

"She's weird."

Michaela nodded. "Oh, speaking of *lost.* Look what I found in one of the stalls at the polo field." She took the bracelet she'd picked out of Rebel's shavings from her purse.

"Oh my God."

"I know. Someone has to be missing this. Can you post a sign up about it, and place a classified ad or something, maybe even call the police and see if anything like this has been reported missing?"

"Sure. Someone has to be missing it. One of my exes gave me one of those once. They cost thousands."

"That would bum me out, if it was mine. I'll hang on to it, and if anyone calls about it, let me know."

"Well, how do we know if they're telling the truth?" Camden said.

"Good point." Michaela looked it over closely to see if there was any way someone could distinguish it. "The only thing I can think of is to take it down to Ed Mitchell's jewelry store and have them tell me what size the diamonds are, and the clarity. That kind of thing. I'll try and get by there and see what it's worth. Whoever owns it should have all of that information on hand, I would think."

"I'd think so, too."

"Good, then that's what we'll ask if anyone comes by or calls saying that it's theirs. And let me know when a box from Horse Jewels gets delivered. I need to get it to Joe for his daughter's birthday."

"Sure. I'll get that sign up and see you at home. I promise I haven't stopped thinking about how to help you out of this mess. As soon as I can get online, I'll start surfing around and see what I can find out."

Michaela needed to get back to her place for Gen's riding lesson. She hadn't cancelled it, because in addition to owing Joe a great deal, she also wanted to try and keep something normal in her life.

Michaela glanced in the rearview mirror to change lanes. An uneasiness floated over her. What was this? If she didn't know any better, she'd say that someone driving a black Ford Explorer was following her.

She had two choices: punch it and try and get away from the Explorer, or pull into a strip mall and see if she was right. *Was* someone watching her, and if so, who? The *whys* she could kind of assume. She'd take her chances. She turned into the first Jamba

Juice/Starbucks/drugstore parking lot she could find. Not too difficult. Even out here in the desert, they seemed to be going up on every corner. She dashed into the Starbucks and peered out the window. The black Explorer was there, parked down the way. From what she could tell, a woman sat inside. She ordered a coffee and then walked out; the SUV was still there. This was not the time to be anything less than ballsy, so she took a big drink of the coffee, hoping to get a good head of steam going. Maybe she'd go kung fu on her *friend.*

She walked briskly toward the car. The driver had sunk down in her seat, but Michaela could still see that someone was inside. Suddenly, whoever was behind the wheel figured out what her intentions were, and before she reached the Explorer the driver cranked the engine, backed out, and tore off. Michaela stood there, coffee in hand, bewildered.

EIGHTEEN

Michaela felt pretty shaken up on the drive home. Why would anyone be following her? She couldn't see the person well enough to recognize who it was. Not all was lost though, because she'd been able read a part of the license plate. Maybe, with Joe's connections, he'd be able to find out who owned the SUV.

She sped home, certain that Joe and his daughter would be waiting for her. Relief swept through her when she saw him getting out of his minivan. After pulling up she walked over to the van and helped Gen out. The girl smiled slightly upon seeing Michaela. Through Gen, she had found many new reasons to see life in a different and special way. The girl's autism had taught Michaela to slow down and feel with all of her senses. And she knew from Joe's feedback and watching his daughter do a little better each week around the horses that she was teaching her something in return. She reveled in working with the ten-year-old.

"Hi. Are you ready to get Booger out and ride?"

"Yes. Yes. Ride Booger."

Michaela smiled. It came easy around this kid; even though things were crashing down around her, she couldn't help but see how precious life could be. When they'd first started working together, Gen rarely ever said a word. But she'd started talking a lot more in the last month, and Booger — Michaela's old gelding — brought the best out in Gen.

"Is she ready? I think she said his name fifty times on the way over." Joe laughed. "How you doin'? Things okay?" he asked.

"No, they're not okay. Now that you two are here though, it's a little better."

"Talk to me. Come on."

Michaela took Gen's hand and the three of them walked to the barn. She told Joe everything that had happened over the course of the last couple of hours.

"Not good. Okay, we put the Nightingales on the back burner. They're trouble soundin', but let's take care of this license plate you got first and then the letter you heard Juliet and Zach talking about. You got an address on this Sterling dude?"

"No."

"Okay, sit tight. I'm gonna see what I can do. It's probably gonna take some time before I can put the license plate thing together with the owner. A partial plate is a starting point. I'll see what I can do, and I'll locate an address on Taber. Right now, why don't you give my pumpkin here her lesson and I'll make some calls. I'm also working on the Sorvino chick. My cousin told me what she said. That was in confidence, you know, but when you took off after her yesterday, I figured I'd better check some things out myself. What I know so far is the girl is a clubber. Sneaks out past her pop and her brothers and heads into Palm Springs for the nightlife when she can. She's trouble."

"That much I am sure of," Michaela replied. She told him about her confrontation with Lucia and Pepe, and how Mario had followed her out of Sorvino's. She also brought up what she'd seen and heard with Ed Mitchell and Pepe.

"I don't like the sound of any of this. They're all trouble and you're wrapped up in it. We gotta take this thing step by step, 'cause one of these loony toons offed Sterling and they have an inkling that you're on the hunt, which you've made no bones about. Well, Mick, you're putting yourself in a risky situation. It's possible that whoever was following you is connected to Sterling's murder. I say you lay low a bit, let me see what I can find out, and then we'll go from there."

"That's easier said than done."

"I know you're antsy and I can't blame you, but you gotta listen to me."

He was probably right. "Deal."

Michaela spent the next hour with Gen and life suddenly felt normal again. The child smiled. The horse did everything asked of him and for a little while Michaela felt a semblance of balance. Then it was over.

With Booger put away and Gen feeding him his treats, Michaela found Joe inside her office on the phone. "Uh-huh. Interesting. Thanks." Joe hung up.

"What was that about?" she asked.

"I put in some calls about the license plate; nothing yet, but I'm not surprised. I'm working on Taber's address. But check this one out: I wrote down a list of all the people you mentioned to me, wanted to see what else I could find out about any of them, and I did."

"You did? What?"

"One of them killed somebody and spent some time in jail."

NINETEEN

"What? Who? How?"

"The makeup artist."

"Erin Hornersberg?"

Joe nodded and leaned back in Michaela's swivel chair, looking pretty darn proud of himself.

"What are the details?"

Michaela sat down slowly on her sofa, taking this new piece of information in. She didn't even bother to ask how he'd found it out. She knew his answer would be something like one of his cousins who works for the parole board or something like that. It didn't matter. Joe knew how to get information and, even better, how to process it.

"What I know so far is, the makeup girly was at a rock concert. A punk rock thing. Word is she was in the bathroom and another girl started giving her some problems, you know, makin' waves kinda thing, and this Hornersberg chick punched her so hard that she fell back and hit her head on the concrete wall and it killed her."

Michaela brought her hand to her mouth.

"She got time for manslaughter and assault and battery. She was supposed to do fifteen years, but her case went back on appeal and the defense was able to produce a couple of witnesses who said that the woman who died provoked Erin and hit her. Turned out it was a case of self-defense. The victim had a rap sheet, and Erin was out after spending nine months in the can."

"Provoked, huh? Self-defense? Even so, I don't know a lot of people who have it in them to kill anyone even in self-defense." Michaela let this jell in her brain. "If she's the kind of person who loses it easily, maybe she lost it just enough with Sterling the other day that she did him in. I need to talk to her. She came by the shop today looking for some makeup brushes she left. When Camden couldn't find them, she said that we needed to pay for them. I've got her address in my purse."

"Hold off and we'll go there together. I can't today. My oldest, Joe, has a concert tonight. Lead saxophone. Kid is awesome." Joe beamed. "Otherwise, I'd say let's do it today. Maybe I could meet Marianne and the kids at the school."

157

"No way. You need to be with your family. I can drop in on Erin myself."

"Mickey, this is a woman who *does* seem like a loose cannon. We don't know all the details of what went on with her case, so you know, I think you better hold off on confronting her. You told me she was a strange bird. I don't want you going there alone."

"Fine."

Gen walked into the office and sat down next to Michaela, who said, "Did you like riding today? Did you have fun?"

The girl nodded. "Fun. I had fun. Booger is fun."

Michaela gently touched her shoulder. Gen tensed under her touch. "Good."

"Mick, I hate to go right now, but the family and all."

"Don't be silly." Michaela waved a hand at him. "You do what you need to do."

"I'll be calling in a bit and checkin' in with you."

"Thank you. And, thank *you*," she said to Gen.

She turned Rocky out into the pasture to play and get some exercise. Then she took out her two-year-old stallion, Leo, and led him up to the arena, where she attached a lunge line onto his halter. Letting the rope out as she trailed to the side of her horse with a long whip in her right hand and the line in her left, she asked him for the trot and then onto a canter, where he was able to get his energy out. She continued to lunge the young horse for several minutes and then she let him off the line so he could romp and play, tearing around the ring. After that she took her older mare, Macy, out and worked her for a good forty minutes, putting her through her paces and enjoying riding an animal who knew how to move and seemed to almost anticipate every move right before Michaela asked her for them. God, it felt good just to get out and be with her horses again. For a while, she'd forgotten about Sterling and this big huge mess she'd become wrapped up in.

After putting the horses up, she went down the row of stalls, making sure that everything was locked up and then fed each one with care, measuring out needed vitamins and supplements and saying good night to each one — her kids.

It was nearly five, and what Joe had told her about Erin nagged at her. She knew what she'd promised him. Maybe she could get Camden to go with her. She'd seen Camden's BMW pull in during Gen's lesson. If she took Camden, she wouldn't be going alone. That made sense to her. What could happen with the two of them together? If Erin were trouble, they'd be double the trouble.

She knocked on the door of the guesthouse, where Camden and Dwayne lived. Her friend opened it. "Want to go see if we can get into some trouble?" Michaela asked.

Camden closed the door behind her. "Since when did you ever have to ask me that?"

A few minutes later, they were turning out onto the highway. "Can you get my purse? There's an address in it," Michaela said.

Camden found it; Michaela could see out of the corner of her eye that her friend was looking at her funny. "This is what you call going and getting into trouble? Come on. This is Erin Hornersberg's address."

"I know." Michaela gripped the steering wheel. "Hear me out." She filled her in on what Joe had told her about Erin.

"You need to turn around and go back home because Joe is right on this one! What are you thinking?"

"I'm thinking that Erin might slip up and say something about Sterling, and if you're with me, we can go to the police and tell them."

"No." Camden shook a finger at her. "You're *not* thinking. That is so stupid. Do you hear yourself?"

"Okay, I agree, it doesn't rank up there in the intellect department. But, come on, I don't know what else to do."

"Wait for Joe. His muscle is enough to make anyone quiver. Besides, think about it: Do you really think Erin is going to slip up and say, 'Oh yeah, I took the dude out'? I don't think so."

"All right." Maybe bringing Camden along wasn't such a good idea, but she wasn't convinced yet that going to see Erin was so dangerous. "Bear with me. We'll see if she's even home and if so, we'll handle the makeup brush thing. That's it. Let's go and see how she acts."

"Ridiculous, but you're not going to let me out of this, are you?"

"No."

"Fine. For this, I may pick one of those ugly bridesmaids' dresses."

"You wouldn't. And I thought I was the maid of honor."

"I would. Hot pink with frills and puffy sleeves à la 1990. And maybe I'll demote you."

"You're a bitch."

"Oh so true, so true."

They started laughing. "You know, I got some snooping done for you," Camden said.

"You did?"

"Told you I would. And I found out some interesting things about Sterling."

"Want to elaborate?"

"Looks like you were right and I am easily snowed. Sterling had some trouble with the law back home in Santa Barbara. I found a newspaper clipping from last summer. All about big money, parties, and a dead girl. She supposedly was one of Sterling's girl-friends."

"Really?"

"Yeah. And there's more." Camden sucked in a deep breath. "Guess who's in the photo with Sterling? His polo mates — Zach Holden and Tommy Liggett."

"So, those guys went to Santa Barbara with Sterling last summer. I talked to Paige Nightingale earlier and she told me Sterling's family tightened up the purse strings with him last summer."

"That's about all I could find. The story seemed to die out. The articles were vague. The dead girl's name is Rebecca Woodson. She drowned after being at a party with Sterling; the article names him as her boyfriend. It also said that the two of them had been arguing and that this young gal left the party, while Sterling stayed and hung out there with his friends. There were conflicting reports. I guess that some party-goers said Sterling followed Rebecca out. Some said they saw him leave with a buddy."

"Wonder if that was Zach or Tommy? It only said *a* friend, or did it say *friends?*"

"I'll give you the articles when we get back, but I'm pretty sure it said *a* friend. Then I found an article from a few weeks after this girl's death; she drowned by falling off a nearby pier. Her family didn't buy it when Sterling was cleared of any wrong-doing, and they filed a civil suit. I can't find anything about it after that."

"Great. This is getting more twisted by the minute, Cam. As if having enemies in the desert wasn't enough for Sterling, the man had people in his hometown who might also have reasons to want him dead. I don't know what you think, but if the Wood-sons think this guy killed their daughter, it seems reasonable to me that someone in her family might have wanted him dead."

"Sounds like a possibility."

"Here's our street," Michaela said. She parked the car in front of a decent-looking apartment complex with nice landscaping. "What number is her apartment?"

"Twenty-three."

"You ready?"

"No."

"Oh, what could happen? It's an apartment building, for crying out loud. There are people all over the place."

Camden gave her that funny look again. "Sure, what could happen, she asks. We're only going to talk to a psycho bitch capable of killing somebody. I don't know, what *could* happen?"

TWENTY

They stood outside Erin's apartment. "Dammit, we're here, knock," Camden finally said.

"I know. I'm rethinking this."

Camden grabbed her arm. "Good, let's go."

Before she could pull her away, Michaela knocked. A few seconds later Erin opened it. "Oh. It's you. I take it that you brought my makeup brushes?"

"Actually, no, we didn't."

"You didn't? Okay, then you're writing me a check or handing me some cash for them?"

"Not exactly," Michaela replied.

"Not exactly? What does that mean? Why are you here then?"

Camden started to open her purse. "You know what? I do have some cash here and I know how important good brushes are, especially to a makeup artist —"

Michaela put a hand on her friend's shoulder. "Okay, before any money is exchanged here, I've got some questions for you."

"Questions for me? I don't know what you might need to ask me and I don't care. Red here wants to pay me for my brushes and that's what matters right now."

"No. What matters to me is that you spent time in jail and you had a beef the other day with Sterling Taber. And I'm sure that you know I've been arrested for his murder — a murder that I didn't commit."

"That's what they all say. My time in jail is none of your business, but if it makes you feel any better, I do understand your problems. I spent that time in jail for something that I didn't do. I sat there for nine freaking months until finally my lawyer, who I paid out the yin-yang, found a couple of chicks who really saw what went down in that bathroom. Maybe you'll get lucky and someone will come forward for you, too."

"I'm not counting on *luck* right now."

Erin postured herself in the doorway. She wasn't a big woman — not tall, anyway. But she was tough. The kind of girl in junior high who Michaela would have steered clear of. Right now, she wasn't even sure where she found her courage, but she was hell-bent on getting the truth.

"I think we should go," Camden said. "I can mail you the check. We'll get out of your hair."

"That's a good idea, Red."

"No. No it's not!" Michaela looked from her friend to Erin. "I know Sterling was a jerk to you, but I'm wondering if you knew him before Sunday."

"I told you, I saw him around. At clubs."

Michaela noticed the woman tightening her fists. Maybe it was a good time to leave. "At clubs. Right. Okay."

"That's it. Now, I'm going to be nice because you two paid me well the other day and you seem to be having a rough time." She nodded at Michaela. "Forget the check. I'll write it off, but also, don't bother me again." She slammed the door in their faces.

"That was a real party," Camden said. "Now can we please go?"

"Yeah, we can go. But she's lying to us."

"What do you mean?"

"I think she knew Sterling. I don't know how, I don't know what the deal is, but my gut says that she's full of it, and I want to know the truth."

"And I want a margarita."

They got back into the truck, Camden wishing for tequila, lime, and salt, Michaela

determined to figure out what Erin Hornersberg hadn't told them.

TWENTY-ONE

When they got back to the ranch, Camden gave Michaela the articles she'd printed up. Camden sipped a margarita while Michaela had a glass of wine.

"I still can't believe that you — I mean *we* — did that," Camden said. "Erin seems real shady to me. You need to be careful."

"Erin *is* shady and I know to be careful." She set the articles back down on the kitchen table. "This is it? This is all you found?"

"Yes. But I think it could be something. Sterling being in trouble with the law might have something to do with what happened to him."

"It might."

"Are you going to his funeral service tomorrow?"

"Sterling's funeral? It's tomorrow? That was fast. Wow. How did you know?"

"It's in the paper."

"I don't know. Maybe. Hey, where's Dwayne? I meant to ask you earlier, but we got *sidetracked*." She wanted to change the subject. Thinking about going to Sterling's funeral at that moment made her mind swirl with anxiety.

Camden brushed her hair back behind her ears. "He needed some time to think. I told him about me and Sterling."

"You did? How did he take it?"

She shrugged. "He's a quiet man. He's philosophical and he understands that I am a changed woman. I'm not the ditz who used to go around screwing anything that looked good in tight jeans. But I think he needed some time to let it settle and then move past it. I want this to be different between me and Dwayne. I love him and I believe that we are meant for each other. I couldn't keep this from him. I know it's my past, and he gets that . . . but my past isn't so great."

Michaela hugged her. "You did the right thing. You're a good person, okay? I love you and he loves you. And I know Dwayne; he's not a jealous type and he's not one to dwell in the past. You're right, he will recognize why you told him the truth and the two of you will be stronger for it."

"I know. I think he went to get something

170

to eat and go a bookstore or the movies. He likes to do that once in a while."

"Yeah. It'll be okay. Well, it's getting cool and if he left earlier, I want to be sure that he blanketed the horses. Thanks for going with me tonight. You're a good friend."

As Michaela reached the barn, she saw Dwayne's truck pull in. Camden stood in the doorway of the guesthouse. She watched as Dwayne hurried to Camden, throwing his arms around her in a tight hug. She knew that Dwayne wouldn't hold Camden's past against her, and a knot of emotion tightened in the back of her throat. That was love.

An echo of whinnies traveled down the barn row when she entered. Dwayne hadn't blanketed the horses, so she went around to each one and took care of it. Leo, her two-year-old, turned and nibbled lovingly on her back as she buckled the straps underneath his belly. She stood up and scolded him. "No, no." He looked injured and went back to the few scraps he had left from his dinner. She knew that his nibble was harmless, but being mouthy like that was a bad habit to let him get into.

Once she'd blanketed the last of her animals, she hung out in Rocky's stall for a few extra minutes. So, Sterling's funeral was tomorrow. She knew it would be scandalous for her to go, considering the circumstances, but she really had to. She wanted to see the faces and reactions of everyone who knew Sterling, many of whom had been there the day he was murdered, particularly those guests she suspected might have had something to do with his death. She also wanted to see if a black Ford Explorer would be in the parking lot.

She turned off most of the lights in the barn and started back to the house as Joe's minivan barreled down her dirt road. He pulled up next to her and rolled down the window. "Go and put some black on — a sweatshirt if you got one, and some pants that you can get around in."

"What are you talking about?" Michaela asked.

"I'll explain after you get changed. Now hurry up."

"Okay." She rushed into the house, did as she was instructed, and met Joe outside.

"Where are we going?"

"First we're gonna drive through a Cotija's taco shop, because Marianne's put me on this diet and it's killing me. I'm wasting away."

"Joe, Marianne would not be happy about

you having a burrito. You don't need to cheat."

"Once. Only once. I do a lot for you, Mick. All I want is a *carne asada* burrito. They can leave the cheese off. And I'll do a diet soda. But I need meat."

She frowned, but let him drive through the taco shop. While waiting for the order she said, "Okay, what is this all about?"

"The letter. The one that you heard Zach and Juliet talking about?"

"Yes."

"We are going to find it."

"Wait a minute. How do we plan on finding this letter?" She stared at him as he turned into a parking lot in front of a row of high-end townhomes. "Oh no, no. I see now. We can't. Is this where Sterling lived?"

"Follow my lead and keep your mouth shut."

"Oh no, we are not breaking into his place. I won't do it."

"You got a better idea?"

"Joe . . ." she implored.

"You coming or what, Mick?" Joe got out of the van and started walking.

Michaela found herself following him with the knowledge that she was about to become an everyday common criminal. But what the hell, she'd already been arrested for murder.

TWENTY-TWO

"Joe, I don't think this is such a good idea," Michaela whispered as they stood outside the front door of Sterling's town house, while Joe took out a tool and jimmied the lock.

"And you think spending the rest of your days in jail is a better idea?"

"I didn't say that I *wasn't* going to do it, but —"

"But nothing, we're in." Joe opened the door and pulled out two small flashlights. "Here, take this one. We need to double-duty this. I'll check the front rooms. You find his bedroom, bathroom, and any other room up those stairs." He flashed his light toward a flight of stairs off to the right. "We gotta be quick, too. Not a lot of people out right now, but it's only eleven, so there may be some night owls coming and going. Lucky this place faces the way it does. No other residences looking in." Michaela took the light. Joe placed his hand around hers. "It's okay. It's gonna be okay. Right?"

"Right." She nodded. Joe had seen her hands shaking. It was *not* okay, but she was here, and his rationale made sense to her for now . . . if anything could make sense.

She took the flight of stairs and found what looked to be a guest room/office. Sterling had good taste, or else a decorator. He'd spared no expense, from little Limoges to elegant tapestries on the chairs and sofa in the office. The rooms had a traditional feel to them, all with a kind of horse/hunting theme. There were pictures of Sterling with just about everyone from the polo club; photos from his modeling and acting gigs; and one of him with Tommy and Zach, which had to have been taken last summer. The three of them were at the beach. It was the same photo that had been in the newspaper. Michaela took that one off the wall and shone the light on it. She studied it for a few seconds — three buddies, hanging out, having fun. Something about it, though. She knew there was more to the story of last summer than what Camden had uncovered. She placed the photo on the desk, hearing Joe downstairs. She ventured into Sterling's tidy bedroom. Sterling had been a neat freak, or else he had a maid — more likely, it had been the latter.

Michaela was curious about Sterling's expenditures. Here was a man who'd been used to living on twenty grand a month. Then last summer, according to Paige, he'd received the slap in the face when his allowance had been chopped in half. Then, he asked Paige for a loan and she'd taken money from her dead son's life insurance to give to him. Living "rich" meant something to Sterling. Was that why he had been dating Juliet? He didn't want to live a life less than he was used to, and Juliet's father was loaded.

She opened up the drawers on his nightstand and found a book, *The Kama Sutra,* as well as a list of acting jobs available in both Los Angeles and Palm Springs. He'd checked some off. There was a ticket stub from the club Sinners and Saints. From what Michaela had heard, this was the new hot spot for anyone who was anyone in the desert. But no letter.

She headed to a matching nightstand on the other side. This drawer was more interesting. In it she found a handful of videotapes. She pocketed them, knowing it was wrong. But Joe was right: What would Sterling care at this point? She walked over to his drawers, feeling creepy looking through his boxers and socks. *Really creepy.* But nothing was out of the ordinary. Next was his closet, and she even found herself digging into his pants pockets, where she found something interesting: an airline ticket. She looked at the date. Sterling had flown to Santa Barbara only two weeks earlier. Had he gone there for fun? Inside the folder was also his information for a rental car. Why hadn't he driven? It was only a half-day's drive. Had he gone to see his family? That had to be it. Had he gone to plead his case? And while there, had he sealed the deal on his fate? The more she dug into Sterling Taber's life, the more twisted and strange it was becoming. Regardless, she had to find out why Sterling had gone home and what had happened there.

Michaela trekked downstairs with her new goodies. Joe stood at the bottom of the stairs. He waved an envelope at her. "Here it is. I read it and you should see what it says."

"Really? You found it?"

He nodded. "Right here in the 'to be filed' stack." He laughed.

"No kidding. What does it say?"

Before he could reply, a rustling noise came from outside the front door. "What was that?" Michaela whispered.

"I don't know." He grabbed her arm as they heard what sounded like a key being slid into the lock. "Come on."

They ran upstairs and into Sterling's bedroom. "Oh God, what if it's the police?" Michaela asked.

"I don't know. Let me think."

They heard the door shut, and then voices — a man and a woman's. Michaela strained to listen. Was it Peters and his sidekick, Singer?

Joe walked to the balcony off Sterling's bedroom. As quietly as he could he slid the door open.

"What was that?" the woman downstairs said.

"I don't know. Stay here and I'll check it out," the man replied.

They heard someone climbing the stairs. Joe motioned for Michaela to follow him onto the balcony. The area overlooked the community pool from two stories up. A palm tree swayed silently in the slight breeze, about two feet away from the balcony. "Hit it, Mick."

"What?"

"No time for questions. Jump onto the tree and shinny your ass on down."

"No way." The man on the stairs was

almost to the top, Michaela figured.

"Do it, *now.*"

Michaela knew Joe was right; they had no choice. Luckily for her she was athletic, so she took the chance and made the jump, then shinnied down the tree. She felt the pain in her hands and on her right knee. She leaped off the tree about five feet from the ground and looked up to see Joe attempting the jump. She closed her eyes. He might have been one savvy guy, but athleticism was not one of his attributes. Somehow, he made it.

They tore out of the parking lot in the minivan. "Shouldn't have had that burrito," he said. By the time they cleared the parking lot, they could not help but laugh. They roared for several minutes. For Michaela, part of the laughter was caused by the reality that she'd made it out of there without getting caught — well, basically — and the release of her pent-up stress.

"Oh my gosh, you should have seen yourself coming down off that tree," she said, tears streaming down her face. "I didn't know that you could move that fast, Joe."

"I didn't either. Yeah, that was classic."

"That wasn't Peters. Was it?" Michaela asked, already sure she knew the answer.

"Nope. I'd bet you it was Zach and Juliet."

"I'd bet you're right."

Joe reached into his back pocket and pulled out an envelope. She took the crumpled paper and turned on the overhead light in the minivan. "Do you mind? Will the light bother you?"

"Nah. I'm cool. Read it."

She read over the words that Juliet had written:

I know what you did. My father knows what you did, because I told him and for your sake, I would get out of town. You are disgusting and horrible and I will never trust you again. My father is out for blood. You've messed with the wrong family.

"Whoa," Michaela finally uttered. "No wonder the two of them wanted the letter. Maybe they didn't murder Sterling, but what if they are protecting Juliet's dad?"

"Yep. It's a good theory, and we can't leave out Pepe Sorvino and his daughter."

"What do you think this all means? It's obvious Juliet wrote it. These are her initials, she and Zach were talking about it out at the barn, and those two are awfully friendly with each other these days. And all this stuff about her and her father knowing what he did . . . Wait a minute, I just had a thought about what Juliet might've told her father."

"What's that?"

Michaela quickly told Joe about the newspaper articles that Camden had found concerning Sterling Taber and Rebecca Woodson. "Follow me. The letter that Juliet wrote to Sterling may have to do with this girl."

"It might. But why wouldn't Juliet just break up with him?" Joe asked. "Why go through the whole deal of telling her dad and all? Sterling was never convicted of killing the girl. You said that the papers reported it to be an accident."

"I don't know. But Rebecca Woodson's family filed a wrongful death suit. They don't seem to think it was an accident."

"Okay. Keep talking. Go back to Sunday at the fashion show. Maybe you missed something."

"Juliet seemed flushed and hurried. Camden had thought she and Sterling were off together because she couldn't find either one of them. She offered Juliet a shot of tequila after she showed up, but she refused and got up on the stage."

Joe nodded. "But what about Zach? Where

was he during all of this?"

"On the runway," Michaela replied. "I saw him up there, and then Juliet came rushing through because she was next. He asked her if she was okay when he saw her stepping up on the stage as he was getting down. She nodded and the show went on."

"One thing we know then is that Zach didn't kill Sterling, so we can cross him off the list, but what we don't know is if he's protecting Juliet. From the sound of it, he's protecting her from *something.* We can also guess they're protecting her father. Strange, though, I don't think Daddy would go and advertise to his little girl that he planned to knock off her boyfriend."

"No. I agree with that. Let's stay with this train of thought, that the murder has to do with Rebecca Woodson," Michaela said.

"Okay, we'll see if we can't peel this back a bit more and give each of them a motive. I know we can only theorize but it might help. Say Juliet felt threatened by Sterling. Maybe the dude did kill this Rebecca Woodson. He might have threatened Juliet for something; maybe she didn't want to see him anymore for another reason. Who knows if there was a lovers' quarrel? Say there was. Taber threatens Juliet Mitchell, who tells Zach, who is their buddy. Now,

Juliet is a pretty girl, and Zach may have had a thing for her. You said they were all kinda lovey-dovey when you spotted them in the stall area?"

Michaela nodded. "Definitely. I would even go so far as to say that they looked to be more than friends."

"Okay. Zach sees an opening where Sterling screwed up with the girl. He's there for her to lean on and she tells him that Sterling threatened her. Zach was in Santa Barbara with Sterling when this Rebecca Woodson died?"

"Yes. And what if Zach knows that her death wasn't an accident and thinks that Sterling might have killed her? He decides to protect Juliet, and one or the other goes and tells her father about Sterling's threat and what happened in Santa Barbara."

"We're like a regular Holmes and Watson, girl."

She smiled. "Sort of, huh? Now, Ed Mitchell hears this and he's not happy. He kills Sterling. Zach and Juliet assume he did it because they told him about Sterling and maybe Ed went ballistic. Now Zach and Juliet feel the need to protect her father."

"Exactly. The kicker is, where does Pepe Sorvino and his clan come in and what's the deal with the ring that you saw Mitchell give to Pepe?"

"A payoff?"

Joe clucked his tongue. "Possible. I'm gonna call around to a few of my cousins and see if the Sorvinos have any ties with one of the families."

"Mafia?"

Joe shrugged and wheeled the van onto her property.

"Wouldn't you know that already? With your connections?"

"You've watched one too many *Sopranos*."

She shook her head. They pulled up in front of her house. Michaela extracted the videotapes from the backpack she'd taken into Sterling's place. "Wanna watch some movies?"

Joe looked at his watch. "Can't. What you got?"

"Compliments of Sterling."

"You little vixen."

"Never know what we might find. I figured I might as well grab them. We've already broken a hundred laws tonight."

"Report back. I told Marianne I'd be back before Conan. We like to watch it together."

"Deal."

Michaela went inside her house. A quiet staleness that she had never gotten used to since her old lab, Cocoa, passed away came

185

over her. She sighed. What it must feel like to come home to a family. Lucky Joe.

She got her video camera out. These videos hadn't been transferred from the camera-type cassettes. She would have to put them through her camera to see, and then run it on her laptop. Maybe she'd make some popcorn for the evening's entertainment. Probably just shots of high-priced vacations that he'd taken. She put some popcorn in the microwave, grabbed a bottle of water, and started watching the first tape while it popped.

The bag remained in the microwave before she ever got to it, an hour later. What she saw on the tapes was not only startling, they also revealed someone who would have one helluva reason to put Sterling in the ground, where he couldn't speak a damn word.

TWENTY-THREE

What Michaela viewed on those tapes was completely scandalous. They were appalling, so much so that she had to fast-forward through quite a bit of it. All she could do was repeat the word *wow* over and over again, and shake her head.

All the tapes, except one, displayed a story of a love affair, if that's what it could be called. More of an *erotic* affair. The stars were Sterling and a woman she had never seen before, and they did things on those tapes together that she had no clue were even possible. One tape featured some other gal with Sterling. Probably a one-night stand. Is this what Juliet had discovered — that Sterling had this disgustingly perverted side to him? Had he taped *her?*

Michaela had never seen an X-rated movie — never had an inclination to — but what she saw on the tapes was likely way up there in that category. It was actually gross. The thing was, it became obvious to Michaela that the woman who was on most of the tapes had no clue she was starring in them. At the end of the last tape, which she assumed was the most recent one taken, Sterling sat by himself at the end of his bed. He slicked back his hair with his hands, sighed, and started speaking:

"As you can see, Carolyn, we've had quite a run, and I'm sure Charles will not be a happy man when he receives these tapes. Don't bother destroying them. I have a few copies in select places. You've been charming and fun and it is obvious that you make an excellent star, but you have not come through for me as you had promised." He raised his voice now, sounding like a madman. Ha! Michaela had always sensed there was something lurking underneath that suave, smooth exterior and here it was, coming out of him as a freakish pervert. "You, my dear, promised to get me back in good with the family and make sure my allowance not only matched what it once was, but was increased substantially. You've failed miserably. I am now giving you, as of today, one week to make good on your promises, or else something tells me that you won't be getting a dime of the Taber fortune once the family sees this. I don't have much more to lose, but you, my dear, have what, forty, fifty million that would slip out of your nasty little hands — which I love, by the way. One week, Carolyn. One week."

With that the tape finished up. The date flashed across the screen. It was almost a week to the day before Sterling was murdered.

Holy flying horse pucky. Who was the woman who had made promises to Sterling that she couldn't keep?

Michaela wracked her brain and went over everything about three hundred times. At least it felt that way. Finally, at about 1:30 in the morning, she started to drift off to sleep, and that's when she heard it. At first it was like the moment when falling asleep as the body drifts into that next stage, almost as if the soul is being shaken loose — the body jerks and then a deep sleep follows. The jerk came, but not the sleep. A noise in the house. She sat up and listened. Had she started dreaming? No. There it was again — in the kitchen. What if someone was rummaging for a weapon — a knife? She quietly slid out of bed and tiptoed over to her bedroom door; she kept a baseball bat behind it. She now realized that she should've been keeping it next to her bed.

What good would it have done her if whoever was down there had made it upstairs
without her hearing? The phone. She
needed to get to the phone and call 911.
Dammit, she'd left the portable phone in
her office. She wished for the day when
phones couldn't travel all over the house,
when they had cords on them and were
stationary. Yes, that would've worked much
better right about now.

She heard a creaking sound. Whoever was
there now climbed the stairs. She gripped
the bat tighter and hid behind the door. She
stood still as she watched a figure enter the
room. It was not a man, but a woman, and
as Michaela switched on the light, she was
stunned to see Juliet Mitchell spin around
and point a gun at her.

TWENTY-FOUR

"Juliet! What in the hell are you doing?" Michaela white-knuckled the baseball bat, poised and ready to swing. "Put the gun down."

"Give me the letter!" Juliet yelled. Her tearstained face was streaked in black from mascara. She did not look well, and if Michaela was right, she smelled of alcohol.

"Juliet, let's talk about this. Rationally. You put the gun down and I'll put the bat down and we can talk. Okay?"

"Give me the letter. I won't let you ruin my life!"

"I don't want to ruin your life. Let's talk."

"No. You don't understand."

"Tell me then, what don't I understand?"

"Juliet, put the gun down!" Zach Holden, standing behind the girl, looked as horrified as Michaela felt. "Please, Jules. This won't solve anything. Let's work together on this."

Michaela wasn't too sure she should be

relieved to see Zach or not, but if he could get Juliet to put the gun down, she at least would still have the bat in her hands.

"Why should I? If anything happens to my dad, then what good is any of this? Especially after what you told me tonight!"

"Juliet, all I was trying to say is that we're young and we don't need to rush anything. This has nothing to do with your father."

"It has *everything* to do with my dad! Everything. You're just like Sterling. All you want is one thing." Positioned between Zach and Michaela, Juliet weaved a bit to the side. Michaela looked for the right moment to pounce. But she had no idea where Zach stood in all of this.

"My dad only wants to protect me and I thought that was what you wanted, too." She turned away from Michaela and pointed the gun at Zach.

"That's not true," Zach replied. "I'm sorry about tonight. You surprised me is all. I thought we agreed to take things slow. The marriage thing, it was out of the blue. You've got to admit that. But, I'm not opposed to getting married at some point."

Michaela saw that Zach was trying to save his skin, but she hoped it wasn't as obvious to the girl. "I believe him, Juliet. Give me the gun and you and Zach can go and work things out."

"Give me back the letter. We know you were at Sterling's tonight. It had to be you. You overheard us in the barn at the polo field." Juliet slumped to the floor, and Michaela and Zach both seized the opportunity. Zach wrapped his arms tightly around her, and shook the gun out of her hand, and Michaela quickly picked it up. She didn't want to aim it at anyone, but she needed the power right now. Still, instead of turning it on either one of them, she simply held it, while Zach wrestled with Juliet, who finally calmed down and began crying into his shoulder.

Michaela had a lot of questions and she was in no mood to not have them answered. "Okay, it's truth time for all of us. I know about the letter and what it says. What you wrote in there, Juliet, is disturbing to say the least. It's obvious to me that you and Zach are protecting your father because he murdered Sterling, and I have been made the fall guy. Frankly I don't care how it was done, but you two are going to tell the police. And — how in the hell did you get into my house?" Her body quickly filled with a heated rage. Tomorrow she planned to start looking for a new four-legged companion.

"The letter . . . yes, Juliet wrote it," Zach said.

"Got that much. Why don't we start with tonight, Juliet? How did you get in here?"

"Your kitchen window was cracked and I crawled through."

Here Michaela thought she'd been careful when she locked up each night. Living in the back forty wasn't apparently as safe as it once was. "Did you actually think you would find the letter and get out of here without me knowing? And you." She turned to Zach. "How did *you* get in, and how do you play into all of this other than wanting to protect Juliet and — from what I gather — keep on jumping her bones?"

Zach sighed. "We went out tonight. We figured that you'd overheard us in the barn talking about the letter and then when we got into Sterling's place, we knew it had to be you who was there. We tried to figure out how we could get the letter from you."

"How did you know that I even had it?"

"We didn't for sure, but we needed to know. Juliet drank more than usual and she was talking nonsense about coming here and confronting you and getting the letter back. I told her that we needed to wait until tomorrow and then we could all have a sensible discussion about it."

"I would've appreciated that, rather than having a gun pointed at me." Michaela wasn't completely buying their story. For all she knew they'd come here to kill her.

"I told her it was crazy, and we argued about other stuff."

"Uh-huh."

"When I dropped her off at home, I had a bad feeling that she might do something stupid, which she did. I called her a few times and when she finally answered she said that she was on her way to get the letter from you."

"So, you drove out here and obviously saw how she'd gotten in, made your way in as well, and here we all are — the three musketeers." She turned to the inebriated Juliet. "You're lucky you didn't kill yourself or someone else in your condition," Michaela snapped. "Okay, the letter. I'm not giving it back, and seeing how I now have the gun in my possession, we're going to call the police and the two of you are going to tell them everything that you know."

"We didn't do anything!" Juliet cried. "We didn't kill Sterling."

"I believe that. But you did break into my house and hold a gun on me, and I think you're protecting your dad, who may have killed him." Michaela tried to change her tone to one of empathy. She understood the need to protect a parent. Over the years she'd shielded her own father, who had fought his gambling addictions on and off, but this was far worse. Juliet was protecting her father from murder and had involved Zach to a point that the two of them could possibly be considered as accomplices.

"She's right, Juliet," Zach said.

"No. We don't know for sure it was my dad."

"Can I ask you what you told your father and why you think he might have killed Sterling?" She looked at Zach. "Does it have to do with Rebecca Woodson's death? I know about last summer."

Zach nodded. "I'm the one who told Juliet about that. I saw her getting serious over Sterling and I knew that his intentions weren't always honest. He was known for telling a woman one thing and then doing another. I thought he was stringing her along like he had Rebecca, and I didn't want her to get hurt."

"Do you believe that Sterling had something to do with Rebecca's death?"

He shrugged. "I don't know what to believe. I was driving home the night of the party. Sterling denies he had anything to do with Rebecca going off that pier, but Tommy

Liggett was there and he confided in me that he saw Sterling follow Rebecca out on that deck. Look, Sterling was a complicated guy and I didn't know if Juliet could trust him."

"You and Sterling were friends, though."

He laughed. "Sterling had a lot of *friends.* He had friends out of convenience. When it worked for him, then it was all good. If there was someone better to hang out with, though, he'd leave you high and dry. People understood that about him. The only real buddy he ever had was Justin Nightingale. When Justin was alive those two were tight."

Robert and Paige's son. That part of the web had not been unraveled enough just yet, but she had to take it one step at a time. "And this didn't bother you? You went and hung out with him for a part of your summer."

"I was only in Santa Barbara for a weekend."

"I feel sick," Juliet said.

"Sit down," Michaela told her and pointed to her reading chair and ottoman in the corner of the room. The danger appeared to be over, and before she picked up the phone and called Peters she wanted to try and get as many answers as she could out of these two, although it looked as if Juliet was going to pass out.

She turned back to Zach. "Why did you go to the coast with Tommy and Sterling?"

"Why not? Tommy had been out there already with him for a month and said it was a blast. Sterling paid for everything. I thought it would be cool, so I went."

"And you met Rebecca Woodson."

Zach nodded. "Everyone met Rebecca. Total party girl, who wanted more from Sterling than he could give, but he fed her lines, you know — stuff like she could come visit him. He even told her he'd get her a place to stay in the desert. Stupid stuff for him to say, because we all knew that he wouldn't live up to it. I left because I was kind of over the scene and his bull."

"Do you think Ed Mitchell killed Sterling?"

"I don't know. I think he's very protective of Juliet and he'd do anything for her."

"And so would you."

"Yes," he replied quietly.

"Even if it meant sending an innocent woman to jail."

"I'm sorry. You have to understand —"

"No, I don't! And now you have to tell the police what you know. As far as the letter goes. I don't think it's necessary for us to tell the cops how either one of us might

198

have it in our possession, but I'm giving it to them."

"You can't give them the letter." He pointed to Juliet, who had passed out in Michaela's chair.

"I don't care about your promises, Zach. I think you're a good man with ethics. I really do, and now is the time to live up to them. If Ed Mitchell is guilty and I go to jail for something that I didn't do, can you honestly live with yourself?"

Zach stood there for a moment, then pulled out his cell phone.

"Who are you calling?" Michaela asked.

"The police."

TWENTY-FIVE

Detective Peters seemed to be as thrilled to see Michaela at three o'clock in the morning as she was to see him, which was not at all. But maybe they could get this mess straightened out and her life back to normal.

Peters questioned Zach over and over on his story. He stayed true to Michaela, but Juliet, when woken, freaked out and blabbed everything.

"She broke into Sterling's house." She pointed at Michaela. "And stole a letter that I'd written to him."

"Is that true, Ms. Bancroft?"

How was she going to get out of this? But Zach cut in. "That's not true. We went into Sterling's house. I found the letter and didn't tell Juliet. I told her that someone else had been there and taken it. I made up the story about seeing Ms. Bancroft there."

Juliet's jaw dropped. "What! I heard

200

someone in his place, too. Why are you lying?"

"You came here in the middle of the night to tell Ms. Bancroft this?" Peters eyed them.

Michaela nodded and shot a warning glance at Juliet, figuring that Zach would possibly corroborate with her about Juliet breaking into her house and pointing a gun at her.

"Where is the letter now?"

Before the police arrived Michaela had taken it from her purse and brought it downstairs. She grabbed it off the coffee table and handed it to Peters.

"This all smells foul to me, Ms. Bancroft." He read it, then said, "If you think that this letter alone merits me waking up one of the most prominent men in this county to be questioned, then you are sorely mistaken."

"What? You're not going to question Ed Mitchell?"

"We've already questioned Mr. Mitchell and he has an airtight alibi during the time of death. He was with a group of people all day at the event and they have all checked out."

"You're not going to look into that then?" She pointed at the letter.

"I'll speak to him about it, but I don't think it has anything to do with Sterling

Taber's murder."

Michaela had no response. If Ed had an alibi then the letter probably didn't mean a damn thing. "Don't you have any more to ask them?" Michaela looked at Zach and Juliet.

"Good night, Ms. Bancroft," Peters replied and opened the door, following Zach and Juliet out.

What a total mess. Had they screwed up by calling the police? At least Zach had defended her. He was a decent guy, or had possibly changed his mind about being head over heels for Juliet when she pointed the gun at him. God, how love was so very blind. Here a man was willing to protect the woman he thought he loved, and her father, and deny the truth, likely sending an innocent woman to jail. Crazy.

If Ed had an alibi, what did that mean for her? It meant that she's just wasted half a night of sleep and risked her freedom — and Joe's — at Sterling's place by breaking and entering. That's what it meant. It also meant that she hadn't figured things out yet.

There were still so many what-ifs, including the mystery woman on the videotapes that Sterling had made, the Sorvino clan, Robert Nightingale's vendetta toward Sterling, and, from Paige's account, his now supposed missing-in-action status. Lest Michaela forget, there was also Erin Hornersberg, who had already killed someone in the past, and who thought Sterling lower than a dust mote. She'd sure clammed up when Michaela and Camden had gone to talk to the makeup artist.

Then there was this bizarre situation with Sterling's old girlfriend Rebecca Woodson, the dead party girl. Michaela should've asked Zach about Sterling's family and what they were like. She would have to talk to Tommy Liggett about that. Tommy had spent more time last summer with Sterling than Zach had. Maybe he could shine some light on what had happened there. And there was the undercover blonde woman in the Ford Explorer who was keeping tabs on Michaela. It all seemed so strange; none of it made sense, but at that point her brain was fried from trying to piece any of it together. She decided to try and get some rest.

Michaela didn't get much more sleep. After tossing and turning for an hour, she got up and made a pot of strong coffee. She didn't know if she'd ever felt so exhausted before. Always an early riser, getting started in the morning wasn't typically a problem. Her life had been filled with plenty of ups and downs, like most people, but before this fiasco she'd finally settled into a peaceful place in her life. Her ranch was a wonderful place to live; she woke up and took care of her animals every day; she taught sweet and special children how to ride; and she thought that maybe there was a possibility with her and Jude. Only a week ago, she'd been able to wake up and be grateful for all that was right in her life. Today, it was hard to do, but she did it anyway, thankful that her animals were there waiting for her and happy to see her. And she was thankful for the caffeine. She was going to need it. Only two hours until Sterling's funeral service; she'd have to psych herself up for the appearance.

She weighed her options. None of them looked too great. Facts were that if she went, all eyes would likely be on her, including Detective Peters, who would surely show up. Wasn't that what investigators did while on a case? Show up at the funeral in case the perp made a wrong move? Oh goodness, she had watched one too many *Law & Order*s. Had Peters really questioned Ed Mitchell? What if Juliet had convinced Peters that Michaela had stolen the letter?

She knew she couldn't continue to lie to him. It wasn't who or what she was, and it could prove to be the final slice in cutting her own throat.

The downside of not going to the service was that she had a gut feeling whoever did kill Sterling *would* be there, and maybe, just maybe, she would pick up on something that the police had missed.

She slipped into a black dress, knowing that she had no choice but to make an appearance at that funeral. She would do her best to make herself nondescript. Maybe no one would notice her. Yeah, right.

Her plan didn't work. As expected, Detective Peters was at the church. He eyed her when she came in. Maybe she was being paranoid, but damned if a lot of people didn't stare at her when she walked in. So much for the nondescript, inconspicuous part. She tried to not allow him to unnerve her. Paranoid. That's all. She was being paranoid.

Then she spotted Robert and Paige Nightingale, which was odd to say the least. Hadn't Robert left Paige only two days before, his anger getting the best of him? And where was Camden? She had chutzpah when it came to the down and dirty questions. Robert's arm was wrapped protectively around Paige's shoulders. Quite a change of heart. Obviously they'd worked out their differences. Or not. Could it be that Paige knew something about Robert that he did not want the world to know? Maybe that he'd killed Sterling out of rage and now he needed her as an alibi? Was it possible that Robert had murdered Sterling over his grief and his belief that he was to blame for his son's death? Paige had replaced her child, in a sense, with Sterling. Loss of a loved one was the worst kind of grief. Michaela knew it firsthand. Maybe Paige couldn't take any more loss in her life, and had told Robert that she'd speak the truth if he tried to divorce her. Michaela had pegged Paige for an insecure woman. Would her sadness and insecurities force her to remain in a dead marriage? If Michaela had learned anything on this path called life, it was that everything was a possibility.

She decided to take a seat at the back of the church to be able to watch as people flowed quietly in and slipped into their seats. This way she'd be able to get a good look at everyone who showed up.

Watching the Nightingales seat themselves, she again thought about Robert's possible reason to want Sterling dead, and she understood it. She could not imagine what it would feel like to lose a child. If Robert truly blamed Sterling for the untimely and horrible death of his son, then she could almost understand his need for vengeance. But what about Paige? She'd been distraught the other day in Robert's office. Did *she* have anything to do with Sterling's murder? These questions needed answers. Michaela was still searching. But what reason would Paige have to kill Sterling? It didn't add up. So for now, she'd cross her off her list. She'd also been able to satisfy her mind that neither Zach nor Juliet had anything to do with Sterling's murder. True, they'd been up to no good, but she didn't think them responsible for killing him. Juliet's father didn't look as if he was a candidate any longer, but what about any one of the Sorvinos? She thought about the ring she saw Ed give Pepe. Had it been a payoff of some sort?

She watched as people continued coming into the church. Zach entered with Tommy Liggett, who Michaela felt could have some answers for her, at least about Sterling's family and Rebecca Woodson. Tommy worked for Juliet's father at the jewelry store. From all accounts, Tommy appeared to be a nice enough guy. But even nice people had skeletons to hide sometimes, and Michaela couldn't help but wonder if Tommy was one of those nice-guy-next-door types who one day went psycho on his good friend for a particular reason — or for no particular reason at all. Tommy had wavy light brown hair, sincere blue eyes, and dimples when he smiled. In a way he looked similar to Sterling, but was cuter, rather than handsome, like his pal had been.

Michaela turned as someone touched her shoulder. "I wasn't sure you'd be here, what with the bad press," Camden said.

"I had no choice but to come. Wish I hadn't though; everyone is looking at me."

"Relax. No one is looking at you. And if they do, I'll stick my tongue out at them."

Music began playing, an indicator that the services were about to start. As several latecomers filed in, Michaela's gaze fell on a man and whom she assumed to be his wife being escorted to the front row. "Are those Sterling's parents?" Michaela whispered in Camden's ear.

"I don't think so. He had told me that his folks were older. Those two look, what, in their forties. At least, the man looks like that. I can't tell with the woman."

Michaela nodded. The woman's head was down and it was difficult to get a good look at her face. "Well, they must be relatives."

"It would figure, but I'm not sure. I didn't know him that well to get his life story."

"You knew him pretty well."

Camden rolled her eyes. "You are mean sometimes."

"I know."

The parishioners listened to the heartfelt service given by the pastor, whom Michaela was pretty sure had never even met Sterling, as he spoke in generalities about the man. Something told her that Sterling didn't frequent church much.

When the pastor finished, he invited any attendees up to the podium who wished to eulogize him. It was strange, but no one took him up on the opportunity. Did *everyone* harbor ill will toward Sterling? After a minute, Tommy decided to go up. Michaela could tell by the way he moved back and forth from one foot to the other that he was nervous being in front of the crowd.

"Sterling was a good guy, a good friend, and all-around good man."

Michaela scanned the crowd and took note that Ed Mitchell had a protective arm around his daughter. Was he as uncomfortable as Tommy looked to be? Then she noticed Zach. He actually appeared almost bored. What a different crowd they all were.

Tommy went on to relate a humorous story about Sterling falling off one of his polo ponies and having to ice his rear. He got a few chuckles from that and then sat down.

Michaela figured they were about finished when the gentleman from the front row took his turn at the podium. All he said when he took the stand was, "On behalf of the Taber family, we thank you for coming today to honor my brother. Sterling's life was amongst his friends, and thus his family has made the decision to have him buried here, where he was loved by so many. Thank you again."

Hmmm. So the older, distinguished guy was Sterling's brother. Okay, so maybe, just maybe, there was an off chance that Sterling's family showed compassion for him by wanting to bury the man in Indio, but she doubted it. Here the brother was the only one making an appearance at the service and that was all he had to say about his sibling? Oh, that made her skin crawl. No, there was more to it. The Taber family wanted nothing at all to do with Sterling. Not in life or in death. That was as plain and simple as it seemed. It made her feel very sorry for Sterling, and actually she started to form a better picture of what appeared to be a lost soul. Not that she agreed with some of the things he'd apparently done or the way he'd conducted his life, but there may have been some deep, dark reasons for Sterling's actions and behavior. Michaela couldn't help wonder if the man's way of life had caused his own demise — a death that maybe his family was behind, wanting to rid themselves of any more scandal he might cause them.

TWENTY-SIX

Michaela's stomach churned as she approached Sterling's brother and his wife. She had no clue what she would say. "Um, why is it that your family ostracized Sterling when he was never charged with or convicted of a crime?" No, that would probably not go over too well. She could not help thinking though that the Tabers had distanced themselves from Sterling because of what had happened to Rebecca Woodson.

She decided on the practical, caring approach. "Um, excuse me, Mr. Taber?"

Sterling's brother turned around. He had slicked-back silver hair and the same blue eyes that, for Sterling, had caused most women to melt. Granted, they hadn't done a damn thing for Michaela, but she appeared to be in the minority. Mr. Taber was of average height and looked to be physically fit underneath what was likely a silk Italian suit specially tailored for him.

Then his wife turned around and Michaela's blood ran cold.

"Yes?" Sterling's brother said.

Michaela tried not to stammer as she made every effort to take her eyes off his wife. She was as beautiful as the brother was handsome, albeit in a sort of "shiny and bright" high-society way. Her obscenely large diamond ring sparkled in the desert sun. But it wasn't the diamond that stunned Michaela, it was the fact that Mrs. Taber was the star of Sterling's videos.

"Yes?" Mr. Taber said again. "Can I help you, miss?"

Michaela reached out her hand, somehow finding a way to string words together. "I'm so sorry for your family's loss. I'm sure it was quite a blow."

"Ah, another girlfriend, I suppose," he replied hesitatingly. He shook her hand lightly, as if she might break.

"No. No, not at all. I hardly knew Sterling. I was on his polo team for a few matches and took lessons where he boarded his horses —"

"Charles, we need to go," the wife interrupted. She looked Michaela up and down.

"I apologize, miss, but our jet is waiting. What did you say your name was?" the brother asked.

Michaela hesitated.

"I know who she is," the wife said coldly. "I've seen her in the news. She's the woman who murdered Sterling."

"No. No, I didn't! I would never kill anyone."

"She's crazy, Charles. I've read the papers. Let's go now."

Charles Taber studied her, his lips turning up at the ends. It sent a shiver down Michaela's backside, as she thought it an evil look. Then he shook her hand again. "Well. If you did it, thank you very much, and if not, as you say, I'm sorry for your troubles."

"Charles, we have to go."

"Yes, Carolyn. Good day, and good luck with your legal woes." The Tabers picked up their pace.

Michaela went after them, all the knots in her stomach gone and replaced by rage. "Wait a minute, wait just a minute. I had nothing to do with your brother's death, and frankly, I find your callousness revolting."

"I knew she was one of his women," Charles said to his wife.

"Dammit, I never dated Sterling. I didn't even like the man, but I didn't kill him and I feel terrible that he's dead."

"That would make sense since you are

charged with his murder."

Michaela stared at these two insolent jerks for a second in an attempt to regain her composure. "You know what, I have to wonder about the two of you. Why are you so relieved that your brother is dead? I know all about the controversy last year out in Santa Barbara. And Mrs. Taber, I could have sworn that I've seen you before? Were you ever in any movies or any type of *film* projects?"

Carolyn's face went ashen. "No! Charles, come on. I told you she was insane! She's a lunatic."

"Maybe it was those home movies that Sterling showed to some of us. I think maybe you were on vacation. I should send you a copy. I'm certain that it was you. I don't remember your husband in them, but yes . . . looking at you now, I'm sure of it."

"We've never been on vacation with Sterling," Charles Taber replied. He looked at his wife.

"I have no idea what you're talking about," Carolyn Taber snapped. "They can't lock you up soon enough! Charles, we have to go."

Carolyn turned and marched away. Charles gave Michaela a nod and followed his wife, who turned around when she reached the car and glared at Michaela. The woman was chock full of secrets that she aimed to expose.

Camden caught up with Michaela, who stood there stunned, watching the Tabers' town car pull away. "What was that all about?" she asked.

Michaela shook her head. "Those people are strange. Really strange, and I have to tell you that Sterling's sister-in-law has some ugly skeletons in her closet."

"All super rich people have stuff to hide."

"No. There's something more here. I've got proof that Sterling and his sister-in-law were having an affair."

"No! Oh come on."

Michaela nodded. "Oh yeah."

"You've got to take it to the police. Michaela, you and your snooping are going to get yourself killed."

Now there was a thought to mull over. Spend fifty years to life in prison or take the chance that she might actually figure this all out and save herself. "You're probably right, I do need to hand the tapes over to the police."

But the other dilemma with that was explaining how she came into possession of the tapes in the first place. If she told the truth it would confirm Juliet's story to the police about breaking into Sterling's place. And once that was affirmed . . . well, it would likely plant further doubt in Peters's mind and could possibly cause her to wind up in jail on separate charges. Plus, would evidence that she'd stolen be allowed in a court of law? Oh jeez, what a mess.

"Yes, you do. Michaela, don't go delving into their lives. It'll be trouble. Look what they did to Sterling. They banned him from the family."

Michaela crossed her arms. "They didn't exactly ban him. They cut his allowance in half. And most of America wouldn't complain about Sterling's ten grand a month. I'm not sure what you don't get about the fact that I was arrested for Sterling's murder. If I don't find out who killed him, Mrs. Robinson . . ." Camden frowned. "Then I am screwed. Totally screwed. No more horse training, no more helping children, no more having margaritas with you as the sun goes down. Nothing, *nada, finito*. Get it?"

"I get it. Okay, let's figure this thing out. What do we need to do?"

"We need to find out exactly what happened last summer and how those two are connected. I want to know why his parents weren't here today, and see if we can find out who else knew about the affair."

"I'm on it. I've got some friends in the jet-set circle in Santa Barbara. Maybe I can call around, see what the gossip is. I need to head over to the shop. Are you going to the polo lounge?"

"I don't want to, but I think I will." The polo team had gotten together and planned a celebration of life after the service. Michaela thought it would be a decent idea to continue poking around.

The event looked to have more people at it than the actual funeral service. The Sorvinos were milling around, of course. Michaela caught Lucia's eye as she served slices of gourmet pizzas to guests and Mario poured drinks. Lucia shook her head at Michaela and rolled her eyes. If there weren't a hundred people milling around, she'd consider strangling the brat. Michaela didn't see Pepe but assumed he was in the kitchen.

Robert and Paige sat at one of the tables with their food and wine. Michaela was beyond caring much what they might think of her. She wanted to know about that invoice, and also how the two of them had made nice with each other. She walked over and sat down with them. No time to be shy. "Nice turnout."

"Yes," Paige said.

"It's also good to see that you two have obviously worked things out."

Robert looked at Paige and then Michaela.

Paige's eyed widened like a deer caught in the headlights. "I . . . told Michaela what was going on between us," she said.

"Oh," Robert muttered. He took a sip of his wine, then set it down as he searched for the right words. "I needed to blow off steam, that's all, and sometimes I lose my temper. I didn't think Paige would take it seriously. I sure didn't think she'd tell anyone."

"I was upset, honey —"

"Anyway, it is nice that you are working it out," Michaela interrupted. So, Paige had not told Robert that she'd been discussing the state of their marriage with anyone. "I can understand why you would have been upset, Robert."

Paige eyed her.

"I think that I would have been upset, too, if my spouse was secretly giving money to a man I thought responsible in some way for my own son's death."

"Michaela!" Paige exclaimed.

Michaela felt bad about saying it. It certainly wasn't her finest moment, but these two had been acting strange and, dammit, she needed to get to the truth here.

Robert sighed. "No, it's fine. I never talk about Justin. Ever. And today, burying Sterling, it has stirred up memories. I understand why my wife did what she did. At first when she told me, I struggled with it. But knowing Paige, she didn't do it out of maliciousness. She wanted to help Sterling and he'd been a link to Justin."

Michaela nodded, encouraging him to continue. God, she really did not enjoy taking Robert on a walk down memory lane. It had to be painful, but maybe through that pain the truth would be revealed.

"What Paige didn't understand was that I had seen the manipulative side of Sterling and, yes, I did blame him in part for Justin's death. But that wasn't Paige's fault, and I don't want to lose her now either."

"Oh honey." Paige took Robert's hand.

Michaela actually believed him. His emotion and sentiment were too real. He did love his wife, but that didn't mean he hadn't murdered Sterling. "I'm sorry to be so nosy, but I have to ask you something, Robert."

"Sure. I think you will anyway."

Michaela smiled. "The day that Sterling was killed and you went and got my mallet, did you see anyone else around your office?"

"There were a lot of people all over the

grounds that day."

"I know, but can you think of anyone who stands out? I know that the mallet was wiped clean before I used it. If you didn't have your gloves on before you handed it to me, then your fingerprints would have been on there, too."

"You're not saying that Robert did this?" Paige asked.

"No. I'm asking him if he saw anyone around that might have stood out. That's what I'm thinking."

Robert swirled his wine around and frowned. "There was one gal who bumped into me and asked if I knew where to get a program. I thought it was kind of odd because they'd been handing them out as people came in. She didn't exactly fit the profile of somebody who would watch a polo match, if you know what I mean."

"No. What *do* you mean?" Michaela asked.

He shrugged. "She had tattoos and ears full of earrings, lots of dark makeup. That kind of thing."

"Purple, kind of magenta or hot pink–colored hair?" Michaela asked.

"Yes. You know her?"

"Erin Hornersberg."

"Who?"

"No one." She waved her hand dismissively. "Um, I don't know how to bring this up, so I am just going to do so. There was an invoice: one to Sterling, on your desk. I saw it. It was there that day, the day he was murdered. It had some not-so-nice words scrawled across it and a letter opener stabbed through it."

"Yes," Robert replied. "What about it?"

"Did you write 'Screw you' across it, or did Sterling?"

"I did," Paige replied.

"Why?" Michaela asked. She hadn't expected that answer.

"Robert and I had just had an argument about Sterling. He didn't know at that point that I was giving him any money."

Robert nodded. "I was upset because Sterling had come into the office and told me that he wasn't able to pay his bill for another week. He was already late. I felt he was taking my generosity for granted. I told him that since that was the case, the event that day would be his last. I didn't know that I was speaking the literal truth." Robert squeezed Paige's hand.

"When Robert told me what he'd said to Sterling, I became upset. In a way, I *did* see Sterling as a replacement for Justin, although now I see how crazy that was. I suppose I've never allowed myself to truly grieve over my son. Robert and I argued. He left and went to do something with the horses. I wrote it across the invoice and left."

"I found her at the charity event a little while later. Remember I told you that I didn't plan to go, but I changed my mind because I felt bad about our fight and I wanted to make it up to her. She told me that she was sorry for the note."

Michaela weighed their story. The two of them were looking at each other with tears in their eyes. She had the gut feeling that neither one had murdered Sterling. They were two sad and hurt people who truly needed each other and not any type of replacement to work through the void in their hearts.

She apologized for her questions and stood up. Turning, she saw Ed Mitchell walking toward her. He had two wineglasses in his hands. Giving one to Michaela, he said, "I understand that you think I'm a killer."

TWENTY-SEVEN

"I don't think you're a killer. I never really did, but . . . I had suspicions to go on." Michaela knew it sounded lame, but this was so awkward. Why didn't she just come right out and accuse him?

"Suspicions or not, you know me. If you had questions about me or my family, you should've come straight to me. I have nothing to hide. My daughter is distraught by your accusations and your sending the police my way. It's no trouble for me. I can handle Peters. However, Juliet is far more delicate and this situation is troubling her."

"Did Juliet tell you that she broke into my house?"

Ed frowned.

Michaela glanced over Ed's shoulder and saw Juliet and Zach whispering at a table in the corner. She sighed. "Did Juliet tell you anything at all about last night? That she threatened me with a gun?" She noticed Ed flinch.

"I think that maybe we should discuss this outside."

She thought about this for a moment. "On the patio then."

Ed gestured for her to lead the way. Once outside they sat down at a small table. Ed leaned in. "Taber was a piece of shit and I don't care that he's dead." He shook a finger at her. "But I didn't kill the SOB. I didn't hire a hit man either, if that's what is going on in your curious mind. What I did was scare him away from my daughter. At least I tried to. Someone performed a service when they did away with him. Do I think you did it? No. I even told Peters that this morning when he rousted me at seven and quizzed me about that ridiculous letter my daughter wrote. Look, I had the guy followed. He was up to no good, screwing around on Juliet with anything that walked. Hell, Sorvino's little brat was on that list. I told Pepe he better keep an eye on his daughter, or else she could also wind up like that girl Juliet and Zach told me about in Santa Barbara."

"Rebecca Woodson."

"Yes. I know Taber got off on that rap, but he was one shady guy and I wouldn't doubt there was foul play involved. The last thing I wanted was to have Juliet carrying on with him."

Michaela didn't know what to say.

"My daughter doesn't always use common sense. I apologize for last night. I'm not pleased with what she and Zach did. I know you're no killer. My daughter should also know that I'm no killer. Saying that she was trying to protect me is ludicrous. I don't need any protection. I was with two other couples the day that Taber was murdered. She didn't know that because she was busy with the fashion show. But that is a fact."

"You say that you had Sterling followed?"

He nodded. "A private investigator."

"And Sterling and Lucia Sorvino were friends?"

"More than that. My guy followed them to the polo grounds, where they were messing around in a stall."

"Really? Do you know, then, why Lucia would finger me as someone who was screwing around with Sterling?"

"She did that?" He laughed. "She's a strange kid, and trouble, too. I have no idea."

"What about Pepe Sorvino?"

He shrugged. "What about him? Good man. Caters all of our parties. I respect his business and his family."

She nodded. "I see. Are you also friends?"

"We do business together."

"What kind of business?"

"You are one nosy woman. I'll indulge you, though, because I like your ambition. I told you that he caters my parties. He did such a wonderful job at our last party that I gave him a ring he wanted to give his wife for their thirtieth wedding anniversary."

That must have been what he'd been doing the day Michaela spotted them after Sterling had been murdered. Mitchell was paying Pepe in jewelry for a job he'd done.

"I certainly hope you get this straightened out, Michaela. If you need any help, let me know. Next time you think I might be involved in something sinister, communicate with me. It'll save you a lot of time and stress. Good to talk and air it out. I've got to go now. I need to see Tommy Liggett. We have a shipment due in this afternoon. I need to be sure that he's headed over there."

Michaela watched him saunter away, reminding her of a character Jack Nicholson might play.

She had pretty much reached the end of her rope and decided it was time to leave Sterling's memorial, maybe take another trail ride, or at the very least get out with the horses. Once again she needed to clear her mind, and the only way she knew how was by taking time out with her animals.

She didn't bother to say good-bye to anyone inside Sorvino's but instead walked to the parking lot. She did make a mental note that Tommy Liggett would be at Mitchell's jewelry store later in the day. She wanted to speak with him about last summer and hear his version of the Rebecca Woodson story.

As she wound down the hill from Sorvino's toward the main road, she spotted a black Ford Explorer at a stop sign in front of her. Sure there was more than one black Explorer around, but her gut told her that this was the same car that had followed her yesterday. She punched it and got right behind the vehicle, but then thought twice. It was the same car, and she knew it was because of the license plate. She'd been able to get the first three numbers and pass them on to Joe; now she read the other numbers and started repeating them out loud to memorize them. It looked to her like she'd found the driver who'd followed her into the shopping center.

She gave herself enough time to get behind a few cars after they turned out onto the main highway. She did note that whoever was driving did not appear to have long blonde hair. That made her wonder if she was on the right track, but intuition urged her on and she stuck with the car for about ten miles, until the driver turned into a residential area. Now she'd have to be more inconspicuous. She slowed her speed way down and figured that whoever was driving hadn't picked up on the fact that they were being followed, or else they would have made an attempt to lose her. At least that was her guess.

The vehicle finally stopped, and she pulled up in front of a house about a block away. Typical desert-style, flat-roofed homes lined the streets, their landscape a mixture of cactus, rock, and lawn. The area was a nice one, so people obviously made efforts to run their sprinkler systems and keep the greenery alive.

A man got out of the car — tall, dark-haired, wearing a suit. She squinted to get a better look at who it was. She knew him. He moved like a man on a mission, holding himself confidently and not really giving a damn what others thought. He shoved one hand into his pocket and headed toward the door. Yeah, she knew the guy — Mario Sorvino.

He walked up to the front door of the

home, which was shrouded by bushes, and a woman came out to greet him. She had long dark hair — not blonde. Interesting. They hugged and kissed, then went inside the house. It had to be a girlfriend. It was the right Explorer, though. Those first three numbers gave it away.

After about ten minutes sitting in her truck and wondering what she should do, she decided to get out and search around the SUV. Sure it might be risky, but it was broad daylight and she'd scream bloody murder if Mario even came close to her. He was probably "busy" inside the house with the woman. She didn't know what she expected to find by peering into the back of the vehicle, or why she felt the need to do so. But she did, and what she saw on the backseat made her flinch: a blonde wig.

She hightailed it out of there, thinking, *Mario Sorvino with a blonde wig in the back of his car.* Mario Sorvino had followed her. Mario Sorvino said that Sterling got what he deserved, which appeared to be the consensus of many. But was Mario Sorvino the killer? Her jaw hurt as she realized she was clenching her teeth. Dammit, if she could tie things together and then take it all to the police, that's exactly what she would do. She needed Joe's help here. She tried to call him but didn't get an answer, so she left a voice mail.

Her phone rang and she immediately picked it up. It had to be Joe returning her call. To her surprise it was Ethan. "Hey, Mick. How are you?"

She didn't want to worry him, so she replied with the standard, "Fine. I'm fine."

"You don't sound fine," he replied. "You sound stressed. Why don't you come by and see your godson and get away for a bit?"

She sighed. "I would, but I'm just coming back from Sterling Taber's funeral and I'm not in the best of moods." She was trying to find some excuse. As much as Michaela would've loved to see Ethan and Josh, she doubted that Summer would welcome her with open arms. Whenever they did all get together there was a definite uneasiness between the two women.

"You went to the service? You are a glutton for punishment. All the more reason why you should stop by. Plus, I bought a new horse I want you to see."

"You did? That's great, but really, isn't Wednesday always your day off? You should hang out with your family."

"Mick, sometimes you can be so difficult. Stop acting like a pain in the ass and come see my new horse. I'd like to put him in training with you. He's a two-year-old, beautiful sorrel animal. Excellent bloodlines. Plenty of Peppy in him."

"Really?" She did like the sound of that. Okay, maybe she could deal with Summer for an hour.

"You're intrigued, I can tell. Come on over."

What was she thinking? She couldn't go to his place. She needed to track Joe down and find out what Mario Sorvino had been after and if he did Sterling in. Time was running out. Her parents would be returning from their vacation next week, and Jude was due back on Friday. She didn't want them to return home to this chaos that her life had rapidly become.

"You're coming, right? Only an hour. Come on, Joshy wants to see you. Me, too. I want to make sure you're as okay as you say you are."

She sighed. "Fine. But I don't have long."

Her stomach sank as she turned into the ranch where Ethan had moved only a little over a year ago. He'd gone from bachelor to husband and father in such a short time. The place belonged to Summer, who like Lance Watkins trained show jumpers. It was an interesting combination, with Ethan's reiners also lining the stall corridor.

Their place was large with both indoor and outdoor arenas, a small pasture, and several boxed stalls. A hot walker sat out behind the stalls, near a set of wash racks. It wasn't one of the larger facilities, but it compared with Michaela's. Summer had sold off quite a few of her horses since Josh had been born and she wasn't doing much training these days. Ethan had told Michaela that she didn't seem interested in the horses the way she used to be, and he'd wondered about it. Michaela figured that motherhood had replaced some of the need to be around the animals as much as before, but she didn't completely buy it. She'd been around the three of them from time to time and, as bad as it made her feel to think it, she didn't believe Summer was the most attentive and loving mother. From what she could tell, Ethan had taken on the brunt of the parenting. Then again, maybe she was simply judging with some jealousy mixed in there.

Summer answered the door in her typical state of perfection — long red hair curled at the ends, flawless ivory skin with makeup intact, a pair of navy slacks, and a pressed white blouse. Summer was so very Summer, and Michaela swallowed hard. "Hi, Michaela. Nice to see you." She fidgeted with her watch and checked the time. "Ethan has been talking nonstop about this horse and how great you'll be at working with him, so I suggested he call you and have you over." She touched her shoulder. "I'm sorry about what you've been going through lately."

Gag. Sure. "Thank you. I appreciate that."

"Come on in. Ethan is in the kitchen giving Josh his bottle." She grabbed a purse from the coat closet next to the front door. "I have to run out right now. Sorry I couldn't visit. Next time."

"Sure, no problem. Nice to see you, too."

Michaela felt relieved. It was so weird between them. Anyone who'd been watching the two of them exchange pleasantries could see that they were both being fake with each other. There was no love lost between them. She couldn't help wonder if Summer's exit had to do with her coming over.

"Mick? That you?" Ethan appeared from around the corner into the hallway of what Michaela referred to as the mini-manor, which was as perfect as Summer — decorated to a tee. Not a color mismatched, not a speck of dust anywhere.

"Hi."

Summer walked over to Ethan and the

baby. "I have to go. See you later. Bye." She gave them each a peck on the cheek It seemed odd for a mother to be almost cold with her son, not to mention her husband. But again, none of her business. "Bye, Michaela." She waved and was out the door, a breeze blowing past as she shut it behind her.

Michaela turned to Ethan. "Everything okay?"

He shrugged. "Oh yeah, fine. Everything's great. How about you?"

"I already told you on the phone that I'm okay. I'm hanging in there." Josh's eyes were at half-mast as he sucked down a bottle. "He's getting so big."

"And heavy to lug around. Come on." He led her into their family room, painted in cream and a soft peach — once again, way too Summer for Michaela. He laid Josh down in his playpen. "Let's go see the horse real quick. He's asleep."

"Will Josh be okay?"

"Sure. I always lock everything up, and he can't get out of there."

She nodded and followed him out to the barn, feeling odd in her heels and black dress, but nevertheless wanting to see Ethan's new horse.

"Here's my boy." They stopped in front of

one of the stalls. The horse padded over to them, his ears pricking forward, his eyes bright and intelligent. He stood about fifteen hands, sorrel in color with four perfect white socks and a blaze down the center of his face.

"He's beautiful, Ethan. Oh my God." Michaela brought a hand up to touch the soft nuzzle on the horse.

"He is. What do you think? Want to work with him?"

"Of course. I'd love to, but Ethan, I can't think much past tomorrow right now. Who knows what will happen with this Sterling Taber thing? I might be going to jail."

"No you won't. That won't happen." He shook his head. "It can't."

"But . . ."

She started to say that it could. He brought a finger to her lips. "No more of that bull about you going to jail. Life is just beginning for you, and this horse will be a part of it. Okay?"

"Okay," she uttered, and for the first time in several days she didn't feel afraid.

TWENTY-EIGHT

Michaela left Ethan's place feeling oddly relieved. He was always the optimist, and spending time with him and Josh had rubbed some positive vibes her way. She hadn't killed Sterling Taber, and justice would prevail. It had to.

Dwayne's truck was gone. He must've driven to the tack shop to help Camden out. She was happy that the two of them had been able to move beyond Camden's past. Once this mess was behind her, she would have to start planning a bridal shower for her friend. She decided to take a break and sit outside with a glass of iced tea, put her head together, and then see about going over to Ed Mitchell's jewelry store to talk with Tommy Liggett.

She changed into a pair of jeans and light sweater. Thankfully the November days were growing cooler. In only a couple of weeks Thanksgiving would be upon them, and God, how she prayed this whole mess would be over by then. She would go to her parents, like she did every year. She and Mom would bake apple and pumpkin pies and have some of Mom's friends from church over. There would be the usual fare of garlic mashed potatoes, turkey, cranberry sauce, green beans, and what Michaela always made best: a black cherry Jell-O dish from a recipe her grandmother had passed down. Grandma had died a little over five years ago and was sorely missed; and then they'd spent the first holiday season without Uncle Lou last year, which had been real tough on all of them. But Camden and Dwayne would be there. Ethan wouldn't. Hell, maybe she should invite Ethan and Summer. She needed to get past the animosity. What about Jude and Katie? She would have to invite them. Why did even the holidays have to be stressful?

She knew Jude would be back tomorrow. How was he going to take all of this? It was strange, but she really hadn't had time to miss him. She'd been so wrapped up in this drama. She had missed the sense of security he provided, and she knew he might've been able to handle Peters's attitude toward her, but she didn't feel that deep sense of longing. It had to be because of the drama that had taken place over the course of the week.

She took a long drink of the tea and closed her eyes, then heard something behind her and sat up. Carolyn Taber stood a few feet away, her hand inside her purse. It took a second for Michaela to register who it was. The woman had raccoon eyes from mascara dripping down her face. "Why did you do it?" Carolyn sputtered.

"What are you doing here?" Michaela asked, standing slowly. Did Carolyn have a gun in her purse?

"Sterling!" she screamed. "Why did you kill him?"

Michaela shook her head. "I didn't kill him and I suggest you leave, Mrs. Taber. You're trespassing."

Why hadn't she gotten a new dog yet?

Carolyn's face turned a dark shade of red, her plastic-surgeoned nose pinching. "Yes, you did. Everyone knows you did. Why?"

"You're insane. You need to leave."

"Not until you tell me why you murdered him."

"Where's your husband, Mrs. Taber?"

"On his way home."

"Does he know about the affair you and Sterling were having? Weren't you supposed to be heading home with him? Is that why you're here? Did my comment about you starring in a film tip him off?"

"No. I told him that I wanted to stay and shop, then go to Los Angeles and do some more."

"Right. I didn't kill Sterling. I know about the affair. I have proof of it, and the police know about it, too." She was bluffing, but maybe by doing so she'd smoke out Carolyn Taber.

The woman looked ghastly, to say the least. "No, please tell me that you did not give those to the police!" She started to pull something from her purse.

"No!" Michaela yelled, but then realized that the woman was opening up a checkbook, her hands shaking.

"Tell me that you didn't give those to the police. I will pay you for them. How much do you want?"

"Yes, I did give them the tapes."

Carolyn's hands shook even more with this revelation. "You had the last set. I talked with Sterling and we worked things out. He said that he'd destroy the other tapes for me. He promised me. I know he did it. I believed him. He loved me! I can't believe that he gave a set of those tapes to you and you gave them to the police. What have you done to me? You've ruined me. You have completely destroyed me! You will

240

pay for it."

Michaela wasn't about to tell her that she'd stolen the tapes from Sterling's house. She didn't figure that would be a good idea. Carolyn Taber spun around and stormed away. Somehow she was convinced that Sterling's sister-in-law would make good on her threat, and she also realized that she now had no choice but to turn those tapes over to Peters.

TWENTY-NINE

Michaela put in a call to Peters, who wasn't at the station. She left a message. What to do? Well, she still wanted to talk with Tommy Liggett. She called the jewelry store, but the woman who answered said that Tommy was on a break and would be back in about half an hour. Frustrated, she slipped on a pair of riding boots and headed out to the barn, where she took Leo out and lunged him for a bit. Watching his smooth, clean lines, his taut muscles move through each pace diligently, was meditative in a sense. His hooves pounded repetitively against the dirt as he moved in a forward circle with each stride. He tossed his delicate head into the air and blew hard, his nostrils flaring as she pulled the lunge line taut and urged him to whoa. His long dark mane lay against his face and neck. She leaned her forehead on his and felt tears sting her eyes. She would get her life back, for her horses and for herself. As soon as she saw Jude she would hand over the tapes and plead for his help. He could help her with this. Thank God he would be home in the morning.

She cleaned Leo up and put him away. Her legs were like Jell-O, and it seemed as if she'd had the wind knocked out of her. This week had torn at a remote part of her soul — so much ugliness, seediness, scandal, and cruelty. If she put feelings on it, vocalized her thoughts, she'd knew she'd break down. Exhaustion engulfed her. She planned to take a shower and then talk to Tommy Liggett.

She stepped under the running water, and once again her mind traveled back to the events of the past few days. The polo mallet. Was the murder premeditated? Or was it a "heat of the moment" thing? Say it was premeditated. No, that didn't jive. Her mallet was a convenient weapon. A premeditated murder would've meant someone would have planned it, brought a weapon, and bam! But that's not what happened.

Who had been angry at Sterling that day? Then again, who hadn't? Juliet was angry. Did she know about Lucia? Oh, and what *about* Lucia? Here was a girl who'd told the cops that Michaela was sleeping with Sterling, which was so far from the truth it was laughable. And Mario's car . . . and the wig? What was that all about? Those two could have been in cahoots, or the three Sorvinos — Pepe included. Ed Mitchell told Pepe that his daughter and Sterling had been fooling around. Pepe would've gotten upset and maybe he went to Mario. What if Pepe confronted Sterling? Followed him into the back office where Sterling was going to change, things got out of hand, Pepe hit him with the mallet, then went to get Mario. Michaela didn't recall seeing Pepe around after she'd found Sterling, and in those few minutes when Mario went to see if Sterling was dead and Michaela called the cops, could Mario have wiped off the mallet? But her fingerprints had still been on the mallet. Pepe could've been wearing gloves. It was a good theory. It fit. The only thing that did not fit was, why would any of them follow Michaela around?

What about Erin Hornersberg? She'd gone looking for Sterling before the match, became angry with him before the show, and didn't care at all when he'd shown up dead. She'd been very uncomfortable with Camden and the women's visit. But this was a woman who did, in all respects, come across as slightly off. Maybe she should consider questioning Erin again, only this time she would take Joe with her.

And what about Carolyn Taber? She hadn't even been at the event. Or had she? Michaela wouldn't have known who she was at the time. There were a lot of people around that day, and if she'd been there she would've blended in with the rest of the crowd. Had she snapped over the videos? Sterling had said on the tape that she didn't need to bother destroying them, because he had more sets. Were the tapes that Michaela had the only ones left? Carolyn had been willing to pay for them. Had she also been willing to kill for them?

These were all angles that she still needed to look into. She rinsed the shampoo out of her hair and turned off the water. Pulling back the curtain to grab her towel, she screamed and jumped back when she saw who was on the other side of the curtain, now staring at her buck naked.

THIRTY

"Jude!" She pulled the towel from the rack and quickly wrapped it around herself. "What in the hell are you doing?"

"I could ask you the same thing."

"Excuse me? You weren't supposed to be back until Friday."

"When Katie and I were in our last port, I called in to the office and heard about what happened. We flew straight home."

"Jude! Why did you do that? You didn't tell Katie, did you?"

"Of course not. She's a little angry with me, though. I told her that I had to get back for work."

"A *little* angry? I don't blame her. I'm angry, too."

"You're angry because I came back to try and help you?" He looked totally incredulous.

He also looked good. How she could think that just then, she wasn't sure, but she couldn't deny that the tan he'd gotten on the cruise highlighted his blue eyes, and his hair had bleached lighter in the sun. She wanted to reach out and touch the lightened waves. "I'm upset, that's all, that you would cut your trip short because of me."

"Come on, Michaela. The woman who I'm dating has been arrested for murder and I'm not supposed to get home as fast as I can to help? Why didn't you contact me?"

"You were in the Caribbean on a cruise."

"There are ways to get messages to passengers, you know. I wasn't off the planet."

"I know, but honestly, I didn't want to ruin your trip."

He sighed. "Why am I not surprised? And why am I also not surprised that this has happened to you?"

"What do you mean by that, 'not surprised that this happened to me'?"

She stormed past him, embarrassed and upset that he had the gall to enter her bedroom, then her bathroom, unannounced, and now he'd seen her in the buff. They'd shared some passionate moments together, sure, but they hadn't ever been naked together, and right now she felt like he had an unfair advantage, which she did not appreciate. And dammit, what *did* he mean that he wasn't surprised about her situation?

"It's not as if you run from murder. You're a modern-day Sherlock Holmes."

She turned on her heel and shook a finger at him, almost losing her towel. "That is so unfair, Jude. I don't go around looking for murder. I can't help what happened in the past and I certainly can't help this situation."

"You still should have called me."

"Oh please. That would've been selfish. You were on your vacation, for God's sake, and with Katie. I couldn't have done that to you, much less to your little girl. I had hoped that by the time you got home this would've all blown over and then we could've laughed about it. Besides, what would you have done if I got ahold of you in the middle of the ocean? You would've gotten on the first plane back home and stormed in here and tried to save me as if I'm a damsel in distress. Thank God you didn't find out until today. At least you had some of the week to enjoy yourself."

"Aren't you a damsel in distress, though?"

"No. I'm a very capable woman. I can take care of myself. I don't need rescuing. I don't need the white horse and Prince Charming. And honestly, that's been a problem for us all along. You seem to feel the need to take care of me."

"Maybe that's because you need a man to take care of you."

"What! Please. You don't know me that well, then."

"What I know is that there is some pretty incriminating evidence against you for a murder that, knowing you as I do, I can't believe you would have ever done. I don't plan to save you, Michaela. Why do you keep fighting me? Resisting me? All I want to do is help. That's what people who love each other do. They are there for each other. But I have to wonder if you even want my help. You're always pushing me away, and this is only the latest incident."

Wait a minute! Love! *Love?* When did that ever come into the picture? He'd let that one slip. Oops, and she decided that she'd let it fly by, pretending that she hadn't heard it, but dammit, why was there a lump of emotion tightening at the back of her throat? She was not ready for this.

He walked over to her. "Michaela, let me help you."

"I need to get dressed," she said.

"You do?" Jude traced the top of her towel with a finger.

"Yes. And we're arguing."

"No, we're not."

"Yes, we are."

"Can we go back to it later?" He kissed her neck.

"Jude, the timing is off. I don't want our first time to be . . . well, make-up sex."

"There is nothing wrong with make-up sex. And I may have been upset with you, but seeing you in the shower and having you yell at me kind of turns me on."

"Yeah, you shouldn't have seen me in the shower. How did you get in? You scared me."

"I'm a cop. I think I know how to get into a home. We need to get you an alarm system. You never know who will sneak in and suck the blood out of you." He sucked on her neck like a vampire. It tickled and Michaela couldn't help but laugh. "I can make you smile even more."

She sighed. He kissed her on her neck again, his fingers traced the edge of the towel wrapped around her. Feelings she hadn't been in touch with for a long time traveled through her, and she stopped thinking. She allowed Jude to keep kissing her as she dropped her towel.

THIRTY-ONE

"You did what?" Jude asked. "Oh this is not good, Michaela! Damn! I could arrest you. I *should* arrest you. Breaking and entering? You stole the tapes? What were you thinking?"

They stood in her kitchen making sandwiches. The afternoon had turned into evening and they were both hungry.

"Arrest me? Please. I didn't want to keep it from you — and doesn't all of this show you that Peters is heading in the wrong direction with this investigation?"

"Maybe, but what you did by breaking into Taber's home was a crime. And you did this alone?" He raised his eyebrows.

That was the only part of the story that Michaela felt she had to omit. She could not expose Joe. He had gone out on a limb for her more than once. He'd given her the opportunity with the riding center and was always there when she needed a friend. No, she could not betray his trust.

"Yes," she replied. "I did it, and I'm not sorry either. What am I supposed to do, Jude? Stand by and let Peters see that I rot in jail? He's not doing anything as far as I know to find out who really killed Sterling. It's me he's after."

Jude stared at her. "This isn't the first time you've gone searching for answers where murder is concerned. The last time you almost got yourself killed."

"I know that. But this is the first time that my freedom is on the line and you and me . . . I mean, *us* . . . aren't we in a relationship? Because it sure felt like it over the last few hours. Like we'd taken that next step. We won't be taking any more steps if I'm in jail. You said that you came home to help me, and now you're thinking I should be arrested for trying to find out the truth."

"That's not fair. I haven't had a chance to speak with Peters yet, but I definitely intend to. I know that you didn't murder Taber. I won't let you go to jail, I promise you that."

"How do you plan to do that, Jude, with your boss so hot and heavy to seal my fate?"

He closed his eyes and shook his head. "I do. Just promise me that you'll stop playing detective for once."

"No. Not this time."

"I don't want you hurt. You have to stop this! It's ridiculous!" he shouted.

"Ironically, if I'm behind bars, who knows what could happen to me? It may be ridiculous, but I don't see another way out right now."

"That won't happen! Do what you do best: Work with kids, train horses, and I'll figure this out." He put his arms around her.

She tensed up. His words sounded good, but why didn't she completely believe him? Was there something in his voice that doubted he could help her? To her, he sounded almost helpless and she wasn't buying his pleas to drop her sleuthing.

"I'll take the tapes with me and get them into Peters's hands. I think you're right, Carolyn Taber seems a likely suspect."

"Peters hates me, Jude. You can't tell him how I got the tapes."

"I won't say how I got them. He doesn't hate you. It's his MO to be a hard-ass."

"MO or not, I'm afraid that Peters will ignore the tapes out of sheer laziness or the mere fact that he sees me as an easy target."

He cupped his hand under her chin. "Peters won't ignore them. God! I can't believe that you stole those tapes. Is there anything else you're not telling me?"

There was plenty, like Mario following her, Zach and Juliet breaking into her place, the threat from Carolyn, as well as the bizarre behavior of Paige and Robert Nightingale. And in the moment that he asked her the question, she wondered why she *didn't* tell him everything. The kitchen seemed to spin as she concluded that she'd made a mistake with Jude. She'd made love with a man whom she wanted badly to trust, to fall in love with, but who admittedly she didn't completely trust. And now she wasn't sure she *could* fall in love with him. Right now she felt weaker than ever before. She'd fallen into a man's arms because she'd wanted security.

"No. I've told you everything. You know, I'm feeling kind of tired and want to go to bed."

"We can do that. We can take our food back to bed with us, and forget all this other stuff for a while."

"No. I want to be alone."

"Michaela?"

"It's been a long week and honestly, I'm feeling overwhelmed."

He tried to hug her but she pulled away.

He looked wounded. "I don't understand."

"I . . . think we made a mistake," she said.

She couldn't believe what she was saying. She typically ran from her feelings. They were far easier to hide from rather than confront. And she had to wonder if by treating Jude like this, she was only doing exactly that. Maybe it was easier for her not to try and love and be loved than be willing to open up and take a chance.

"I'm only trying to protect you. I don't want you getting hurt and I am planning on taking all of what you've told me, plus the tapes, to Peters."

"I know. But I still need some time to be by myself."

"Okay." He nodded and tossed up his arms. "If that's what you want."

As Jude left, tapes in hand, Michaela stared out the front window for a long time, not knowing at all what she wanted.

THIRTY-TWO

Michaela didn't sleep much after Jude left; the next morning, life seemed even more complicated than the day before. Being wishy-washy wasn't her style, but that's where she was in this game. Wishy-washy with Jude, her theories, everything but her horses. *Solid ground* would be nice.

She didn't trust that Peters would interview Carolyn Taber about the videotapes, and she had questions for Tommy Liggett, who might have met Carolyn and could enlighten her further. He might also know something about Sterling and Lucia. The brat certainly wasn't going to talk to Michaela. She needed to chat with Joe about the Sorvinos. Maybe one of his cousins had some information for her. Plus, Tommy could possibly fill her in on what happened in Santa Barbara to Rebecca Woodson.

She decided to head over to Ed Mitchell's jewelry store and have a talk with Tommy.

First, she checked to make sure that the bracelet she'd found at the polo grounds was still in the zippered pouch in her purse. Maybe Tommy could take a look at it and tell her what it was worth and see if she couldn't get it back to the rightful owner. So far no one had called on it. The main reason for going to the jewelry store was because she needed answers; she headed over midmorning, hoping to find Tommy there. The buzzer rang, announcing her entry. The store was upscale, painted in a light gold, and several small love seats stood next to large windows, which looked out onto the main shopping district of Palm Springs. Classical music played through the surround sound. A couple looked at engagement rings, happily trying on possible contenders. Tommy was helping them.

"Be right with you." Tommy glanced up. "Oh hey, Michaela."

"Take your time. I'm not in a hurry."

He nodded. Michaela looked around at all of the beautiful trinkets, with their expensive price tags. There were gorgeous necklaces, bracelets, watches from the finest watchmakers in the world. This store was for the wealthy. She liked jewelry enough, but most of what she owned was simple. Fine pieces like these would never fit into her lifestyle.

Tommy handed the couple glasses of champagne, and they sat down on one of the sofas, continuing to admire a ring they obviously were considering. He walked over to Michaela.

"Hey, are you okay? I heard the news." He shook his head. "Everyone at the field knows you would never hurt anyone. One of the detectives questioned all of us, and I told him that there was no way you killed Sterling. I hope they catch the bastard who did it. You don't deserve this."

"Thank you," she said.

"What brings you in here?" He rubbed his palms together.

"I'm not here for jewelry."

He gave her an odd look. "Okay. How can I help then?"

"I appreciate you putting in a good word for me. Since you believe that I didn't kill Sterling, do you have any ideas as to who might have done it?"

He shrugged. "You know that people who met him either loved or hated him."

"How did you feel about him?"

A shocked expression came over Tommy's boyish features. "He was my friend. What do you think? I loved the guy. We hung out all the time. What happened to him was wrong. He had his faults, you know, there's no getting around that. Kind of a narcissist and egomaniac, but he was funny . . . funny as hell. We joked a lot and women loved him, which didn't hurt me at all when we hung out. He could reel them in and, well, I'd kind of get the chicks he didn't want."

"Ah, the buddy system."

"Yeah, I guess."

"Speaking of women, what do you know about him and Lucia Sorvino?"

"Lucia? She's a kid. He toyed with her a little, but Juliet suspected something was going on and he dropped it."

"I'm sure that didn't make Lucia happy."

Tommy shrugged. "I wouldn't know. I don't know her too well. Like I said, she's young, and I actually told Sterling to leave her alone. Her brother is a hothead."

"Hot enough to kill Sterling?"

"Maybe, I suppose. I know he can lose it, though, because I saw him yelling at his sister just last week. He laid into her real good. She was in tears."

"Where was this at, and when?"

"I had to pick up some menus for Ed because he's planning a shindig at his place next month and Pepe always does the catering. When I swung by, Mario had his sister cornered and cowering like a dog. I don't know what it was about. They stopped, and Mario turned into Mr. Suave when he spotted me and that's pretty much it."

"Do you think they could've been arguing over Sterling?"

"It's possible. I don't trust Mario, though. He kinda looks mean, if you ask me."

"Yeah."

"Why all the questions about this?" Tommy asked.

"I'm sorry. You have to realize that I am under a lot of stress with all of the scrutiny. The police don't seem to be listening to all the people out there insisting that I didn't do it. I'm trying to do what I can to find out on my own. I'm trying to clear my name."

He nodded. "I understand."

"Thanks. I was wondering if maybe you could tell me about last summer?"

"What do you mean?"

"Last summer Sterling went to see his family in Santa Barbara, and you went?"

Tommy nodded. "I went with him for a couple of weeks. Zach came down for a few days, too. We had a great time, but his family . . . a bunch of uptight jerks, if you want my opinion. We didn't hang out much at their place. That brother of his runs the show. His dad passed away not that long ago and their mom is pretty ill, I heard."

"How about Carolyn Taber? Did you meet her?"

"Sterling's sister-in-law? Briefly. She was a snob, too."

"Did Sterling ever say anything about her to you?"

"No. He couldn't stand Carolyn or his brother."

"Really?"

"Yes. Why?"

"I have reasons to think that maybe there was more to Carolyn and Sterling's relationship than what he might've let on."

"No way. He thought she was a total bitch."

"He never said anything to the contrary, like maybe he wanted to sleep with her? I wasn't born yesterday. I know guys talk like that, and she's an attractive woman. I saw her at the funeral yesterday and, I don't know, there was something that I picked up on that made me think she had more than just a sisterly type of interest toward him."

Michaela didn't want to tell him about the tapes. She wasn't sure she could trust him yet and she thought she'd let the police see them before she said anything.

He laughed. "Look, Sterling liked women. He liked a lot of women, but I can guarantee that his sister-in-law was not one of them."

This line of questioning was getting her nowhere. Obviously Sterling hadn't found Carolyn too off-putting, but he hadn't let on to Tommy that he was involved with her. Or maybe they hadn't gotten together until after the summer, when Sterling's stipend had been cut in half. "How about Rebecca Woodson?"

"You read some old papers." Tommy frowned. "I met her." He shook his head. "Talk about a wild one. Once she hooked into Sterling, man, she wasn't about to let go."

"She was not from a well-to-do family?"

"Not that I was aware of. My impression was that she'd gotten connected with a group of rich kids out there and glommed on to the party scene with them. The rumor was she had some old guy who was keeping her in the cash as long as she was keeping him happy. He was supposedly married, so he didn't have much say as to what she did on her own time."

"Did you ever get the name of that guy?"

"No, why would I? I really didn't care. She was a party girl, a kind of . . . you know . . . how do you say it nicely? I mean, she put out pretty easily."

"So Sterling wasn't really dating her?"

He laughed. "Like I said, she put out. Sterling was a guy. She was hot. Problem was, as soon as they connected and she found out how loaded his family was, I think she saw a better deal than having to pay homage to the old guy. You know, I shouldn't be talking about her like that. It's not cool. If you read the paper, then you know that the poor girl died, too. She drowned."

"I heard that. Sterling was there that night, wasn't he?"

"We both were. It was a crazy party out at some mansion on the beach. Tons of people."

"What happened?"

"Like I said, it was crazy, you know, like out of the movies. Rebecca and Sterling . . . well, everyone was drinking a lot. I was super buzzed. There were a lot of drugs, too. I'm not into that, but I had my share of booze. They got into a fight. He wanted her to back off and leave him alone. It was a pretty nasty scene. She left the party, and the next thing we know the police are at Sterling's house the next morning because they found Rebecca washed up on the beach near the party house."

"Was it an accident?"

Tommy shrugged. "I think it probably

was. She had a bump on her head, they said. Her body was found right off the pier. It looked as though she'd leaned against some old railing, it broke, she fell, hit her head, and rolled into the water off the embankment, then drowned."

"But the cops thought there might have been foul play?"

"I know you're trying to clear your name, but why all the questions about Rebecca and Sterling and what happened in Santa Barbara? The police finally closed that case, said that it was an accident."

"But there's still speculation that it wasn't. And Zach told me that Sterling's family nearly disowned him after this took place, because the girl's relatives brought a civil suit against Sterling, and his folks didn't want the media attention or bad publicity."

"That's true. But still, why are you asking? I mean, are you going anywhere with this?"

"Honestly, I'm not real sure. But I have to wonder if maybe someone in Rebecca's family or even Sterling's own family didn't have something to do with his murder, and if it doesn't all lead back to the night that she died. Or is it even possible that the older guy who was paying for her company might not have sought revenge?"

"Oh. Wow. That's a good point." He nodded. "Yeah, Rebecca's family went berserk. Like I said, I never knew who the old man was that she hung out with. I'm sure some of the kids we partied with might know."

"Do you know anyone that I might be able to call?"

"Jeez, I don't know. I'd have to check my book. You know, that was just a party scene. It wasn't like I was making lifelong friends out there. I might, though. I met a couple of girls out there and took their numbers. I can call you if I find them."

"That would be great."

"What about Rebecca's family?"

"I wouldn't know how to get ahold of them. I know that she had a brother who came over a few days after they found Rebecca and tried to beat on Sterling, but he was arrested. I think his name was Ryan. Not sure. It was an ugly scene and I went home that afternoon, actually. Once Sterling was cleared by the police he came back here, and we never talked about it."

"Excuse me," the woman on the sofa called out. "I think we want to look at the first ring again."

"I'll be right there," Tommy said. "Hey, sorry, I've got to help these guys out. And then Ed wants me to run some errands."

"No problem."

"Hope I helped."

"You did. Thanks."

Tommy nodded and went back to assist the customers. As Michaela started to leave the store, her eye noticed a display of bracelets. She peered in through the glass and spotted what looked to be an exact replica of the tennis bracelet she'd found. She needed to ask Camden if anyone had come forward to claim it. It seemed odd that no one had. She could turn it over to the police — to Jude. Maybe not her best option, albeit logical, if she wasn't already in over her head.

She decided to wait around a few more minutes for Tommy. She wanted to ask him the price of the bracelet.

A saleswoman approached. "Can I help you with anything?"

Michaela looked at Tommy. He and the couple were engrossed in their business. She didn't know how long he might be. "Yeah, sure, you could help me. That tennis brace-let: How much is it?"

"This one?"

She nodded and the gal pulled it out. "Eight grand. Gorgeous, isn't it? I would love to have one of these."

"It is beautiful." Michaela reached into

her purse and pulled out the bracelet. She'd hadn't gotten a chance to ask Tommy about it, but maybe the woman could help her. "I had no idea they cost that much. Can you take a look at this for me? I'm curious what it's worth."

"Let me take a look," the woman said. She held it up to the light and then placed it on a black velvet fold and studied it through a jeweler's loupe. "This is a great fake. Excellent really."

"What do you mean, fake?"

The woman looked again and nodded. "Yes. These are high-quality CZs. Cubic zirconium. Really nice, though. Didn't you know they weren't real?"

"No, I didn't. They look like the ones there in the case. I found the bracelet, so no, I didn't know. I placed a classified because I was sure someone would be missing it."

"I would think that someone would claim it, though. I know they're not real, but they still aren't cheap. Like I said, it's a great fake. That's what is so cool about good CZs. No one would ever know that they're not real, unless you have a trained eye." The woman handed the bracelet back to Michaela.

"Mitchell's doesn't carry cubic zirconium

jewelry then?"

The woman smiled. "Are you kidding? Have you ever met Ed Mitchell? The man is super particular. Only the best of everything. Best for his store, best food, best clothes, best cars, best for his family."

The buzzer rang and an older, elegant-looking woman walked in. "Good luck with that," the saleswoman said and turned her attention to the new customer.

"Thanks." Michaela looked back at Tommy to say good-bye, but he was still busy with the couple.

Thirty-Three

"I don't think Rebecca Woodson's drowning was an accident," Michaela said. She'd called Camden to see if they could meet in town for a late lunch. "Have you found out anything on your end? Did you get ahold of anyone you know in that Santa Barbara jet-set circle?"

Camden nodded and set her iced tea down. "I talked with this gal whose family owns a big winery up there. She knows a lot of the gossip. She told me that the Tabers are real secretive."

"No kidding. But there must be someone who knows what they're about."

"She knew a few things. The scoop is that Charles, Sterling's brother, is a control freak and runs the entire family. After the dad passed away, Charles took over. They are filthy rich and everyone knew that Sterling was the black sheep of the family. Always has been. The thing with Rebecca Woodson was a big deal there last summer, but the Tabers have paid a lot of cash to keep things as low-key as they could. This friend of mine said that the rumor is they even paid off someone in the police department. When her family filed the civil suit, the Tabers settled with them out of court. Sterling came back here, and word was the family didn't want him around ever again, and they stopped giving him money to live on."

"Ten grand a month, though; he was still getting that. They didn't cut him out completely," Michaela said.

"When you're talking about a family with the kind of status and money the Tabers have, then I can see where Sterling was coming from, why he might have been disgruntled."

"This I have to hear."

"Think about it: Here's a guy who has been spoiled and has a sense of entitlement. Take it away from him, even if he'd done something to cause it, and he throws a temper tantrum."

"Imagine that." Michaela clucked her tongue.

"There's more." Camden rubbed her palms together briskly.

"You're scaring me. I think you're enjoying this in some perverse way."

"As if you aren't."

"Trust me, I'm not. It's a necessity. You like the gossip angle of it."

"Maybe a little . . . but listen, so there's been talk that Sterling had been in trouble with the law when he was a kid. He even spent some time at juvenile hall. His dad couldn't get him out of that one and his brother wasn't running the show at the time."

"What did he do?"

"I don't know this for a fact, only what my friend told me. She said that he was a thief. He stole. He would hang out at friends' houses and take any money lying around, that kind of thing. But he got popped supposedly for stealing some rare emerald off someone's nightstand."

"Seriously? Why would a kid with that kind of money need to steal?"

"For the same reason any kid does anything negative: attention. His parents were busy jet-setting, his brother was the golden boy, and Sterling had to lash out to get noticed. So he did it by becoming a petty thief . . . but it wasn't so petty."

"He was really screwed up. It's a shame." Michaela shook her head.

"You think he killed Rebecca Woodson? You know, it's so weird, because I knew him, and I never figured him for the patho-logical type."

"Your hormones knew him."

Camden shrugged. "You're right. What do we do now?"

"I don't know. I need to talk to Joe. He seems to know how to dig and get direct answers."

"What are you looking for exactly with this Rebecca Woodson thing?"

She frowned. "I can't pinpoint it, but I think Sterling's murder goes back to his past. There are people here who didn't like him and aren't sad to see him gone, but I can't help feeling like either he was killed because someone here was afraid of his past, or of him directly. I wish I could find out more about Rebecca Woodson. Or Carolyn Taber."

"Oh yeah, her. I wanted to tell you this, too. She's a manipulative one. She wormed her way into Charles's life. I guess she doesn't come from big money and she's been the one dark spot for Charles. The parents weren't keen on her, and she had to become Miss Perfect to get her hooks into him."

"She also got her hooks into Sterling. I guess he wanted to cement her situation all the way around. But it looked like it backfired on her."

Camden nodded. "I hate to run, Mick, but I've got to get back to the store. By the way, that necklace you wanted to give Joe's daughter for her birthday came in."

"Oh good. I'll be by to get it. Thanks for helping me with all of this."

"No problem. See you at home."

Michaela paid the bill and looked at her watch. She needed to go and work horses for a while. If she was going to get any further with finding out who'd done Sterling in, she knew she'd need some help. There were tons of loose ends; she just wasn't sure how to tie them up.

The fresh air, and working with her animals, might help clear her mind, but when she pulled onto the ranch, she knew that wasn't going to happen. To her dismay, another visitor had shown up. Detective Peters leaned against his car, waiting for her.

THIRTY-FOUR

"Hello, Detective. I'm surprised to see you."
Michaela hoped he wasn't here to arrest her
for breaking into Sterling's place. What if
Jude had told him the truth about how he
had come into possession of the tapes?
Would he do that to her? Especially after
yesterday? She didn't think so, but she also
didn't like the mere fact that she was
questioning it.

"Good afternoon, Ms. Bancroft." He
crossed his arms and shifted from leaning
against his car.

Oh no. What was this all about?

"Some new evidence has come to light in
our investigation regarding Mr. Taber."

"New evidence?" she asked. He *was* here
about the tapes then.

He nodded. "I'm here to let you know that
Carolyn Taber, Sterling's sister-in-law, committed suicide this afternoon and left behind
a set of incriminating tapes, along with a

letter that has led us to believe she was involved in her brother-in-law's murder. I'm afraid that you were a victim of circumstance. My apologies."

"Suicide?" She shook her head. No, that didn't add up at all. Carolyn Taber was off — that much was a given — but she hadn't appeared suicidal. Michaela could buy into the possibility that she'd murdered Sterling, but not that she'd kill herself. The tapes. She rubbed her forehead. "Um, you said tapes? What do you mean?"

"Ms. Bancroft, this is an ongoing investigation and I'm not permitted to discuss it with you." He leaned back against his cruiser.

Rage suddenly boiled under the surface, overtaking her sense of shock. "*You can't discuss this with me?* After all the grief you've caused me in the past week, going after me like a pit bull, and you can't at least let me in on what you've found?"

"That is correct. The case against you was shaping up to be circumstantial, and it would appear after our forensics team went over the polo mallet again that there is another set of partial prints on there. I do apologize for any inconvenience this has caused you."

"*Inconvenience?* All I have to say, *Detec-*

tive, is that if I were a vengeful person, I'd have a lawsuit smacked down on the police department and you personally so fast that you wouldn't have time to shove another donut down your throat! This has been the most poorly conducted investigation." She shook her head. "I think it would be best for you to leave now."

She stormed off toward the barn as Peters drove away. *Now* they found partial prints other than hers on her mallet? Of course: Because she'd handed over the tapes, the investigation took a different turn. She kicked the dirt with her foot. "Damn!" She went into her office, grabbed a bottle of water out of the fridge, and sat down at her desk. The tapes. Peters had said that Carolyn had a set of tapes with her when she killed herself. But she'd pleaded with Michaela for *her* tapes. Sterling had told Carolyn that he'd destroy the tapes, or at least that had been her story. He hadn't destroyed his set, that much was for certain. Michaela had turned that set over to Jude. And Carolyn had presumably destroyed the set that Sterling had sent her. He told her on the tape not to bother destroying her set because there were others. Someone had another set of those videos. But who? Had Carolyn killed herself because she felt there was no hope? Maybe she thought that if her husband found out, things would be over between them and the gravy train would stop running. Again, though, how had she acquired a set of the tapes? Where was she when she'd supposedly taken her life?

Michaela wanted answers, because she wasn't buying the idea that Carolyn had killed herself. Women like Carolyn Taber bounced back, even after ugly divorces and scandal.

She needed to talk to Jude. Would he give her the information she wanted? Or would he tell her to go and do what she was best at — train horses and teach kids? Wasn't that what he'd told her? She hit her desk. Here she should be thrilled. She was off the hook. No one suspected her of any wrong-doing and she was free to get her life back on track. But still, what good would it do if she felt in her gut that Sterling Taber's killer wasn't dead but still out there? Sure, Sterling and even Carolyn weren't exactly pillars of society, but they *were* people, and they didn't deserve to be murdered. And Michaela knew that Carolyn Taber had been murdered. She just knew it.

She got up from her desk and headed into the house. She had withheld one of the tapes from Jude, the one with another woman in it — which she'd assumed was a one-night stand. She hadn't thought it mattered the other night when she'd seen it, and then she really didn't think it mattered when she connected Carolyn to the other tapes. But *did* it matter, though? Could the mystery woman have had a set of the tapes, too?

As much as she hated to do it, Michaela put in the other tape. She watched all forty minutes of it and was thoroughly sick to her stomach when it was over. She saw nothing. Well, she saw something all right, but she couldn't find anything odd. The sound effects consisted of some grunts and moans and Sterling finally yelling out the woman's name — Sheila! Yuck.

Nothing there. Michaela paced inside the family room — usually a place of comfort and warmth, it now felt like four walls closing in on her. There were holes in all of this, and she was going to take them one by one and plug them up. She called Jude but he was out of the office, so she left a message. She was determined to learn what he knew about Carolyn Taber's apparent suicide. Since she couldn't start with Carolyn, she'd begin with Rebecca Woodson's fall from the pier in Santa Barbara last summer and her subsequent death. Everything about what had happened last summer smelled foul to her. She didn't believe the story that Rebecca had fallen by accident. She'd seen Sterling in action. The man had an anger management problem, plus he was a narcissist and complete egomaniac. He'd do anything to cover his ass. Both Zach and Tommy had witnessed Sterling and Rebecca drinking, then arguing, and that was all they knew until the next morning when the police questioned Sterling. Then, Rebecca's brother came by to beat *the truth* out of Sterling about what had happened to his sister. Then, the Woodsons filed a wrongful death suit that Charles Taber quietly made go away with a large sum of cash to the Woodsons. After that he'd cut down his brother's share of the family fortune and suggested that he leave for good; thus, Carolyn Taber and Sterling's desire to get back into his wealthy family's deep pockets.

Michaela got on the Internet, hoping to see if she could find out any more information about Rebecca Woodson. After about an hour of skimming articles and scouring phone information pages, she found the man she believed to be Rebecca's brother. She had to speak with him and find out what the family thought happened that fateful night. She picked up the phone and hit pay dirt.

Rebecca's brother, Ryan, hesitated to say anything at first. "Who is this? What do you want? You from the paper?"

"No. I'm not from the paper." Michaela explained who she was. She told him about Sterling's murder, the investigation over the past week, and why she felt the need to talk to him. Amazingly, the man didn't hang up on her.

"I'm not surprised that bastard is dead. You know, Becky was my baby sister. A good kid. Sure, she was a little wild sometimes. She liked to party, and if she hadn't gotten all caught up in that rich-kid crowd, she'd still be here. But that Sterling dude, he was no good, you know? Strung Becky along like he was dangling a carrot in front of a rabbit. Creep. I hear he done that with lots of girls. Liked to give them jewelry and things, you know, make sure they believe he was into them. Crazy, too, 'cause a guy like that didn't need to do no convincing girls to be with him, you know? A guy like that only needed to snap his fingers and there you go, the girls come runnin'."

"He liked to give women jewelry?"

"Oh yeah. Gave Becky a diamond ring, like he was gonna marry her or sumthin'. Please. That ring, she had it on when they found her." He started to choke up. "I know this is gonna sound real awful of me, but I needed money to investigate those people. Them Tabers are loaded and when Becky was killed — and she was killed, I know — it broke my mother's heart. I made a vow to get those people. I took that ring to hock it and get some cash to pay this guy I know who's a private eye, and the ring was a fake. Fake fucking diamond."

"Fake?"

"Huh. Yep, fake. Just like that guy was."

Michaela asked him about what he thought happened the night his sister died.

"I think Becky and what's his name, can't even say it, got into it. My sister was feisty and I think she figured out what he was all about, and they started in and he pushed her off the pier. He ran home and hid behind his family's dough. Money talks."

"I hate to ask you this, but what about the rumor that Becky had a sugar daddy?"

"That's bull! I never heard that. She wouldn't do that."

"What about the wrongful death suit your family filed?"

"I can't talk about that. The Tabers did pay my mother some cash and we decided to leave the situation alone. Too painful."

"Did you ever talk with Sterling again?

After your sister's death?"

"Once. Dude actually called me three weeks ago. He had the gall to call me and tell me that he wanted to talk to me about Becky and what happened that night. I told him that unless he planned to admit that he murdered my sister, we had nothing to talk about."

"What did he say?"

"I didn't let him say nothing. I hung up on him. He came into my work a few days later but I wasn't there. I don't know what the hell he wanted. It's probably a good thing for him I wasn't here. But looks like I won't need to be worrying about Sterling Taber dropping in on me ever again."

Michaela talked a few minutes more with Ryan, thanked him, and hung up. Tommy was pretty certain that Rebecca had a wealthy older man keeping her in diamonds and pearls and that she played him on the side, but her brother claimed he had no knowledge of it. Was it pure rumor started by a group of wealthy, spoiled young people, or was there a secret life to Rebecca that her brother either didn't know about or denied? Either way, as far as she was concerned, she'd acquired two interesting pieces of information from Ryan Woodson. The first tidbit was that Sterling had gone to see Ryan when he was in Santa Barbara. Why? What was it that he wanted to tell Ryan about his sister's death? He surely wasn't going to admit any wrongdoing. The visit itself was a mystery, but could it be tied into Sterling's own demise?

The other fascinating thing she'd learned was about the ring that Sterling had given to Rebecca — a fake. It caused Michaela to think about the tennis bracelet she'd found, and Sterling's juvie stint for stealing an expensive jewel.

Before she had time to explore that train of thought, her doorbell rang — repeatedly. Oh God, don't let it be Peters with a change of heart about things.

"Okay, I'm coming!" she yelled. Whoever was on the other side of the door certainly wanted her to open it.

She was surprised when she opened the door and came face-to-face with Ethan's wife, Summer, holding Josh. It took Michaela a moment to even register who it was. She immediately recognized little Joshy, but — hold the horses — Summer was not in her usual state of yuppydom with carefully applied makeup and perfect outfit. "Summer?"

She handed Josh to her. "I have an appointment and I couldn't find anyone to watch him and I knew you'd probably be here and it's important, and you are his godmother, so watch him for me for a little bit, okay?"

Michaela nodded. "Sure. Are you okay? Is everything all right?" Was this for real, Summer asking her to help with the baby? Never in a million years would she have thought this would happen. Something had to be wrong. "I'm . . . well . . . uh . . . are you sure?"

"Yes, I'm sure," she snapped. "I don't have a choice. Are you going to help me out here or what?"

"Yes, of course, I'll watch Josh. Everything is okay, right?" she said again.

"Everything is perfect." Summer took a step back and stood up straight, brushing her hands across her tight, black satin pencil skirt and lacy white blouse cut down to . . . well, pretty low, and the hair — no longer the pretty copper that Michaela was slightly jealous of. No, it was magenta almost, and not pulled back, but down, long and wavy. If Michaela didn't know better, she might think that Summer and Ethan had some kind of hot date planned, because she looked every bit the seductress. "There's formula in here." She handed her a blue diaper bag. "And diapers, wipes, and a jar of food. Actually there's a few jars of food. He likes the sweet potatoes."

How long did she plan to be gone? Not that Michaela minded. She loved being able to spend time with her godson. "What time will you be back?"

"I left a message for Ethan, letting him know to pick him up here. My appointment could run late, so Ethan will be by."

"Okay." So they didn't have some afternoon delight thing planned. Strange, but Michaela was relieved, which was stupid, because it wasn't as if Summer and Ethan didn't sleep together. And now she herself seemed to have a sex life again. Sort of.

"Bye. Thanks." She gave Josh a kiss on the cheek. The baby smiled at his mom but didn't reach out for her as he leaned his head against Michaela's chest. Her heart quickened. She couldn't deny her desire for a baby, especially while holding Josh.

Summer rushed toward her Mercedes. She turned around at one point and seemed to hesitate, but then waved again. Odd. Actually beyond odd, but Michaela wasn't going to fight it. She was going to spend some time with Josh and she couldn't be happier to see his cherubic face and big blue eyes. "Hey, little babe, what are you doing?"

He cooed and smiled at her and she

thought her heart would melt right there. To have a child — amazing. If she could feel this much love while holding her godson, then what would it be like to have her own baby? That thought brought her back to Jude and made her wonder if she should consider taking their relationship further. She knew that he wanted to. Could she allow herself to fall for him, completely and totally? He also had told her that he desired more children and he didn't mind that it looked as if she couldn't conceive. That if they ever did commit to each other then adoption might be a good option. They'd only briefly discussed it when he'd asked her about kids. She'd told him that she hadn't been able to get pregnant while married to her ex-husband, Brad. She'd endured a series of fertility treatments, which her insurance didn't cover, and at the time had caused her to go deeply in debt — this right after Brad took off with an ex–rodeo queen.

Michaela laid out Josh's blankie and some of his toys, then took each stuffed animal and made voices and faces to go along with it. The baby laughed and it was probably the sweetest sound Michaela had ever heard. They made silly voices, endured one diaper change, and then they lay on their backs and stuck their feet in the air, grabbing their toes — well, Joshy was able to grab his toes. Michaela wasn't quite so limber and wound up twisting and falling over to the side, laughing at herself. She hadn't had this much fun in ages.

Josh started to wind down and fuss. "I bet you're hungry. Auntie Mickey will fix you a bottle." She got up and took his bag into the kitchen.

As she started back from the kitchen she heard a noise. What was that? She came around the corner to see that Josh had pulled her purse onto the floor, spilling all of its contents. This quickly reminded her how disorganized she was, seeing everything from receipts, gum wrappers, and even an empty raisin box on the floor. She cringed and ran over to where the baby was putting a business card in his mouth. He'd just started rolling over and he must've pulled on the purse strap. Dammit, she should've moved her purse off the chair. "Oh no, no, you cutie-patootie. What do you have there?" She took the card from his mouth and shoved it in her back pocket while quickly cleaning up the mess on the floor so Josh couldn't get into anything else. She laid him back down on the blanket and handed him his bottle. She watched him for a minute, then reached into her back pocket to see if the card he'd had in his mouth was important, like her coffee card from the Honeybear. She was only one stamp away from a free cup.

The card *was* important, but not because it entitled her to a free cup of java; it was Erin Hornersberg's card. The card had the makeup artist's name on it with her title, but it also had the name of the shop — The Sanctuary — and beneath that it read, *OWNER: SHEILA ADDISON.* Sheila! The tape. Michaela turned the card over and her jaw fell. She remembered what Erin had said to her when she gave her the card. "Sorry, there's an address written on the back here, but I don't need it anymore."

Michaela had blown it off. No biggie. But looking at the back side of the card for the first time, she realized something: She recognized the address. She'd even been there. It was Sterling Taber's.

THIRTY-FIVE

After Josh sucked down his bottle he started to fuss, forcing Michaela, for the moment, to forget about her questions regarding Erin Hornersberg and Sheila. She knew that she should drop the whole thing. Move on. She was clear of any wrongdoing. Her life was hers again. Why did she feel the need to pursue this? Maybe because she knew that there was still a killer among them. She had to get it off her mind.

Josh started to whine. "All right, little love, what's the problem? You've been changed, played with, fed . . ." He rubbed his eyes. "Ah, but you haven't been cuddled to sleep." She picked him up and wrapped a thin blanket around him, deciding to take him out to the back patio, where she had a wooden rocker next to the pool. Maybe the waterfall that flowed into the pool would soothe him. Nothing she'd ever experienced before was more comfortable than rocking and cooing to the baby.

She watched crystalline droplets of water flow into the black-bottom pool, which Uncle Lou had built to look like a lagoon. She sure did miss him. Green foliage surrounded the pool and area, along with an array of tropical flowers that flourished in the desert heat and dry air.

The beauty surrounding her and the baby in her lap brought a deep sense of contentment, despite everything else on her mind. She twirled Josh's fine brown curls in her fingers. His hair smelled of baby shampoo. He looked so much like his daddy. Ethan and Summer were lucky to have him. She couldn't help but nod off.

She didn't know how long they napped like that, but she was awakened by the touch of a hand on her head. She blinked several times.

"Hey, sleepyheads," Ethan said.

"Hi." She looked down at the top of Josh's head. He was still asleep. "How long have you been there?"

"Long enough to know this was the most peaceful that I've ever seen you."

She didn't know how to respond, but she knew that she didn't want him to lift Josh off her lap. "Summer call you?"

He nodded. "Left me a message. Did she

say where she was going?"

"No. I thought that maybe she was meeting you."

"Uh-uh. I had a full day. I've tried calling her but I keep getting her voice mail."

"I don't know."

Josh stirred and as soon as he realized his dad was there, his mouth grew into a wide toothless grin. "Hey, buddy," Ethan said.

Josh reached his arms out for him. Michaela handed the baby over. "You are such a good dad."

"Thanks, Mick. I know you'll be a mom one day. I know it. You'll be awesome."

She didn't reply.

"I better get going. I've got horses to feed and this guy to take care of."

"Hey, Ethan, everything okay at home?"

"Sure. Everything is fine."

Something in his voice made her wonder if he were telling the truth. "Yeah?"

"Yes. Why?"

"I don't know, I guess I found it odd that Summer would drop Josh off with me and . . . well, you seem kind of distant; I don't know."

"I'm tired, that's all. Summer dropping the baby here . . . well, you're his godmother and I'm always suggesting that we have you watch him. Looks like she took my suggestion."

"Yeah. Okay." She gave Josh a kiss on the cheek.

Ethan took her hand and squeezed it. "Thanks, Mick."

"Anytime. I love having him here. Hey, did you hear? I've been cleared of the murder charges against me."

He grinned and hugged her with his free arm. "I knew you would be. No way in hell were you going to jail." He thought a moment. "Hell, you probably *could* get away with murder. Everyone loves you and people know you wouldn't hurt a soul."

She smiled at him, helped pack up Josh's bag, and walked them to the door. She was sad to see them go. Did Summer have a clue as to how good she had it?

THIRTY-SIX

Evening was settling in as a full moon started to rise over the mountains and waves of pink and orange floated through the desert sky. Dwayne would've fed the horses tonight. Michaela contemplated making a drive over to the shop where Erin and her girlfriend worked. She wasn't going alone, though. She gave Joe a ring.

"Oh hey, Mick, Camden give you my message? Why didn't you call me and tell me that the cops are off your back? My cousin Anthony got a call from Peters today about it. That's great. You probably wanted to tell me about it tonight, right? Do you need any help getting all that stuff over here?"

Michaela smacked herself upside the head. How could she have forgotten Gen's birthday? They'd even talked about it when they'd gone over to break into Sterling's place. "Of course I'm coming. I told you that I wouldn't miss it. And, yes, I did plan to tell you about the case, but there are a few unanswered questions."

"Drop it, Mick."

"I'll tell you about it when I see you." She looked at her watch. She was supposed to be at Joe's in less than an hour. "I've got to go by the tack shop and get Gen's gifts loaded. Sorry for the delay. Nothing is wrapped."

"No, no. You been under a lot of pressure. I was gonna come by earlier today and grab them, but Marianne needed my help around the house. I got a few minutes to spare now; why don't I meet you down there and I'll help you get everything together. I appreciate you ordering all that stuff on short notice."

"I can do it, Joe, don't worry about it."

"I'll see you in, what, a half hour?"

"Okay." She sighed, knowing that it was no use arguing with him. She changed her blouse because the other had wound up streaked with baby spit, ran a brush through her hair, and darted out the door. She wanted to get to the shop before Joe did and see if she couldn't get a few things wrapped. Thank goodness Camden had thought of everything when she stocked the tack shop — including horse-themed wrapping paper.

When she pulled into the parking lot, it was obvious Camden had already locked up and gone home for the day. She stood in front of the double doors and unlocked them. Joe hadn't arrived yet.

She flipped a light on and punched in the code on the security alarm. Suddenly she felt anxious about being there. It was nearly dark. She turned back to lock the front door and as she did she stopped. Her heart raced and fear coursed through her as she stared into the eyes of someone in a mask, dressed in black. Blood rushed through her ears.

"Wh-what . . . do you want?" she stammered. "The money is in a safe. It's . . . it's not much, but you can have it."

The figure started toward her and she knew that whoever was behind the ski mask was not there for any money, but rather for her. She darted toward the door and he lunged in front of her, reaching out to grab her. She pulled back and raced in the other direction, toward the rear door. She could hear steps close behind her. Running between a row of English saddles, she turned to push a set of them down as hard as she could. The intruder tripped over them and grunted, then rose and started after her again. She was at the door, her hands shaking, and turning the dead bolt, when she felt something hard hit the side of her face. She screamed as she fell to the ground. Her assailant pulled her by the arm and dragged her away from the door. Michaela knew that her life was about to end. She looked up and saw evil in the eyes behind the mask. Then she saw a polo mallet in the one free hand. It rose above her. She screamed and twisted away as a voice from the front called out her name. The intruder turned, dropped the mallet, and ran out the back door.

"Joe! *Joe!* He's getting away!"

"What?" Joe approached her, clearly aware that something horrible had just happened. He sprinted past her and out the back door. Michaela stood, rubbing the side of her head. She could now see what the killer had initially swung to knock her down — a twisted snaffle bit. Her hands shook and her body felt numb. She tried to get up but could only sink back to the floor, stunned.

A minute later, Joe came back in and knelt by her. "You okay?"

"I . . . think so. What happened? Did you see him?"

"I'm sorry, Mick. The bastard got away."

THIRTY-SEVEN

"Let me get you some ice." Joe bent down. "Looks like you got a bruise there across your cheek. That ain't so good. You got some in the freezer, don't you?"

"Yes — wait, don't leave me!" Oh no. Michaela didn't like sounding so needy. She prided herself on her independence and, yes, even courage. But right now the last thing she felt was courageous.

"Don't worry, Mick. No one is gonna hurt you. I'll kick the shit out of 'em."

She smiled at his retort. He was right. One look at Joey P. and the bad guy would be off and running.

A minute later, Joe brought back a small bag of ice and placed it on the rapidly swelling lump on her face. "That jerk say anything? Take any money? Anything?"

"No. He was here to kill me."

"What?"

"Yeah. I offered cash, but he chased me

through the store, swung that metal bit at my face, and then tried to bash my head in with the mallet. Thank God you showed up when you did."

"You sure it was a man?"

"Seemed like it, I mean whoever it was, was pretty athletic."

"Yeah, but not a big guy. I got a good look at the physique; we can't assume it was a guy yet, but we gotta call the police, Mickey."

"What? No way, Joe. The last thing I want to do is call the police. I've had enough of them. I don't want to answer any more of their questions."

"What about Jude?"

"Not even Jude." She didn't want to say *especially* Jude. He was the real reason she didn't want to call the police. She knew that he'd come unglued.

"Don't be stupid here. Someone tried to swing that thing at you and you don't want to bring in the police?" He pointed to the mallet.

She shook her head. "Okay, okay, but look, you've got to go and be with your family. Next thing I know it'll be Marianne swinging a mallet at me and I wouldn't blame her."

"Ah, Marianne knows you're like a sister

to me. She loves what you do for our kid. Don't go worrying about that. Let's call the police."

"Okay."

Joe made the call and within ten minutes a black-and-white arrived. Shortly after, Jude rolled in, his face strained with worry.

Michaela sat on the sofa in her office drinking the water Joe had gotten her. After Joe told the police what had happened from his perspective, Michaela insisted that he go on home. She told him where Gen's gifts were, and one of the officers helped him carry them to the minivan, while Jude sat down next to her. "You're going to give me an ulcer," he said.

"It's not as if I ask for this stuff to happen."

"I know." He reached for her hand. "Let me ask you, what do you think this was all about? You say it wasn't a robbery. Do you think this was some kind of copycat killer?"

"What do you mean?"

"Like Sterling Taber's killer."

"That was no copycat killer. That was *the* killer."

He shook his head. "No, Michaela. Peters is certain that Carolyn Taber hired someone to murder Sterling, if she didn't do it herself. She was found at the Marriott. She hung herself. She left a note for her husband, apologizing for the grief she'd caused, and for Sterling. Her husband says that last Saturday she told him she was going to a weekend yoga retreat, but we checked, and she never went there."

"I don't think Carolyn killed him. She came to see me about the tapes."

"What? You didn't tell me this." He let go of her hand.

"I know I didn't."

"Why?"

"I didn't think it was important. I gave you the tapes and I figured that was enough."

"No. That's *not* enough. That's you keeping important information from the police. From me. When are you going to stop playing detective? When are you going to trust me?"

She didn't reply.

He sighed. "What else? Is there anything you want to tell me about when Carolyn Taber came to see you about the tapes?"

"She tried to pay me for them. I told her that the police had them."

"Did you ever think that might be why she killed herself?"

Michaela sat up. "Wait a minute. You're not blaming me for Carolyn Taber's death, are you? I had nothing to do with that. She . . . she tried to threaten me. That woman didn't kill herself. There was another set of tapes somewhere, and whoever had them, that's your killer."

He stood and again reached for her hand. She didn't take it. "Come on, let me take you home," he said.

"No. I have a little girl's birthday party to go to. Do you need anything else from me?"

"Yes, I do. I need you to be honest with me. I need you to be a civilian, not a cop. I'm the cop. My guys are still dusting for prints. Now, let me take you home."

She tossed him the keys to the shop. "Lock it up for me. I have to go." She reached her truck and brushed away tears, wincing at the bruise on her cheek.

THIRTY-EIGHT

Joe's family doted on Michaela. Marianne and Joe had five kids, and they weren't without their tribulations — Gen dealt with autism, little Joe with anger management issues. Vincent, who was thirteen, seemed well behaved and mild mannered, and the twins, Giorgio and Isabel, were rambunctious toddlers who kept their mother hopping. But there was a lot of love inside this home, and Michaela enjoyed being there eating birthday cake with them while Gen opened her presents, with Vincent's help.

Gen smiled widely when Vincent took out the therapeutic riding saddle for her. "That's your very own saddle," Michaela said.

"It's just for you." Marianne stood behind Gen, placed her hands on her daughter's shoulders, and winked at Michaela.

Marianne mouthed "thank you" to her. Michaela nodded and smiled. Her head still ached, but being around the Pellegrino family helped. Their house was one of the newer tract homes and had that Southern California feel combined with Mediterranean flair that so many contractors were trying to emulate in the area. It looked like Marianne probably needed help with the housecleaning. There were toys pretty much everywhere, and the twins appeared to be messy marvins, as they were busy strewing the wrapping paper all over the floor.

The adults steered clear of discussing Sterling's murder and anything related to it while the kids were around and instead talked about horses, TV shows they liked, and even the weather — anything light. They took special care in avoiding what had happened earlier. Marianne had taken Michaela into the kitchen and given her an earful when she arrived.

"You and Joe been getting into some trouble. He's worried about you. I'm worried about you. He told me what happened and that's not good. Are you okay?" Marianne rested her hands on her hips. She was a thin, petite woman, but Michaela knew that when Marianne Pellegrino meant business, she wasn't one to mess with.

"I'm fine. I'm sorry. I know I've been a pain, and I'll leave Joe out of this from now on."

"Oh no you won't. You'll get yourself killed if Joey isn't around. But I don't need my Joey getting himself killed either. Promise me you'll start carrying some pepper spray or something. Joey makes me carry it. No more dead bodies either. This business of you and murder . . . well, it's not good for anyone. You need to be teaching my kid and the other kids how to ride, and settling down."

"You're right." As if she really enjoyed coming across dead bodies. But she wasn't about to argue with Marianne, who at that moment played the part of a perfect mother hen.

"Of course I'm right. Now go and have some cake."

But once Marianne suggested that the kids get ready for bed and they all told her good night, Joe clapped his hands together and said, "What do you think? Should we put our heads together on this?"

"What do you mean?" Michaela asked.

"I mean, you know and I know the cops don't have this thing figured out. Someone tried to kill you tonight and we gotta find out who it was."

"I don't think that's such a great idea," Michaela replied.

"Why not?"

"Marianne had a little talk with me and I don't want to step on any toes."

He waved a hand at her. "Mare is all bark, no bite. I gotta help you and she knows it."

"No, you don't. Why do you want to anyway?"

He yawned and stretched. "Makes me feel kind of like that dude on that old TV show — *Magnum P.I.*"

Michaela laughed. It made her head hurt, but she couldn't help it. "Tom Selleck? Oh Joe, you'd have to lose some weight and grow some more hair."

He touched the top of his head. "You cut so low sometimes. You noticed I'm losing hair, too, huh? Marianne said something about it the other day. Used to have a ton of it only what, last year or so. Shit, this getting old stuff sucks."

"I'm sorry. So, if you're Magnum, that means I must be the pain in the butt Higgins."

He pointed at her. "Ain't that the truth. Wanna beer?"

"No. I have to get home."

"Uh-uh. Marianne and I talked and you need to stay the night until we get this all resolved."

"I can't do that. The horses need me and your family doesn't need the intrusion."

"Mickey, you *are* family and you got Dwayne and Camden to take care of the animals."

"That's right, which means they're there with me and I'll be fine."

Joe smiled. "Them two are too busy these days from what you say, being holed up in the love shack."

"True."

"So you'll stay."

Marianne walked into the family room. "Of course she'll stay. And I know you two are up to no good, so you are going to deal me in. If you're going to do your little private investigating then you better include me."

"Ah, Mare, come on. You wouldn't be any good at this."

She shook a finger at him. "Joey, I'm in and there's nothing you can do about it. I think three heads are better than two, so you two start from square one and fill me in. It's obvious by the bruise on your face, Michaela, that you're in trouble. So talk."

She looked from Marianne to Joe and nodded. Joe shook his head. "Women."

"I don't think you're going to win this one, Joe."

"I never win."

Michaela started from the beginning, going over the day of the match, what happened before it, after, and then the days following.

Marianne raised her brows when she revealed that she and Joe had broken into Sterling's place. She shot her husband a dirty look. He shrugged and looked chagrined. "You think that maybe this makeup artist had a set of tapes? Or that her friend Sheila had the tape she was in?" Marianne asked.

"It's possible, but it doesn't make sense that she would kill Carolyn Taber," Michaela replied.

"No, but we don't know for sure that the woman didn't kill herself," Joe said.

"She didn't."

"You still got that bracelet you mentioned?" Marianne asked.

"Yes, it's in my purse. No one's claimed it yet." She took out the bracelet and handed it to Marianne.

"Pretty. Looks real. I have some of these fake diamonds, the cubic zirconium like this, and no one knows the difference. You mentioned the Sorvinos." She looked at Joe. "You know that the Sorvinos are related to Diamante Pizzini."

"The Pez?" Joe asked.

Marianne nodded.

"Where did you hear that?"

"You're not the only one who has cousins." She smiled.

"Can I ask who the Pez is?" Michaela said.

"He's a low-life thug. He's been in and out of jail for stolen goods. Last time he got out, I heard he went into business with some wealthy guy in Palm Springs. He runs that Sinners and Saints club."

"The place that Lucia likes to hang out at?" Michaela asked.

"That's the one, but I didn't know they were related. You sure about that, Mare?" Joe asked.

"Sure I'm sure. I ran into my cousin Nancy last year who knows Diamante's ex-wife's brother and she said that the Pez is a bastard son of Pepe Sorvino's brother."

"Pepe has kept that one under wraps, hasn't he?" Joe said. "Not surprised. Pepe likes to act like he's all about being on the up and up, and as far as I know he is, but I do find it interesting that he's related to this guy and that his daughter hangs out at that club."

"If you want my two cents," Marianne said, "I'm betting that Lucia and her brother, Mario, had something to do with the murders and now tonight with Michaela."

"But why go after Carolyn Taber?" Michaela asked.

"That's a good point, and I don't know why, but we need to trap that little brat and get her to talk," Marianne said.

"And how do you plan to do that?" Joe asked.

Marianne thought for a few seconds, and then a smile spread across her face. "I got an idea."

THIRTY-NINE

They stayed up late into the night talking and planning. Marianne had a good idea to get Lucia to talk, but it also involved some delinquency on everyone's part. Joe was surprised by his wife's sneaky side and by the way Joe patted her on the butt when they finally went to bed, she got the feeling that Joe wasn't only surprised by his wife, but that it also had ignited something else in him.

Michaela camped out on the couch. She awoke the next morning to four big, round brown eyes staring at her. The twins were up early. It wasn't quite seven and Isabel was touching the side of Michaela's mouth, which was open, and she realized that she'd been drooling. Oh, thank God they were only two. She swallowed and realized how badly she needed to brush her teeth. Instead of waking Joe and Marianne, she found bowls and some cereal and gave the twins breakfast. Vincent came padding out as she brewed a pot of coffee.

"Thanks," he said.

"For what?"

"Making the twins something to eat."

He was a good-looking boy with dark hair like his dad, and light green eyes like his mom. "It didn't take much. Just poured some Frosted Flakes into a bowl."

"I know." He smiled. "But it's still cool. My mom is tired a lot and it's good she's sleeping in. My dad, too."

Michaela felt a nudge of guilt. Had Joe spent too much time trying to help her? And now Marianne was involved. "You know what? Why don't you and me surprise the two of them? Your dad mentioned something about their wedding anniversary coming up. Why don't we send them away for a weekend and I can stay with you guys?"

"Really?"

"Yes."

"Are you sure you'd want to do that? The twins are crazy and Gen is a lot to handle sometimes. And have you ever seen little Joe throw a tantrum? It's ugly."

Michaela touched Vincent's shoulder. "And what about you? You look like trouble."

He smiled sheepishly. "I try to be good."

"I think you've got it handled. So I'll make some plans for them and then we can surprise them on their anniversary."

"I think that's cool."

"I think you're cool. Listen, I've got some things to do. Will you let your mom and dad know that I'll call?"

"Sure."

Michaela cleaned up and left Vincent with the twins. What a good kid . . . and spending a weekend with Joe and Marianne's family was the least she could do, given all they'd done for her.

She made a quick trip home, where she fed the animals, cleaned up, and got back on the road. This morning she was going to find out what the truth was between Erin Hornersberg, her girlfriend, Sheila, and Sterling Taber. She wanted to be sure all of the bases were covered before the planned attack on Lucia Sorvino went down.

FORTY

Michaela found the salon that Erin Hornersberg worked at and Sheila owned. It was definitely one of those posh spa places where all beauty services were rendered. The sound of ocean waves played over the speaker system, and the scents of patchouli and rose filled the air. Camden would love this place. Off to the right of the beige marbled flooring and peach faux-finished walls were a couple of manicurists and their clients. They spoke in hushed tones as they lacquered the nails of their cucumber eye-patched patrons, who sat in neck-massaging chairs.

A receptionist dressed in a white lab coat, as if she were a doctor of some sort, eyed Michaela as she walked up to the desk and asked for Erin.

"Oh, Erin hasn't been in for a few days. She must've quit."

"Did she call?"

"No." Another woman slid in next to the receptionist and looked at the appointment book. She had long golden hair, which cascaded down her back, a flawless complexion, and bright blue eyes. Her nametag read SHEILA.

"Sheila?" Michaela asked.

The young woman looked up. "Yes? Are you my next client?"

"No."

"She's looking for Erin," the receptionist said.

"Funny. Me, too."

"Oh?" Michaela wasn't sure what to say.

"Can I ask why *you're* looking for her?"

She leaned in and lowered her voice. "It has to do with a murder investigation."

"Are you a cop?"

"No, I'm not. Erin did a job for me last weekend. I'm sure you've heard about Sterling Taber's murder in the papers?"

The receptionist looked up. Sheila grabbed Michaela's arm. "Tell my client when she shows up that I'll be back in a few minutes. Come on."

"What?"

"Come on. I'll get you some tea."

"I don't want any tea."

The girl practically dragged her into a rear storeroom. She closed the door and crossed

314

her arms. "What the hell do you want?"

"I told you that I wanted to talk to Erin. Can we keep the door open?"

"No. This is a place of business and I run a professional operation. I don't appreciate you coming in here asking nosy questions about Erin."

She should've brought Joe with her like she initially planned; she hadn't expected to be dragged off into a storage room. She didn't like this one bit.

"Wait a minute." Sheila snapped her fingers. "Did you and some other woman stop by Erin's the other night?"

"Yes."

She nodded. "Uh-huh, then you're the reason she took off."

"What? I have no idea what you're talking about. I'm here because a man was killed and she might know something about it. She had his address written on the back of her business card, and now another woman associated with Sterling is dead. I know that Erin was probably jealous of what happened between you and Sterling."

Sheila played dumb. "What do you mean?"

"Come on. Erin even told me that you went home with him."

"Who are you?"

"I am the woman who was accused of murdering Sterling. He was killed in my office."

"Oh, I see, and you think that Erin did him in because she was jealous of me and him."

Michaela shrugged. "Why don't you tell me?"

Sheila shook her head. "Erin had that address because the morning after I was with that jerk, I needed a ride home. Yes, it bugged her what I did, but we got through it."

"Did you know that Erin was looking for Sterling the morning of the polo match?"

"I told her not to bother. Look, the guy was calling and harassing me. He made up lame stuff like he had me on video and he was going to show his friends and anyone else who wanted to see. Erin wanted to track him down and tell him to leave me alone. She found out he was going to be in that match, so she went looking for him. Then she wigged out when she realized that she would have to do his makeup."

"She told you all of this?"

"Yes, she did. We don't keep things from each other."

"What if I told you that Sterling wasn't lying to you about you being on tape?"

"What?" Sheila looked truly horrified. "How do you know this? Are you sure?"

"I'm sure, and it's a long story," Michaela replied.

"Oh my God. I thought he was only trying to get me to come back over to his place. He was such an ass. Oh jeez. I never in a million years thought he was that sick."

"Do you think Erin knew about the tape?"

"No way. How would she?"

"I don't know, maybe Sterling said something to her about it at the show. You know, she came really unglued because he was harassing her about you."

"No, and you know what? Contrary to what people think about Erin, she's not a bad person. She's had some rough experiences and she's pulled through them."

"But you're looking for her?"

"Yeah," Sheila replied. "After you and your friend stopped by to talk to her the other night, she kind of freaked out. She called me and said that you were asking a lot of questions, and she was afraid that after the argument she and Sterling had on Sunday that the cops would come back and press her about it. Cops aren't exactly Erin's favorite people. She spent nine months in jail for a crime that she didn't commit. So she packed up and split, and I've been calling around looking for her ever since."

"I'm sorry." Michaela could understand how Erin might've felt. The police had been on her back since Sterling's murder, and even though she had nothing to do with it, Peters had been relentless. "You mentioned something about Sterling and his harassment. You figured that it was all just talk."

"I guess I was wrong."

"Do you know who his friends might be?"

She sighed. "No. I only spent one night with the guy, but I remember who he was partying with the night I went home with him."

"Who?"

"This one guy, middle-aged Italian dude, thought he was Al Pacino or something. I think he runs that club — Sinners and Saints. What a jerk — but Sterling told me that he did business with him. There was this little chicky there, too. I never caught her name, but she didn't like me hanging around with Sterling. I got the feeling she was hot for him. She looked kind of stupid, though. I'd seen her before."

"Stupid?"

"A wannabe. I know she had a wig on. Too dark a complexion for blonde hair. I don't know, maybe she dyed it, but it looked like a wig to me because she had one of those Britney Spears kind of beret hats on and she just looked dumb. I think she knew the Italian guy, too, because he kept whispering something to her."

"Were they there as a couple?"

"I don't think so. I think they could've been related. Then this other kid came in. Kind of a cute boy-next-door type with dimples, but trying to be a bad boy, you know. He wore a tank, looked like he had a new tattoo, and wore earrings."

"Earrings? What kind?"

"Diamonds. Big freaking ones, too."

"What was his name?"

"I don't know. I know they talked about playing polo."

"Was it Zach or Tommy?"

"Like I said, I don't know. I wasn't paying attention. Look, that's all I know. I went home with Sterling. He was an ass at about five in the morning, kicking me out. That's when I called Erin to come rescue me."

"Thanks. Hey, I'm sorry about Erin," Michaela said.

"Sometimes she likes to spend time in Big Bear, when she needs to think. She'll be back. We've had our issues before, but we always get past it. I might drive up there if she's not home in a day or two."

The receptionist tapped on the door.

"Sheila, your client is here."

"Thanks. I better go."

Michaela eased out of the storage room and headed to her truck.

So, Sterling, a middle-aged Italian guy, and a younger Italian woman with a blonde wig had hung out. It hadn't been Mario wearing the wig after all, but more likely Lucia Sorvino, hanging out with her cousin Diamante Pizzini. What kind of craziness had they all been up to together? And the other guy? It had to be either Tommy or Zach. They both were good-looking and played polo. Michaela was banking that it was Tommy hanging out with them that night.

It was time to talk with Lucia Sorvino.

Her cell phone rang, snapping her out of her thoughts. Joe said, "Hey, thanks for feeding the twins and hanging with Vince this morning. Me and Marianne were kind of beat, I guess."

"No, thank *you.* I should've waited until you woke up, but I wanted to try and question Erin Hornersberg some more. It looks like she's skipped town."

"Interesting. Well, I may have something on the Sorvino girl. Can you meet me? I've got to take little Joe to soccer practice. Wanna come to the field?"

"Definitely. I'll be there in twenty. I found out some other things, too."

"Can you bring me a soda and maybe a bag of chips or something? I'm kind of hungry."

"Who do you think I am, the errand girl?"

"I'm your Magnum P.I., remember? Yeah, you must be the errand girl."

"I thought I was Higgins."

"Same diff. That dude always catered to Magnum."

"Ha! I'm not getting in any trouble with your wife. She told me about your blood pressure."

"She did? Damn."

"I'll bring you a bottled water and some fruit."

"Some friend."

"You'll thank me when you lose that extra fifty pounds and maybe start to resemble Tom Selleck."

"Fine."

Twenty-five minutes later she parked her truck next to Joe's minivan. "Hey, Magnum."

Joe waved her over to the soccer field, where a group of boys chased the ball up and down the field, with parents on the sidelines screaming their brains out as to how the game should be played. She never did understand the whole soccer-parent mentality. It seemed like a form of cruel and unusual punishment for the kids, or at least emotional abuse.

"I wish I'd never made that remark about Magnum. You're never going to let me live it down, are you? You know I love that show? I got all of 'em on DVD."

"I am not surprised. Okay, so tell me what you found out about Lucia Sorvino."

"It's not so much her, but it's her cousin the Pez."

"Yeah?"

"Yeah. Check this. You know how Marianne and I told you that he's spent time in and out of jail for theft. Well, some years back, one of the guys who works for him went to the big house on charges that he was taking real jewels like rubies, emeralds, diamonds, the good stuff, and replacing them with fakes, which he was selling to a high-end jewelry store."

"No kidding?"

"No, but it gets better: The jewelry store was in Santa Barbara. And Diamante was using rich kids in the area to steal for him as well — on the side. Didn't you tell me that Sterling got popped as a teen for stealing jewels and spent time in juvie?"

"I sure did."

"Uh-huh. Well, it's all connected. Sterling knew Diamante for the last eight years or so, and who knows how long and who they've been scamming. Sterling did his short stint in juvie, got out, and moved here soon after. His folks didn't send him away. He was a delinquent. He followed Diamante and I bet lived his life conning and stealing and soaking it all up. The guy in jail for the initial crime won't talk. Word is he knows that Diamante is connected and he got framed for the crime, 'cause it's really Diamante dealing in switching out fakes."

"You think that maybe the bracelet I found in the stall — which we know is a fake — is connected to this Diamante character and somehow connected to Lucia, who may have been involved with Sterling?" Michaela said.

She filled him in about what Sheila had told her about the Sinners and Saints club and who Sterling had been with. "I think Marianne was right last night when she said that Lucia has the answers. I had to try and talk to Erin to satisfy all my theories, but this really does come down to Pepe's daughter. Lucia is looking like she's a big part of this, and now I know why she told the cops that I was screwing around with Sterling: It's because she knew that people had seen him with a blonde woman, and because I refused Sterling's advances. She might have murdered him and framed me because it was easy to do. But still, why did Lucia need to go out with the disguise?"

"Pepe Sorvino. He wants his sweet little daughter to save her *virginal* self for marriage, and if he had an inkling that she's the little tramp that she is, he'd blow a gasket. I bet she was driving her brother's car the other day when she followed you. She was trying to figure out your next play."

"Why?"

"She's a dumb-ass kid, that's why. They do stupid things. Maybe she thought you suspected her of being involved and wanted to know what you were up to."

"I can buy that, I guess," Michaela replied. "But Lucia is not the mastermind behind all of this. She didn't come after me in the tack shop last night. What should we do next?"

He shook his head. "I don't know."

"Let's backtrack. Lucia's uncle could be trading out real jewels for fakes, turning around and selling them on the black market. Where is he getting the jewels, and how is Sterling connected?" Michaela said.

"Beats me —"

"Wait! You know what, I think I might

know who is behind all of this and why, and also why Carolyn Taber was murdered as well."

"You do?"

"Yes. You ready to catch a killer?"

"Do you have to ask?"

FORTY-ONE

The next day Michaela, Joe, his cousin Anthony, and Marianne all met at Joe's house. Camden and Dwayne had agreed to watch the Pellegrino kids, which Michaela was sure would prove interesting, while they put their plan of attack into action.

Phase one began as they pulled up to Sorvino's with Anthony driving and Marianne in the passenger seat. Michaela was in the back covered by a blanket. Joe had called to find out if Lucia would be working, and what her schedule was. He'd asked the hostess these questions under the guise that he was a friend who needed to drop something off for her.

Joe was also in the backseat and made sure that Michaela couldn't be seen. Michaela didn't really need to be there for the plan to work, but she knew she had to be for her own sanity. She'd dragged her good friends into this and wouldn't miss it for the world.

She knew that it was likely going to be through Lucia that they would catch a killer — one who had possibly framed Michaela and then attempted to kill her as well.

They waited for Lucia to end her shift, which luckily was the lunch shift, because there was still much to be done, and the first thing they needed was to get Lucia Sorvino to cooperate with them.

When she emerged, she headed toward the black Explorer. "You ready?" Joe asked Marianne and Anthony.

They nodded and got out of the car. The night before, they'd all rehearsed how this was going to go down. Anthony was as eager as Marianne as they'd sat around the kitchen table.

"With the attorney general's office, eh?" Anthony had asked. "Don't you think when she looks at my card, she might ask why it don't say nothing about being employed by the attorney general?"

"It says attorney on it, doesn't it?" Joe said.

"Yeah, it says *tax* attorney, though."

"That's fine," Michaela said. "If she asks about it, then tell her that stealing jewels is not only considered theft, it's tax evasion."

"She's going to deny it," Marianne added.

"Of course she will, and that's where you

come in," Joe said. "You are an undercover police officer and you're there to help her. If she goes with the two of you, then her father or brother will have to know about it."

"I like it," Marianne replied. "Playing a cop. Cool. Do I get to carry a gun?"

"No," Joe said. "No guns."

Marianne had frowned.

Now, Michaela and Joe watched as they approached Lucia. Would their plan work? They saw Lucia take Anthony's card, then look back and forth between him and Marianne. "Do you think she's buying it?" Michaela asked.

"We'll see."

Marianne then slipped her hand around Lucia's arm and escorted her to the mini-van. "Nice move," Michaela said.

"That's my girl," Joe replied. "I knew she could do this."

Michaela ducked down in the backseat. Joe had moved up front, behind the wheel, and as Anthony and Marianne opened the side door to the van, Marianne got in first. and Lucia sat between her and Anthony. Joe started the car and locked the doors.

"Who's that guy?" Lucia asked.

"The driver," Anthony said.

"Driver? Do I need a lawyer?"

"I am a lawyer," Anthony said.

"I didn't do anything wrong. I didn't," the girl protested.

"We want to help you," Marianne said. "Here is what we know. We know that your cousin Diamante Pizzini, also known as the Pez, has been trading out valuable jewels for fake ones."

"I don't know nothing about that," Lucia said.

"Really?"

It was all Michaela could do to lie in the back and stay quiet. They needed Lucia to talk. They didn't want her to know that Michaela was there — not yet.

"Yeah, really."

"Huh, well that's not what Diamante told the feds."

Marianne was good at this.

"Diamante? What do you mean, he told the feds? What did he say?"

"He said that you're the one who gives him the real jewels and sells them direct to the jewelers."

"That's not true! No. I don't do that. Sterling did that, not me."

"Sterling who?" Anthony asked.

"Taber."

"The man who was murdered last weekend?" Marianne asked.

"Yes. Him."

"So he was trading your cousin real jewels, swapping them out for the fakes, but who was cashing in? Who was Sterling selling them to?" Anthony asked. Joe kept on driving and Michaela laid low.

Lucia didn't say anything for a while.

"Lucia, it's your word against your cousin's, and we can help you if you talk to us. We may even be able to keep your father out of this," Marianne told her.

"And Mario, my brother? If he knew, he'd be so ashamed of me," Lucia said.

"I think we can arrange that," Marianne said.

"Fine, I'll tell you what I know if you promise me that my dad and brother don't need to know."

Marianne opened her cell phone and dialed. Michaela had no idea what she was doing until she spoke into it. "Okay, Miss Sorvino has agreed to work with us. Yes. On the condition that her family is not made aware of the situation. Yes. Okay. Sure. I'll tell her. Yes, sir. Good-bye."

"Who was that?" Lucia asked.

"The attorney general. He says he'll do what he can for you, but he can't control what your cousin might say or do. However, I'm sure that whatever your cousin may say, you can convince your family that he's a lunatic. Especially if you have my help."

Priceless! Michaela wanted to nominate Marianne for an Academy Award.

And then Lucia spilled her guts.

FORTY-TWO

An hour later, after Anthony and Marianne had versed Lucia on her role, they were ready to go. Michaela's back hurt from being driven all over town in such an uncomfortable position. She'd wanted to whip back the blanket covering her, jump over the backseat, and strangle the brat when she'd said that she only told the police Sterling said he was sleeping with Michaela because she was afraid that, if she didn't say something, the cops would find out about the jewelry scam.

"I had nothing to do with his murder," Lucia protested. "I was scared because I knew what we were doing was wrong. Looks like the police found out anyway."

"That's our job," Marianne said. "We think we know who murdered Sterling and why, and because it involves the jewels, it's up to you to get a taped confession. That is, if you want to stay out of jail."

"Wait, no. I can't do that! I don't know how to do that," Lucia said.

"So I'm going to tell you." Marianne went over everything that she and the others had concocted. "Make the call."

"Okay," Lucia replied, sounding shaken.

She dialed a number. "It's me. I need you to meet me at the club. Diamante called and needs us there. No, I don't know why. But you need to be there. Now. I'm on my way. I'll see you there." She hung up the phone. "The club won't be open right now, you know."

"We know. Everything can take place outside the club. You'll be wired and we'll park around the corner."

"Wired?"

"There's nothing to be afraid of," Marianne said. "We do it all the time."

"Fine, but you better not let me go to jail and you better be right about this."

"We are."

Michaela crossed her fingers. What if her theory was wrong? No harm, no foul, other than one irate Lucia Sorvino. It was a risk, but she figured that if they didn't take it, she might eventually wind up dead. Sterling's murderer was ruthless, and after the other night, Michaela feared that the killer still intended to see her wind up the same way.

The car stopped. Michaela heard everyone get out. Joe helped Marianne wire Lucia. "Play by the book, Miss Sorvino. We'd hate for this to all go wrong for you. Pretty girls like you don't last long in jail," Marianne said. Oh, she was good!

A minute later, Joe opened the back hatch. "She's around the corner."

Michaela pulled off her blanket and blew a piece of hair out of her face. "Oh my, you are so brilliant, Marianne. I could kiss you."

"I *was* good, wasn't I?" Marianne replied.

"What about me?" Anthony asked.

Michaela patted him on the shoulder. "Excellent, all of you."

"Yeah, well, it ain't over yet," Joe said. "C'mon, get back in the car, let's see what we can hear."

"Do you think she'll run?" Michaela asked.

"No. Her family is here, and we've got her on tape now. We've got plenty of leverage on her, and my wife scared her witless. She won't run. Shh, here she is. Listen."

"Hi."

"What's this all about? I don't like this. Where's your car?"

"I parked around the corner. I don't know

what it's about. Diamante just wanted to see us."

Michaela and the others exchanged looks. Joe turned up the volume on the scanner. Michaela was wondering, as she was sure they all were, if Lucia would blow it, or if Tommy would press her about where she'd parked.

"It better be good. I had to make up some lame excuse why I had to leave work. Ed Mitchell gets a whiff of it, we may not have a jewelry store to use for this stuff. And I need this. We haven't reached our goals. Mitchell thinks I'm so dependable, that's why he likes me. If he knew I was robbing him blind . . . oh God." Tommy's laughter rang through the scanner.

Michaela winced. She had no idea the man was so completely calculating and cold-hearted.

"I'm going to tell Diamante that I don't want to do this any longer," Lucia said.

"What? Why? You're kidding. How much money have we made at this in the past few months? What, a hundred grand each? Come on. Don't be stupid. What's all this about?"

"Sterling."

"Honey, we've talked, and even though he's not here any longer we can still go

335

forward with our plans. Come on, you're being ridiculous."

"No. I'm scared," Lucia replied.

"Why? There's nothing to be scared of. We have dreams, and this is the way to get them."

"What about Michaela Bancroft? I followed her, you know, and she's been talking to everyone about Sterling and I don't think she did it."

"Of course she didn't. Haven't you heard the news? The cops are saying that Sterling's sister-in-law did. We've got nothing to worry about. Michaela Bancroft won't be snooping around any longer."

"What if she does? She might find out about the jewels."

"She's not going with the script," Michaela whispered. "What's the deal? I thought she was only supposed to focus on Sterling."

Marianne shrugged. "I don't know. Maybe she knows what she's doing. She better."

"You know she found my bracelet," they heard Lucia say.

"What?" Tommy asked. "That was *your* bracelet? You're an idiot."

"What do you mean?"

"She came into the store the other day and the other salesperson looked at it and

336

told her it was a phony. Luckily, she told me about it. Quit worrying about her. I'll take care of Michaela."

"What does that mean?' Lucia asked.

Joe raised his eyebrows.

"Nothing. You need to quit worrying so much and do what you're told. Now, where the hell is Diamante? I don't have time for this shit!"

"I'm out. I can't do this anymore. I just can't. I'm gonna tell Diamante when he gets here. You and Sterling had dreams and I went along with all of this because you told me that you could convince Sterling to be with me and that he'd fall in love with me."

Joe and Michaela eyed each other. "I thought so," Michaela said. "I figured there was something going on between those two. Ed Mitchell indicated it as well."

"Shh!" Joe said. "They're still talking."

"Oh babe, love is overrated. Plus, you and I have had some fun together. We got enough cash stored away right now to run off to some Caribbean island and have a party."

"I don't want to party with you. I want Sterling back!"

"That isn't going to happen. Now what the hell is wrong with you? You didn't seem all broken up about Sterling after it happened."

"How could I be? Of course I was, but I couldn't show it. I had to think quick. I was afraid the police would think that I did it."

"Well, you didn't."

"Like I just told you, Sterling's sister-in-law looks like the bad guy now after killing herself. They think she hired someone to kill him. We can still make our deals, and like I said, we can go have some fun in the sun. And if that's not your thing . . . well, no problem, babe. I'll take my share and go have some fun. Don't be so fucking stupid!"

"You know what scares me is that I still think there's a killer out there. What if it's Ed Mitchell? He could have found out what was going on, and he'll take each of us out one by one. Or that daughter of his."

"Juliet? Please. The cops think it was a hired gun, and they don't go after people like us. They get paid, they do the job, and they take off." Tommy laughed. "Look, neither Ed nor Juliet had anything to do with it."

"How do you know? I don't like this. I don't believe that Carolyn Taber hired anyone. How do I know that it's not someone we know? Maybe it's even you."

"You are acting like a sick little bitch!

You're gonna do what you're told to do because that's the way it is! We brought you in on this because we needed you to convince your cousin to work with us. After what happened with Sterling in Santa Barbara when he was a kid, Diamante wasn't too keen on working with him again, but you helped with that, and now you're the middleman since Sterling is fucking dead."

There was a rustling noise.

"What are you doing?" Lucia exclaimed.

"Get in the car!"

"No!" she screamed.

"I said, get the hell in the car. I don't like where this is going, and I don't think Diamante is on his way. I don't know what you're up to, Lucia, but get the hell in the car and start talking because we're going for a drive."

"No! Let go of me!"

"I should have killed you, too. Dammit. I knew you were trouble."

"What do you mean . . . ow!"

It sounded as if Tommy was hurting her. They heard a car door slam.

Joe cranked the engine on the minivan as Lucia screamed, *"No!"* again.

They squealed around the corner. Marianne and Anthony fell on Michaela as they scrambled for seat belts.

"Joey!" Marianne yelled.

"Get my piece from the glove compartment," he said.

Marianne did as he said.

"Anthony, you know how to use a weapon?"

"Hell no, Joe. I'm a tax attorney."

"You're also a Pellegrino!"

"I can use it, honey, I know how," Marianne said.

"No, Michaela knows how to as well. I need you to drive. Here, trade."

Michaela watched in awe as Marianne slid under Joe, who moved over to the passenger seat while keeping his hands on the wheel and foot on the gas until Marianne could take over. "You two are scaring me. You're like a regular Bonnie and Clyde," Michaela said.

"In my bag, in the back, grab the other gun. You remember how to use it?"

"Yes," Michaela replied. Joe had taken her to the shooting range several times over the past year after her uncle had been killed.

Marianne spun into the parking lot as Tommy and Lucia took off in his jeep. They all heard Tommy say, "What the hell? Who is that, Lucia? Who the fuck is that?"

"I swear I don't know. I don't!"

"Should have never trusted you. You

should've kept your questions to yourself!" Tommy screamed. "I'll kill you just like I did Sterling and that stupid sister-in-law of his!"

"What? No!"

"Oh my God," Michaela said. "He's spilling it all."

"She hasn't lost the wire yet," Joe said. "This isn't good. Are you willing to use the gun, Mick?"

"I . . . don't know," Michaela said.

"No time for 'I don't know.' I think this guy plans to kill her," Joe said.

Marianne punched the accelerator.

"Lucia!' Tommy screamed. "Tell me! Who is following us?"

"I don't know," she cried.

"I'm going to kill you, Lucia, just like I did Rebecca Woodson! And frigging Sterling got all greedy on me and was gonna tell that stupid chick's family that I did it, all because he wanted all the cash from the jewels. Know what? He probably would've figured a way to have ousted you, too. He was a snake, Lucia, and you're being a moron! I'm willing to share with you and now you go and rat me out. Didn't you?"

"No! No! Diamante did!"

"He did kill Rebecca," Michaela said.

"What! What the . . ." Tommy turned

341

down a one-way street, his tires screaming around the corner.

Marianne stayed right behind him. Tommy emerged on the other end, but just before Marianne got there, a huge semi started to pull in front of them.

"Oh shit!" Joe exclaimed.

Michaela held onto her seat belt.

"Oh Mary, Mother of God," Anthony muttered.

Marianne floored the gas and circled around the semi's cab, barely missing it.

"Around that way!" Joe yelled.

She followed his directions and they again got behind Tommy's gray jeep. "Now, Mick, now! Can you take out that left rear wheel?" Joe yelled.

"I don't know."

"Try!"

They rolled down their windows. Joe stuck his gun out the front window, Michaela the back, pointing it as best as she could at the tire. They were heading toward the freeway and traffic increased as they weaved between cars. The last thing Michaela wanted was for anyone to get hurt.

Anthony had his phone out. Michaela heard him calling the police, which at this point was an excellent idea. He reported an abduction and gave a description of the car.

Tommy went down another street, away from the freeway and toward suburbia.

"Take the shot, Mick! You've got a better vantage!" Joe said.

She aimed and fired. The jeep squirreled out and then zipped around a light post, finally straightening out. "I think I got him!"

The jeep started to slow. Michaela watched as Tommy leaped out. "Stop the car!" Joe yelled.

When Marianne did, Joe scrambled out and started after Tommy. Michaela followed. What happened next seemed like it took place in slow motion. No one figured Tommy had a weapon on him, but he turned around and fired, and Joe went down. Michaela sprinted to him as Tommy ran off.

"Asshole got me in the knee." Joe winced. Marianne was by Joe's side in seconds, with Anthony behind. "Go check the girl. Make sure she's okay," Joe told Anthony.

"Oh no, Joey, Joey!" Marianne cried.

He reached a hand out for her. "I'm fine, sweetie. It hurts, but I'll be okay. Now, where did that SOB go?" Joe said, his face paling as the pain hit him hard.

"He got away. Again," Michaela said and took Joe's other hand.

FORTY-THREE

Michaela leaned against the cold, hard wall of the hospital corridor, coffee in hand and thoughts racing through her mind. Joe was in surgery, having a bullet removed from his knee. This was not how it was supposed to happen. Detectives were questioning Lucia, and Michaela was afraid that all of them would be facing some sort of criminal charges.

Marianne was in the waiting room; Anthony had gone down to the cafeteria. Michaela had no idea what Lucia would tell the police. If she told them what Marianne and Anthony had said, then, yes, they would all be in a lot of trouble. She didn't know if Lucia was even aware of her involvement in the car chase. Once the police had been called and emergency crews arrived, it all happened so quickly. The area had been sealed off and a manhunt for Tommy ensued, with no results. He had definitely eluded the authorities.

She turned to see Anthony walking down the hall. He held out a cookie for her.

"No thanks," she said. "What do you think will happen?"

"Joe is gonna be fine. He's tough."

Michaela nodded. She prayed that his knee would be okay. "How about Lucia? What do you think she'll tell the police?"

"She's not going to tell them anything. That's why I was looking for you. I just got a call from her and she has refused to talk until she sees me. She told the police that I'm her attorney." He smiled. "I better get on downtown. Don't worry, I'll handle everything."

Michaela had no idea what Anthony had up his sleeve. But the one thing she'd come to know about the Pellegrino family was that if anyone could get out of a sticky situation, it was them.

After Anthony left, she went into the waiting area and joined Marianne. She took her small hand. "I'm sorry, Mare."

Marianne turned and looked at her, her eyes red from crying. "Sorry? Sorry? Oh honey, don't be sorry. Are you kidding me? Joey is gonna be fine and we all knew what we were signing up for with this deal. You don't need to be sorry. I have to tell you, that was the best damn time I've had in years. Please don't apologize. The only reason I'm upset is that I know for the next however long it takes for Joey to heal, I've got to play nursemaid." She started to laugh. "Okay, so maybe I'm a little worried, but honestly, Joe is not a good patient."

"I imagine not." They both laughed. "I really do hope you know how sorry I am about all of this."

"Dammit, Michaela, you say that one more time and I'm gonna knock you across the room. Just stop it."

Michaela gave her a hug. When she pulled away she looked up and saw Jude heading toward them. Her stomach sank.

"Hello, ladies. Michaela, I think we need to talk."

She nodded. Marianne excused herself and Jude asked her not to go far, as he planned to question her as well. When she left the room, he turned to Michaela. "Do you want to tell me why you and your friends were chasing a car that Tommy Liggett was driving with Lucia Sorvino inside it? Oh, and don't leave anything out, especially the part where you shot out Tommy's tire."

He wasn't happy with her and she didn't know how she was going to get out of this.

"We spotted Lucia being dragged into a car by Tommy and it didn't look good, so we followed them and could tell she was in trouble. I shot out the tire because I was afraid he was going to kill her."

"And why would you think that?"

"Because I found out that Sterling and Tommy were dealing in stolen jewels. Lucia had connected them with her cousin Diamante Pizzini, and then Tommy murdered Sterling, because last summer the two of them were involved in the death of a woman in Santa Barbara."

Jude placed his head in his hands. "Oh God. Go on."

"While Detective Peters was busy pointing the finger at me, and you were off on your cruise, I didn't have much choice but to try and figure out who really murdered Sterling Taber." She told him everything she'd found out about Rebecca Woodson and what she surmised had happened last summer on the pier. "I think Tommy was there, and whether or not it was an accident, either Tommy or Sterling pushed her. Then, I think they agreed to cover for each other. I spoke with Rebecca's brother this week and he said that Sterling had tried to get him to meet with him. He told him that he had information about his sister's death. I believe that Sterling was greedy and planned to tell Rebecca's family that Tommy had killed her. Tommy found out about this and so he killed Sterling — because Sterling was about to betray him and also because of the jewels they were dealing in. Sterling wanted all the profit. He wasn't the type to share."

"Interesting. If you have that all figured out, then why don't you tell me what part Carolyn Taber played in all of this."

"I think Tommy killed her. I think he had a set of tapes that Sterling probably gave him. When he saw that there might be holes in the case against me, he knew he'd need another fall guy and he chose Carolyn. She was easy to frame. I bet that if you run a handwriting analysis on the suicide note, it won't match Carolyn Taber's handwriting."

"Maybe you should become a cop."

"Funny." She smiled at him but he didn't return the smile.

"You know that Anthony Pellegrino, who is your friend Joe's cousin and who was in the minivan with you and the others, is now downtown with Lucia Sorvino, *representing* her."

"He's a good lawyer."

"He's a *tax attorney*, Michaela. I know there are blanks to fill in here. You haven't been forthright from the get-go. But honestly, I don't think I want to know everything anymore, because I've got a bad feeling that if I did know, I'd have to arrest you. And I don't want to do that. You better hope that the holes in your story don't get bigger and that none of your partners fill in the blanks."

"Yep." She took a sip of coffee. It was all she could say. A minute later, Jude stood. She asked him, "Have they found Tommy?"

"Not yet. But we will. I've got to get back to the station. Tell Mrs. Pellegrino that I hope her husband is better."

"You aren't going to talk with her? I thought you said —"

He held up a hand. "Like I said, I don't think I want to know. I've got enough to file a report and keep you out of jail. But we do need to talk. We really do. Just not now."

She nodded. Jude left the room and she watched him walk down the hall to the exit. She got up and paced the hall. A few minutes later Marianne came back and said, "Where's the cop?"

"Gone. He says he hopes Joe feels better and he changed his mind about talking with you."

"Huh. Okay. Well, Joey is out of surgery and the doctor says it looks good."

"That's great. Can we see him?"

"They say he's in recovery and it'll be a while. You know, why don't you go on home and I'll call you. I'm kinda worried about the kids anyway. I'm sure Camden and Dwayne have their hands full."

"Of course. Sure. Yes, call me."

Michaela headed home with an empty feeling inside. Her friend was hurt, and she'd done a dumb thing by trying to take down a madman. Jude was right: She needed to stop playing detective. She didn't have the skills for it.

It was getting dark and all the lights were on at Dwayne and Camden's place. She walked in and was pleasantly surprised by what she saw. On Camden's lap sat a sleeping Isabel; Dwayne was playing Monopoly with Vincent and little Joe. Gen was drawing and Giorgio was watching a TV show. Wow.

"Hi, Michaela," Dwayne said. Camden smiled at her and brought a finger to her lips. Who knew that Camden could be . . . domestic? A wave of comfort came over her and she wanted to sit down and start crying, but she knew that would raise too many questions, and the last thing she wanted to do was break up the peaceful scene. She went over to the table where the Monopoly game was going on. "Sorry guys, it took us a little longer than we thought. Um, and I think the kids will probably stay for a little while more. I'll go out and feed the horses and then take the kids off your hands and give them dinner."

"No, no. I be making some burgers for them. I got the grill fired up already and Cammy girl made the patties earlier for us," Dwayne said. "We all be good. You sure 'bout the horses? I can feed 'em."

"No. You look like you're having a good time." She glanced at Camden and smiled. "Look at you," she whispered.

"I know," she whispered back so as not to wake the toddler. "I know." She smiled.

Michaela left them and headed to the barn. She piled flakes of hay onto the wheelbarrow and began her rounds. She fought back all of the emotion that ate at her, which ranged from anger, frustration, sadness, and fear to the other end of the spectrum after seeing Camden and Dwayne with the kids — which had given her a sense of peace and happiness. She'd had her doubts about those two getting married, but any lingering questions had been wiped away in the last few minutes. They were going to be married and start a family and Michaela wanted all of that and more for them, because it was her strongest desire to have a family, too. If she couldn't have one then her best friend should, and she could share in their joy.

Her stallion, Rocky, snorted as she passed. Here was her family. He tossed his head as she started to open his stall door. "Okay, okay, easy. I'm getting it," she said.

Rocky pawed the ground. He was always eager when it came to dinnertime, but there was something off about him tonight. She pushed the stall door open a little farther as Rocky sent a shrill whinny echoing through the breezeway. It all happened in seconds, but Michaela felt something go around her neck. She reached her fingers up, clawing at the object. Someone was strangling her. Rocky reared up inside his stall. She could see the whites of his eyes and his nostrils flare, fear emanating from him. She kicked and struggled. She knew who had her: Tommy Liggett had come to her ranch and hidden out, waiting to strike.

As she felt the lead rope tighten further, she heard Tommy telling her what a stupid bitch she was. "You didn't have to keep snooping around. I killed Carolyn Taber for you. I actually liked you. I didn't want you to go to jail. Then I thought Carolyn would be a perfect killer to pin this all on and you'd be free. But no, you had to keep after me, send in Lucia and the troops. What the hell is wrong with you?"

Michaela, still struggling, grew dizzy. She knew she was losing the fight. And as she faded, Rocky shoved his stall all the way open with his head and charged at Tommy, who dropped the rope. Now on the ground, Michaela rolled quickly to her side. Rocky reared up again and came crashing down, knocking Tommy onto his back. He screamed, but it was too late; Rocky's hooves came down on Tommy's chest. Michaela sat up. Her horse had just saved her life.

FORTY-FOUR

It was over. It had been a week since Tommy Liggett was taken away in a body bag from Michaela's ranch. The police closed the investigation after running the handwriting analysis, as Michaela suggested. Lucia worked with the police in fingering her cousin in the jewelry scam and told them what Tommy had said to her in the car about killing Sterling. She did not, thankfully, tell the police about Marianne's and Anthony's role in any of it. Anthony was able to get her a deal if she cooperated with the cops, and no one was the wiser about how things had really occurred the day they chased Tommy down.

Jude and Michaela finally had that talk, and both came to the conclusion that maybe they weren't right for each other. She knew that Jude had been hurt by her dishonesty with him, and she'd been hurt by his lack of faith in her. She had to wonder if she'd ever find the right man and start a family. Joe was back home with his brood, and she'd taken food over for them several times and run errands for Marianne, wanting to help out as much as she could.

Dwayne and Camden had gone back to putting all their efforts into planning their wedding and running the tack shop.

Rocky was her hero, and every day she'd gone out to see him with an extra handful of carrots. As horrible as Tommy's death had been, Rocky had saved her life and she was grateful.

Michaela sat out back, her eyes closed, listening to the waterfall pour into the pool. She thought about Ethan and wondered how everything was going with him. He'd called when he heard what had happened, and wanted to come over. She'd insisted it wasn't necessary. She knew that the two of them needed to have some space between them. Summer was not her favorite person in the world, but Michaela knew her feelings for Ethan were wrong, and she needed him to stay away. She needed to move on with her life, and thankfully tomorrow would be the beginning of that as she went back to giving riding lessons. She got up and went inside to make herself some dinner. Camden and Dwayne had gone out for the evening, and although she thought she'd relish having time to herself after all she'd been through, she felt pretty alone.

She seasoned a chicken breast and put it in the oven to bake. As she started fixing herself a salad, the doorbell rang. *Who could that be?*

Ethan stood on the other side of the door, little Josh in his arms. He looked distraught. "Ethan? What is it? What's wrong?"

He walked past her, put Josh down on her family room floor, and handed him a set of plastic keys to play with. He grabbed her arm and took her into the kitchen, where in a lowered voice he said, "She left."

"What?"

"Can you believe it? Summer. She just left us. I was at work. The baby was at day care. I had to go down to the Helen Woodward Center in San Diego yesterday. Then, I got this call from the day-care lady, who said that Summer never picked him up. She'd called yesterday and asked her to keep him overnight, but then she didn't show up today."

"What?"

"Yeah, so I raced home and picked him up and came home to an empty house. She even took her horses."

"No, Ethan. No! That's not true."

He handed her a letter. "Read this."

Michaela took it. Summer's letter detailed how she couldn't handle being a mother, that she thought she'd loved Ethan but now she didn't think so, and she didn't want the life. She wanted a different life. The words were crazy and unfathomable. *How could a woman leave her baby?* The letter further stated that she'd met someone, and for Ethan to expect divorce papers and that she wouldn't fight him in a custody battle.

"Oh my God, Ethan. No. Look, you have to find her. Maybe she's going through some type of postpartum depression like we talked about, and she needs help. Women don't just leave their children. They don't do it, and I know she loves Josh. I've seen her with him."

"Find her? No way. She left her son and me. You read the letter. And you don't know the half of it. I didn't want to say anything. You've had so much going on," Ethan said.

"I don't understand."

He took her hands. "Summer. She has not been a mother to our son. I'm so exhausted. I come home from work and he's either hungry or needs to be changed. I don't know what to think. I'm the one who found the day care because I was so worried about him. I tried talking to her and she would

357

scream at me and tell me that she was fine."

Michaela shook her head. "I had no idea. This is all wrong. She'll be back. This is crazy."

"No *she's* crazy. I don't want her to come back. She's found another man, and you know what, the whole way over here, Michaela, I kept running it through my mind. The day she left me at the altar and then wormed her way back into my life, and the way she has tried to keep us from being friends, and I know why. It's because she's seen all along what the two of us haven't, and as far as I'm concerned this is a blessing."

"What?"

He leaned in and kissed her hard, wrapping his arms around her. The world, her life, all of it swirled into a blur, as if she was in a dream. But it was real. And it was more than nice and more than special. It was a connection so profound that it brought tears to her eyes, and although she was confused by all of it, at the same time, she felt more clarity in those seconds than she'd ever known. He pulled away from her and said, "It's been you, Mick. Always has. It's that simple. It has always been you and I'm tired of pretending or denying it. I won't do it anymore. Will you? I mean, we want to be in your life and I think there's a future here for us." He looked at Josh and then back at her. "The three of us. Don't you?"

Emotion caught in the back of her throat and she couldn't respond for a second. Ethan didn't take his eyes off of her. When she was finally able to express herself, she replied, "You don't even have to ask that. I think you already know the answer." She wiped her tears and kissed him back. ///

We hope you have enjoyed this Large Print book. Other Thorndike, Wheeler, and Chivers Press Large Print books are available at your library or directly from the publishers.

For information about current and upcoming titles, please call or write, without obligation, to:

Publisher
Thorndike Press
295 Kennedy Memorial Drive
Waterville, ME 04901
Tel. (800) 223-1244

or visit our Web site at:

http://gale.cengage.com/thorndike

OR

Chivers Large Print
published by BBC Audiobooks Ltd
St James House, The Square
Lower Bristol Road
Bath BA2 3SB
England
Tel. +44(0) 800 136919
email: bbcaudiobooks@bbc.co.uk
www.bbcaudiobooks.co.uk

All our Large Print titles are designed for easy reading, and all our books are made to last.